THE SURVIVORS BOOK THREE
NEW WORLD

BY

NATHAN HYSTAD

Copyright © 2018 Nathan Hystad

All rights reserved.

No part of this publication may be reproduced, distributed, or transmitted in any form or by any means, including photocopying, recording, or other electronic or mechanical methods, without the prior written permission of the publisher, except in the case of brief quotations embodied in critical reviews and certain other non-commercial uses permitted by copyright law.

This is a work of fiction. All of the characters, names, incidents, organizations, and dialogue in this novel are either products of the author's imagination or are used fictitiously.

Cover art: Tom Edwards Design

Edited by: Scarlett R Algee

Proofed and Formatted by: BZ Hercules

ISBN-13: 978-1719502016

ISBN-10: 1719502013

Also By Nathan Hystad

The Survivors Series

The Event

New Threat

New World

The Ancients

The Theos

Red Creek

ONE

*T*he familiar hum of the FTL drive stopped as Mary pulled us out of hyperdrive. I was mentally prepared, but after traveling across our system toward Proxima for the last two months, the smallest noise difference caught me off-guard.

"Scan the area," I said, and Slate went to work on his console, looking for anything that would show up on our sensors. We'd elected to pull up short of the colony planet, in case there were any surprises waiting for us. If the Bhlat were there, or some other complication cropped up, we wanted to be aware of it before we were detected. "Stay cloaked."

We were at least six hours away, at our in-system speed: a stroll into our new home to get our bearings of the area.

"Slate, you're telling us that all the press about Proxima b being inhabitable was a lie?" Clare asked once again.

The big man nodded. "General Heart said it was a backup plan. We had probes sent to all the corners of space we could."

"Where'd they get that technology?" I asked.

He shrugged. "Beats me. I don't think the general NASA employees knew about them."

A shiver ran down my spine. Government conspiracies about space were nothing new, but FTL satellite probes being sent to the far reaches of the universe? That sounded suspiciously like alien technology to me.

"The stories about the atmosphere being too weak to sustain human life?" Clare prompted.

"I don't know much; I'm just a soldier. Heart said it was a bunch of bull set up between the leaders of the science community and the governments. They had top-secret meetings about all sorts of things: Mars colonies, liveable stations, Proxima, and countless others," Slate said, still scanning the area, this time casting his net wider as he zoomed out on his console's map.

"They've made elaborate space stations, but not without help from our Kraski databases. I wonder how they expected to do them prior to the Event?" Clare asked, ever curious about anything to do with engineering.

I sank back into my chair, seeing the back of Mary's head at the helm as she guided us through the system. The viewscreen showed us nothing but space. Proxima's star hung in the distance, a red-hot omen. *A star can mean life or death. It depends how you use it.* The old words from my father came to mind. Where he'd gotten that saying was beyond me, but he'd used the reference to tell me that not everything was black and white.

"The video we saw of New Spero looked like paradise," Nick said, walking onto the bridge, holding a cup of coffee. We were running low on a few supplies, but coffee was still prevalent. One of life's small miracles.

"For all we know, that's also a lie Earth's telling. Maybe they didn't even make it there." I said the words but didn't believe them. If Magnus, Natalia, and Carey hadn't made it there, I had no idea what we would do. They were the goal at the end of the journey, and I hoped they were still there with open arms. It had only been a few months for us, but I missed them fiercely, especially my little furry buddy. Seven years for them. A lot could change in seven years.

"Then it's a good thing we're sneaking in," Slate said. His vote had been for stealth, and I had to agree. To fly straight into a potential trap would be foolish.

"Maybe we should have tried to contact them," Mary said.

"We discussed this. If New Spero is there, General Chen and President Naidoo would have told them of our arrival. And I suspect it wasn't a message to greet us with medals." I stood up and started to pace around the bridge. It felt good to get some blood flowing through my body. I could almost feel the hybrid plasma still inside me. Mae's blood... no. Janine's blood. The urge to hit the onboard gym coursed through me, but instead, I strode back and forth like a caged animal at the zoo.

"Boss, sensors are picking up something," Slate said as the lights started to flash red, a warning klaxon echoing in time with each flash.

I crossed the room to stand behind Slate, seeing a blip appear on the screen, then another, and another. Soon there were six of them surrounding us, each a few hundred kilometers away.

"Looks like we weren't as sneaky as we thought. Any way to tell if they're ours?" I asked, proud my voice didn't convey the nerves I was really feeling.

Clare went to work on her console, and in less than ten seconds, she had an answer for me. "They're not doing anything to hide their IDs. They aren't in our database, but they're using the same number format as our ship, and the ones from Earth's base. They're ours."

"Can we contact them?" I asked.

"Message arriving. In audio," Clare said.

"*Uncloak the ship, deactivate your weapons, and follow along.*

Do not attempt to contact us. There is no negotiating this." The message ended. Clare played it again.

"Do we know that voice?" I asked, trying to put a finger on it. It was a man's voice, but the message was so monotone, the Deltras' lack of inflection came to mind.

"It could be Heart," Mary said. "Dean, are we going to obey?"

What choice did we have? Something felt off about the whole thing, but if we tried to run, where would we go – if they didn't blow us to smithereens on the way out? "Do what they ask."

She nodded and soon we were visible to the outside world, weapons off, and flying toward Proxima b, or as our people were calling it, New Spero. I only hoped our new world was a friendly one.

It was a nerve-racking hour later that they sent another message. We tried to stay calm and keep the speculation to a minimum, since we couldn't control what was going to happen to us. The planet had come into view some time ago, and with every minute, it grew larger on our viewscreen. The message alert came as we spotted the station hovering in space over the planet. It was much smaller than the one near Earth, but along the same design.

"Play the message, please," I said to Clare, who tapped the console, and we heard the same clipped-speech voice over the speakers.

"Follow the lead ship to dock. We've reached our destination."

"I don't like this," Slate said. "If they led us planetside, I'd feel better about it. Up here, they can do anything to us, and no one down there" – he pointed to the floor – "would ever know."

He made a good point. We didn't have many options. Either we complied or we made a run for it, leaving the system or heading for the surface. Any of those options could get us killed. Mary looked at me, eyes hard, and there was only one real answer. "We follow them in. We haven't done anything, and if this is the colony, like we think it is, they'll know us and listen to our story."

Slate's eyes still burned, but he didn't push his opinion any further.

"Going in." Mary eased the ship behind them, and five minutes later, she was entering a docking station on the far bottom of the station.

Slate was heading for the storage room already. I knew what he was doing and wasn't sure if I should stop him. I closed my eyes, taking a deep breath. What was the answer? I saw Mae fall, her wound instantly fatal, and Slate's massive form there. *Target down*. I went after him.

"Slate, we can't go in guns blazing," I said, catching him strapping a pulse pistol to his calf.

"No, but we can be prepared for anything. Being prepared keeps us alive."

I couldn't argue with that. The rest of the crew made their way to the bay. Mary stood there, arms crossed and a frown creasing her forehead. "I'm with Slate. Let's at least have something to give us a chance."

I nodded solemnly. Even though they looked to me to lead them for some reason, I wasn't a dictator, and they were probably right. "Small weapons. They'll most likely take them from us anyway, but it can't hurt to be cautious." Everyone concealed some sort of weapon: me a knife, and even Nick, who used to be scared of handling a gun, pocketed a pistol with confidence. Two months on a small ship, and we were all trained and more fit than we'd ever been, thanks to time and Slate's willingness to teach us.

"They're waiting, I imagine," Clare said, standing near

the ramp. We hadn't lowered it yet.

"Let's make them wait another minute," I said, suddenly feeling like we should have made a break for the planet. If they knew who we were, Dalhousie would have sent a greeting party instead of the curt messages and show of power.

It must have been five minutes before I nodded to Clare to hit the icon, lowering the ramp. She looked relieved as it sank to the floor of the hangar.

"I'll go first," I said, Mary holding my hand and walking up front with me. Slate stuck close behind, always on alert. We walked down the ramp, our boots clanging on the metal. I wasn't sure what I'd expected, but it wasn't what we found. At least twenty guards in black uniforms greeted us, and instead of handshakes and hugs, we had pulse rifles in our faces.

"Stand down," I whispered to my crew through clenched teeth. I raised my hands in the air, and the rest of the team followed suit. "Who's in charge here?" I asked the soldiers.

"I am," a voice echoed from the far end of the room, but we couldn't make out a face past all of the guns still pointed at us. Footsteps clinked on the floor, and in a minute, the guards were stepping out of the way, making a path for their leader. When he arrived, I was surprised to see I didn't recognize the man. Seven years was long enough for a shift in power.

He stood there, not speaking as he silently assessed us. The man was wearing a suit, tie included, a fashion I didn't expect us to hold on to on a colony planet. His black hair was slicked, and his dark pupils judged us through a squint. I instantly didn't like him.

"Come with me," he said, turning his back on us. No questions, no patting down, just an order; not that we had a choice, with twenty weapons pointed at us.

"What do you think?" I asked Slate behind me.

"We do what he says," Slate replied softly, "for now."

I stepped forward, and we followed the man, twenty feet behind him, until we were out of the hangar. From there, only three guards continued on the trip with us, the rest presumably staying behind to watch our ship. I had the urge to go back and raise our ship's ramp, but I knew if they wanted in, they would get in.

The halls we were in were built to be corridors only; they were just metal studs and support beams, visible wiring running through them. Nick must have been dragging behind, because we heard a grunt from him, and I turned to see the rear guard shoving him with a gloved hand. This wasn't what I'd expected our arrival at Earth's first colony to look like.

Nick and I made eye contact, and I moved my head a bit to the side, to tell him to hurry and let it go. I'm not sure if it translated, but his gaze went to the ground and his feet sped up.

The lead guard stopped as their leader entered a sliding door to the right. I followed him in and found myself in a large open space, with tables and chairs like my university accounting classroom. It felt out of place here.

The man sat down at a table near the front of the room. It had stools all the way around it: one for each of us, and an extra. They hadn't known how many of us there were. That might have been a good sign.

We each took a seat, with me closest to the man in the suit. It felt like five minutes before he spoke but was probably only thirty seconds. "Why did you come here?"

It was a simple question, but one that felt loaded in many different ways. "We came to see our friends." The answer was short, but the truth.

He nodded to that. "And just who are your friends? We have a lot of people here on New Spero."

"General Heart. President Dalhousie." I almost smiled when I saw his eyes go wide at my reply, but I kept my composure. I was going to be a better poker player than him.

"Interesting choice of friends. Here's what I do know. We received a message from World President Naidoo a while ago. Apparently, you threatened her and were in possession of a genocidal weapon. When confronted, you escaped and ran here."

"Then did she tell you who we are?" Mary asked, obviously getting tired of this charade. I didn't blame her.

He nodded once again, more slowly this time. "She did tell us who you claimed to be, but it's impossible. Those Heroes of Earth are long dead. The Bhlat sent Naidoo video evidence. They attempted to attack an outpost of the Bhlat and were expunged from space for their efforts. That leaves me with some questions. Where did you get this ship? Did you steal it from the old base in America? Why take the most famous," he paused, "or infamous people on Earth to imitate?"

I was getting tired of it too. "Listen here" – I motioned for him to say his name, but he didn't – "fella. I don't know what the Bhlat showed Naidoo, but it wasn't us dying, and frankly, I don't give a crap about your power trip, or whatever this is. Let me speak with General Heart or President Dalhousie, and let me speak to them now." I tried to keep the anger out of my voice, but it was impossible to conceal.

"You keep saying those names, but I'm sorry to say, neither of them can help you now."

"Then I want to talk to Magnus Svenson." I said the name slowly.

New World

He didn't hesitate. "I'm afraid that's not possible either."

"Why? Why is that not possible?" Mary asked. "If you claim we aren't the Heroes of Earth, then let's bring the other two up here, and let them identify us."

He shook his head. "I'm under orders to hold you for your crimes on Earth. Possession of alien weapons and conspiracy to murder the World President."

I stood up, fists against the wooden tabletop. "Wait a minute! We did nothing of the sort. We went to talk, and she was ready to kill us for that alien weapon you talk about. She's already in bed with the Bhlat, who'll come and destroy every last person on Earth."

"That's what anyone would say to save their own skin." His words were firm, but fear escaped his eyes. Hearing that she was working with the Bhlat probably sent some alarm bells ringing, especially after already knowing she had video from them. What was their arrangement? The man stood, and Slate moved between him and the doorway. The rest of the crew looked ready to spring into action, but I couldn't let that happen yet. We were at a disadvantage.

"Let him go, Slate," I said, the fury leaving me with each breath.

Slate stood firm, and the man had to go around him. I loved the power move by my large friend, but we weren't in a position to intimidate either.

The door slid open, and I spotted a few guards out in the hall with weapons in hand. We were being quartered here for the time being.

"What the hell do we do now? Has this whole colony gone to shit?" I asked.

"Maybe there's been a regime change, or," Mary stood, "the station is run by that slimy man, and he's in

Naidoo's pocket. That would allow them to control who arrives, or who leaves the colony, with the surface never knowing."

It made sense. "I think you're right. We need to get back to our ship and down to the planet."

"How do we do that with all of these guards around?" Clare asked.

Slate had a twinkle in his eye as he came back to the table. "Do you all have your pins on?"

We each felt our collars, where the small metal pins sat that would lift us to the ship if needed. "It looks like we do," Mary said.

"You know what that means, right?" Slate asked, and it clicked.

"But how will we have enough time? They have ships at the ready," Mary said.

"Then we distract them. We have to get to the surface, and then we can straighten it all out," I said, not fully believing my own words one hundred percent, but giving them a good chance. I looked around the space for signs of cameras or listening devices. They were undoubtedly watching us. I raised a finger to my lips in a "be quiet" gesture. We moved to the corner of the room that was most inhospitable. If any part of the room wasn't bugged, it was that dark unfurnished corner.

The plan formed faster than I'd thought possible. We felt like a real crew at that moment.

TWO

"Come on, I have to use the bathroom!" Nick called to the guards on the other side of the door. It had only been an hour, but we weren't going to sit around waiting for them to convince themselves to dispose of us.

Clare must have sensed that Nick wasn't getting anywhere, so she went to join him. Maybe a woman in need would pull on their macho soldier hearts.

"Me too. I can't go in here. Don't you guys have any compassion?" she asked, layering in a thick sad tone to her voice.

After a minute or two, the door slid open, and a guard motioned for them to step through. It was tough to see, but even from across the room, I spotted the glint of the screw as Nick placed it at the base of the door, feigning tying up his shoe in front of the guards.

We hadn't been counting on two of ours getting separated, but it was in motion now, and we couldn't turn back. Slate was already moving for the door, which had slid shut but not all the way, as the six-inch-long screw stopped it from sealing so that it wasn't locked. Clare had seen the blueprints on the original station plans, back on Earth at the base she'd spent a year working at. These doors had almost a faux lock; a precautionary thing for safety, not really meant to keep anyone in. Only prison cells would have the real locks that would alert someone if the door wasn't sealed properly.

"Two guards, minimum, had to go with them. It looked like we only had three or four watching us, so I say we all go, swing the ship back, and grab the other two," I said to Mary and Slate, the only others left in the room with me.

Slate nodded, gun already in his hand. I wished I'd seen this coming, because the knife in my grip didn't give me the confidence a pulse pistol would have.

Slate stood at the door, three fingers raised. He lowered them one by one, and when his count was at zero, he gripped the handle and pulled it inward with a grunt. It slid open, and two guards were there, talking between themselves.

Before they could react, Mary was on one of them, disarming him and pointing her gun to his head. "Drop it," she told the other one, and I bent down, picking up the pulse rifle from the ground.

"Do it!" I called to the last guard still holding his weapon. He lowered it, letting go, the metal clanging on the floor. "Mics," I said, holding my left hand out. They looked at one another, and the smaller of the two took an earpiece out and set it in my hand. The other guy followed suit. "Thank you. So you know, we *are* the Heroes of Earth, and when this all shakes out, come down to the surface and I'll buy you a beer."

They looked at us, wide-eyed. "I told you it was them," the smaller one said, grinning as we led them into the room we'd recently vacated.

Slate pulled the screw from the door jamb, and we left, locking them in.

"Let's go before the other guards come back," I said, wishing we had Clare and Nick with us. Even though we had a plan, leaving anyone behind was a chance I didn't want to take.

We knew the way back, since we'd walked these very halls over an hour ago. Foot traffic was nonexistent; I wondered how many people lived on the station, and what exactly it was they did up here. I hoped I'd eventually learn the answer.

"This way," Slate said as we heard footsteps coming from down the hall. We ducked into a side room, the door sliding shut as the steps reached us. We waited in the dark as the sound echoed away from us. My heart was hammering in my chest, and Mary had gripped my hand, a gesture of worry and comfort.

"Let's go," I said, heading back into the hall. The one good thing about function over fashion was that we could hear anyone coming from a hundred feet away on the metal floors. Twice more, we ducked into empty rooms before continuing on our way, soon making it back to the hangar. As we paused in the hall leading to the docking station, alarms blared loudly, getting the attention of the guards lingering inside the large room.

One of the guards held his hand to his earpiece, trying to hear commands over the noise, and he pointed to the door we were standing near. The three of us ran the other way, turning in time to see the guards from the hangar heading down the hall, toward the room we'd escaped from.

"Time to shine," Mary said, rushing back to the hangar. There were only a couple guards left in the room, the rest likely sent to assist in searching for us. Mary ignored them and ran straight for our ship, which still had the ramp lowered. I followed her while Slate threw some covering fire at the guards' feet and made for one of the other ships docked inside the hangar.

The guards didn't even have time to fire back, which

was a good thing. We had no intention of killing anyone today. They were doing what they were told, like any good soldiers.

Our feet clanged on the ramp, and I hit the button as I entered the storage area on our ship. Slate was still firing, and I caught a glimpse of green light emanating around him as he lifted into one of their ships. I still hadn't seen a guard fire at us.

"Time to go!" I yelled as Mary ran to the bridge, firing up the engines.

Our viewscreen showed Slate's ship leaving, erratically flying like a madman. We followed him out, and when he went left, we went right, back toward the middle of the station. It was only moments later that two ships came after us, but Slate was on them, firing at their shields, making more of a show of it than actually trying to harm them. It was enough of a distraction that the two ships focused on him rather than us.

"Come in, Clare," I said after slipping my comm-device in my ear. The sound crackled, and as I thought they might not have been able to conceal the earpieces, her small voice came through.

"Dean, we're down the hall in an office, about a hundred yards down from the room we were in. I can't talk, they…" Her voice cut out.

"We're coming now. Be ready."

There was no reply as I told Mary the directions. When we thought we were above the section of the station they were in, I told Clare to activate the pins. The energy changed slightly in the room, and I ran to the storage room where the beam drive sat. Clare entered, and she was crying.

"They spotted it right before you came. Nick's still down there," she exclaimed.

"This complicates things," I said, wondering if we should head to the surface now and hope we could deal with getting Nick back after. It might be the smartest move, but I hated the thought of leaving one of us behind. There were too many unknowns.

"That's not going to matter, because you're all going back," a voice said, coming from the far side of the ship where the rooms sat. The black-haired man in the suit emerged from the dim hall, gun pointed at us, a sideways grin covering half his face.

The training Slate had engrained in us over the last few months took over, and I assessed the situation. For now, I would keep him talking.

"Find anything you like, or were you having a nap?" I asked, my voice level.

A flicker of annoyance passed his eyes before he smiled again. "Those quick to joke are covering their own insecurities."

I wasn't sure if he was quoting someone or just making up something stupid and irrelevant, but I played along.

"I heard that men who wear suits all the time are covering their own soft desk-job bodies." I shrugged, and he raised his gun, this time pointing it at me.

"Dean, are we good?" Mary called through the ship's intercom system.

"Tell her to join us back here," the man ordered me.

I shook my head. "Why would I do that?"

He moved the gun to the side, firing at Clare, who saw it coming and rolled out of the way. "Because if you don't, I'll kill this one." He fired again, but Clare was already pulling her own gun from the strap on her leg. She shot the man as his beam struck her in the arm.

It hit him in the leg, and he stumbled, dropping his

gun. I lunged at him, tackling the shorter man to get him away from the weapon. Clare groaned but walked over to us, holding her pistol in her left hand.

"What's going on back here?" Mary's voice carried across the room.

"I'm dealing with a stowaway," I said while getting off the man, leaving my knee on his chest.

Mary came to my side as the man cursed me, tears falling from his eyes. I wasn't sure if it was from the pain or the humiliation.

"What are we going to do with him?" Clare asked, her voice grim.

"Collateral." Mary and I got him to his feet, half-carrying him toward the bridge.

"You won't get away with this!" he yelled, but I was beyond caring what this man said. I only wanted to get to the planet.

"Where's the colony located?" I asked him as we entered the bridge. We half shoved him into the communications seat, and he almost slid out, his leg wound obviously painful. I took his tie from around his neck and used it as a tourniquet on his leg, cutting off the flow of blood. He screamed as I twisted it a little more than I needed to. "Where is it?"

"On the eastern coast of the largest ocean," he said, head slinking down. He called out some coordinates, and Mary quickly moved us toward the planet.

"Clare, are you okay?" I asked, and she nodded, holding her arm.

"It's just a flesh wound. I wish Nick were here to fix it," she said, and I agreed.

"We'll have him back sooner rather than later. I swear." I hoped I could follow through with the promise.

The planet approached quickly through the views-

New World

creen. It was a beautiful sight. Having followed the hybrids to another planet, and having seen Earth a few times from space, I knew I'd never grow tired of seeing a world from this vantage point. It was awe-inspiring.

Still, no ships followed us, and that meant Slate was up there causing all sorts of issues for them. I took a seat at the helm and checked the radar. Four ships followed a single one that was unpredictably flying away from the planet. I silently wished him luck as we entered New Spero's atmosphere. The ship shook slightly, and then we were heading down toward the location our now-passed-out friend had given us.

The comm-device beeped, receiving a message. "This is NS-001. Your ship is untagged. Identify yourselves."

Mary looked at me for guidance. "No point in hiding it. Take us in slowly." I reached over to the console and tapped the reply icon. "NS-001, this is Dean Parker, Mary Lafontaine, and Clare LeBlanc coming at you from the past, requesting clearance to land this bird."

There was a pause from the other end before a crisp message came back. "Dean Parker, we're sending you the landing details. Over."

Mary keyed them in, taking us over a desert landscape at five thousand feet, slowly descending as we neared the landing pad. The terrain changed as small mountains jutted out from the ground, the land growing greener as we went. Eventually, we were able to spot structures, and I let out a whistle. When I'd first thought of a colony, I pictured straw huts and campfires. I wasn't prepared for the small city we saw.

There were no high-rises in sight, but a few multistory buildings popped up all over the area. A city full of residential areas, commerce, and agriculture was evident as we flew over it all. My heart pounded in my chest. We were here. New Spero.

The landing pad was a few thousand feet long. Dozens of different types of vessels sat idly, and we chose a slot as close to the outbuildings as we could. If we needed a fast escape, we wouldn't have to traverse the long runway.

"How's the readout?" I asked, knowing Clare was working on gathering data from the probes we'd shot as we entered the atmosphere.

"Perfect. It's warm, like a spring day in California. Within two percent of Earth's atmospheric blend. This is amazing." She stared at the screen, her pain all but forgotten as the scientist in her took over.

The ship settled down. "We better bring him," I said, indicating the groggy suited man in the chair. I tapped his cheek with my palm a few times. "Time to wake up," I said, unsure of how our first steps on the colony planet would go. We might need him as a bartering chip.

Mary and I lifted him by the shoulders, mostly dragging him back to the bay, where Clare hit the ramp icon to lower it. "Remember, we're survivors. Whatever we find down here, we'll make it. Together."

Mary smiled at me, blowing a kiss in front of the dead weight we were carrying around.

We stepped down the metal ramp, warm air blowing against us. I held a pistol in my right hand, Mary had one in her left, and Clare was in front of us, a pulse rifle raised and ready. I suddenly wished Slate was there with us.

We reached the ground, which was some sort of sandstone-like rock, a good place for a landing pad when you didn't want to waste a large amount of concrete. No one was there to greet us.

"That was a little anti-climatic," Clare said, lowering her rifle slightly and scanning the horizon.

New World

We set the wounded man down, which gained a few groans from him. He needed medical attention; he had lost a lot of blood before I'd used the tie on his leg.

A slight hum came from the direction of a nearby warehouse. I spotted a cart, like the ones from the base on Earth, coming toward us.

"Get ready," I said, holding my pistol up, ready to look for cover if I had to.

It closed in on us, and I couldn't believe my eyes. It was Magnus. The cart stopped twenty yards away, and a woman in uniform stayed in the driver's seat as my old friend came rushing toward us. Clare still held her gun up, and I called at her to stand down. She'd briefly known the man, but he did look different. She listened and stepped out of the way as Magnus came crashing into me, his wide arms crushing me in a bear hug.

"Dean, you son of a bitch! Oh my God, it is you!" He held me back, gripping my shoulders tight. I saw his face then, the youth from his thirties gone, wrinkles creased around his eyes as he smiled at me, gray lining his hair and stubble. Tears were streaming down his face, and I found myself crying too. "Mary! I can't believe you guys are alive." It was Mary's turn to be picked up and swung around by Magnus, and she squealed, matching tear for tear with the big man.

"You have no idea how good it is to see you, Magnus," Mary said, wiping her face with her free hand.

"Magnus, before we do anything, I need you to call up to the base and tell them to stop chasing our friend, and to take it easy on Nick." I didn't want to break up the reunion, but I couldn't let anything happen to my new friends.

He looked at me, confused, before cluing in. "No problem. Laura, comm the station." The woman had been within earshot, and soon we heard her convey our message.

"They said Andrews is missing," she called back to him. Magnus' gaze found purchase on the body slumped on the ground. "The ships are calling off their chase."

"I think I found him," he said, grinning at me like old times. "We have a lot of catching up to do."

THREE

"Is he going to be okay?" Mary asked.

Magnus nodded. "He's fine. Already up and walking. Modern medicine has changed a lot since we last saw each other." He waved his arm in front of him. "Even in this backwater planet we call home."

"I'd hardly call what you have here a backwater anything. It looks like paradise to me," I said, following the man down the street. People walked by on the sidewalks, heading into different stores. They were labeled with basic names – *clothing*, *grocery*, *seeds* – and I couldn't shake the feeling we were in some sort of science-fiction socialist regime. I wasn't going to judge it, because under the right circumstances, it had every chance to thrive. The problem was, humans rarely allowed for the right circumstances.

"I know we're going to wait to get to my house to really talk, but, guys, how is it you don't look any older? What the hell happened out there?" Magnus asked, leading us past the stores.

"It's a long story. One Nat's going to want to hear too. How many people live here?" I asked. I had a general idea, because a lot of them had left Earth.

"This city? About half a million, but we're spread out over two hundred square miles. We have places set up all across the world. Different things grow in different biomes, and we have each city manufacturing various supplies. That way, we can trade and keep everyone gainfully employed and productive. It's quite the setup." Magnus looked happy about it, but I could tell he was dying to know our story.

"What's your main export?" Mary asked.

"Agriculture. We have the planet's best soil, and grow everything from food, to hemp for clothing, to bamboo for various things. I bet you didn't ever think I'd be a farmer."

I laughed. There was no way he was being serious. "Are we almost there?" I asked, curious to hear if Nick and Slate had made it planetside yet.

"Not quite. That's why we're taking this." He led us to a camo-covered Jeep-like vehicle, and we hopped in. Mary took the front seat, I grabbed the back. I sat in the center of the rear bench, watching wide-eyed as Magnus fired up the engine and drove down the dirt road. We left behind what constituted cityscape on New Spero, and in a couple minutes, we were away from any signs of humanity. The only evidence anyone had been here before were the tire tracks in the grass we were driving in. "See all this? It's mine."

I looked around us, seeing acres upon acres of farmland, crops growing in the summer-like afternoon. At least it felt like afternoon. I really didn't know what time it was and realized I knew next to nothing about the planet we were on. It was remarkable. If I took a deep breath, there wasn't anything there to tell me I wasn't on Earth, in middle America, somewhere much like the state I'd grown up in. I suddenly felt homesick, but for what or where, I wasn't sure. It was just a feeling gnawing at my stomach.

We kept going for a few minutes. Soon Magnus

New World

turned right and drove down a dirt road leading up to a cabin. It wasn't big, and smoke poured out of a chimney on the left side of the structure.

"Home sweet home," he said, his words adding to the aching feeling in my gut.

"This is amazing, Magnus," Mary said, her voice cheerful. I hadn't seen her so happy in months and tried to picture me and her living in a similar place, quietly farming, minding our own business. No more intergalactic strife to deal with. I wasn't sure how we'd manage, but I was willing to try.

"It's not much, but it's home. I know I didn't have time to tell you anything, but we have a few surprises of our own." He parked the vehicle and we got out. The ground felt soft under my feet, and it did feel alien for a moment. I quickly forgot all of that when I heard a bark. A dog barking, on this faraway planet, brought normalcy back to me in an instant. It woofed again, and my heart sped up. I knew that sound. It was from someone that had become my best friend during the Event.

"Carey!" I called. My hands were shaking as I looked for him. Another yap, and I spun to see him running at us from the house. Natalia was at the door, her hand covering her eyes, trying to see who was with Magnus. He'd wanted us to be a surprise. Carey bounded at us, and I ran toward him, so excited to be back with the little guy. His ears flopped up and down as he raced to me. "Carey!" I said again. He seemed to know it was me.

I fell to my knees, and the dog jumped on me, licking my face with fervor and love. I couldn't recall a time I'd felt more relief or pure joy, and I sat there petting and talking to him, trying to explain why I'd left him. He didn't seem to care at that moment, and we just shared that time together as equals on the ground. After everything we'd been through, this was exactly what I needed.

Once we'd both settled down, I noticed how different he looked. He'd aged well, but at eleven, he was heavier than he'd been, and his eyes didn't have quite the same glow to them.

"Thank you for being there for him," I said to Magnus, who I could tell was behind us by the large shadow. My voice was thick with emotion.

"Dean, we love that dog. It was our pleasure, really," Magnus said, walking over and giving me his hand. I took it, and he pulled me up off the ground. Carey rubbed his head on my shins, and I heard more barking. Natalia was walking toward us, two other dogs in tow. They were cockers like Carey, one brown, and the other buff like the older dog.

"Magnus, who's with you?" Natalia asked as she neared us. Our backs were to her, and Mary and I turned to her, tears already falling down Mary's face.

"Nat," Mary said, stepping over to our friend. It was then I noticed there was a small boy clutching on to Nat's leg.

Natalia cried out in anguish. I almost reached for a gun before it clicked that she was just surprised by us.

"How? How are you here?" she asked, her eyes instantly red, puffy, and adorable at the same time. She embraced Mary, holding on tight.

"If you have a cup of coffee, we can tell you," I said, and she turned to me, grabbing hold of my arms and pulling me into a big hug. She was so warm, and I hugged her back, telling her how glad I was to see her. "Who's this?" I asked, crouching to be at eye level with the boy. The three dogs came over and played, rolling on the grass between us.

"These are Carey's little ones," Magnus said. "Charlie,

the boy, and Maggie, the little troublemaker there." He pointed to the brown one, who gave him a bark. They looked young, but they weren't puppies any longer. "And that," he nodded to the brown-haired hiding boy, "is Dean." Magnus looked at me, a twinkle in his eye.

"We didn't think we'd ever see you again. It had been four years. We wanted to... remember you," Natalia said, sniffling as she held Mary's hand.

It was quite the reunion, and I felt like I'd been through an emotional wringer. "Hi, Dean," I said. He peeked out from behind her leg and looked at me, the perfect little combination of Magnus and Natalia. I was so happy for them. "Look at what you guys have accomplished out here. It's amazing. It's... kind of the dream." I felt the loss hard. They'd had seven years together, building a family and taking care of Carey, and we'd just been on a journey across space for a few months. It was hard to wrap my brain around.

"It's been nice," Magnus said, and I hardly heard him.

"Let's go inside," Natalia said, her accent still thick, but her voice softer than it had been.

We started the walk to their cabin, the dogs sauntering along. Carey stuck close to Magnus but looked back to make sure I was coming. I knew whose dog he was now, and to say it didn't hurt would be a lie. I was glad he was a happy dog who'd had the opportunity to lead a safe and healthy life. I wasn't sure if I could have given him that security.

The smaller brown cocker followed along behind me, playfully romping through the grass, her bark trying to get me to play along. I knelt and scratched her ears, which she rolled over for, kicking her back legs out for a stretch. "Well, Maggie, it's nice to meet you. I think there might be some treats inside the house with your name on them." At that word, she perked up and ran ahead into the house as Magnus held the door open.

Mary stayed behind after the other three entered the home. "Are you okay?"

"I think so. It's just... a lot. How about you?" I asked.

She smiled. "I'm happy to see them. It's just so weird. With the snap of a finger, we missed years of our friends' lives. It'll just take some time. Let's go share stories and have a night where we don't have to think about the next thing."

We did have a lot of explaining to do to the powers that be; Andrews, the suit Clare had shot, was just the beginning. Our friends inside were high-ranking officers, and they were able to pull some strings to get us acclimated to their world before we got grilled the following day. I was grateful for it, but as I entered their house, I hoped the other crew were being taken care of.

"Any word on Slate and Nick?" I asked, taking in the cozy décor of their small home. It was sparsely furnished with homemade wooden furniture, a dichotomy to the futuristic screens on the walls and counters. Lights came on automatically; a clear screen above the mantel acted as a television. I recognized signs of Kraski technology everywhere.

Magnus keyed something into a screen in the kitchen, and a face appeared. He asked the man a few questions and was told the two men from the station were on New Spero, and that Clare was with them. We'd left her at the complex to wait for the rest of our team.

"We've built hotels for visitors from other cities to stay. Your friends are in the suites saved for city leaders. Much better than being cramped up on a ship for months, I tell you," Magnus said after he ended the call.

"Thank you, Magnus," Mary said. "Your home is perfect." She walked around the living room and back to the kitchen. "Dean, maybe we can have something like this." Her words were soft, hopeful. Little Dean came over to me, and I saw he was holding a wooden train.

"Of course you can," Magnus said. "We'll get right on it. I don't want to speak out of turn, but there's house a couple acres over if you want it. Share the land, so to speak. We built it…back then, hoping you would come claim it."

It was all happening so fast, and I didn't know how to reply. On one hand, it sounded amazing, but we had just arrived and had no idea what New Spero was really about. "I think we might like that." I smiled at Mary, and she returned it. I knew Mary loved the idea right now, but her taste for adventure might kick in after a few weeks of feeding chickens and weeding a garden.

"Time for your nap, *malen'kiy*." Natalia took her son's hand, and he let her lead him into another room without complaint.

"What a cute kid. I can't believe you have a son. The last night we saw you, you were just getting married," I said, seeing his shoulders slump all of a sudden, like my words took the air out of him.

We sat in the living room, the smell of coffee flowing through the air toward us. I realized how tired I was then; sitting on the soft cushions, I had the desire to lie down and sleep.

"Dean… Mary," Magnus said quietly, "we thought you were dead. Patty kept asking for word from you, from Earth, and eventually she stopped talking to us about you. I don't think she stopped asking, but she could tell it was getting too hard for us to hear about you after those first few years."

Carey looked up at me from the floor, his head turning sideways. "Come here, boy." I patted my lap, and he jumped up, setting his head on my leg, letting out a sigh that he must have been holding for me for seven years. Soon his breath slowed, and I just rested my hand on his back, letting him know I was there.

"He's yours, by the way," Magnus said, looking at Carey from the other couch. Mary sat beside me, petting Maggie. Charlie was at Magnus' feet.

I shook my head. "I can't take him now; it's been too long. He has his home now, his pack." It hurt to say, but it was true.

"Tell us everything," Natalia said, bringing a tray with coffee and cups from the kitchen.

"Where do we begin?" Mary asked.

"At the start."

"You were married, and Mae arrived, beaten up. The hybrids escaped." I said Mae's name, and I could see they were aching to ask after her, but they knew she was dead. It was all over their faces.

We told our tale to them over the next few hours. The sunlight dimmed in the room, and soft lights automatically came on as we spoke. Natalia got snacks and we drank coffee, them on the edge of their seats at times, while at other moments, tears flowed freely from their eyes.

They learned about the Deltra still living on another planet. Magnus nearly stood as I talked about getting the smaller version of the Shield, and about Mary almost dying by the Bhlat warriors on that lone station far out in the universe. They sank into the couch and held hands as I told them about killing everyone at a Bhlat outpost. Natalia let out a cry as I told them the gut-punch of Mae really being Janine, the woman I'd fallen in love with. It

New World

hurt to bring it up and relive the story. Hearing that Slate had shot her took the wind out of their sails, and neither of them spoke for a few minutes.

When we got to the part about World President Naidoo communicating with the Bhlat, and how we thought she was going to kill us, Magnus turned red. "That bitch! We're going to straighten all of this out tonight."

"I think that Andrews guy is in her pocket," Mary said.

"He has to be. If anyone ever shows up in our system, the station's supposed to relay it to us and await instructions. Evidently, Naidoo asked Andrews to ignore our protocol and take you himself. I'm glad the slimy little slug got shot." Magnus was still red, but Nat's calming hand on his arm seemed to be working.

"That's quite the story," Natalia said. "Mag, I think its our turn."

He nodded. "First, I need something." He left the room, coming back with a bottle and four small glasses. He set them down on the large coffee table. I recognized the brand of Scotch as Magnus' favorite from back on Earth.

"Is that…?" I started to ask.

"The one and the same. I've been saving this for something special. I'd say this constitutes something special, wouldn't you?" The sparkle of my old friend was back in his eye. "Do you remember that day? We got the rings from that guy with the German shepherd."

"And half a truckload of booze. Don't you have distilleries here?" I asked, vividly recalling the day. It was only six months ago to me.

"We do, but there's nothing like a bottle of twenty-year-old Scotch, aged a few more for good measure. God, I wish things had worked out differently that wedding night. I'm going to miss Mae." He poured the liquid into the four glasses, passing one to each of us. "Even though she screwed us over a few ways to Friday, she was something." He raised his glass. "To Mae."

"To Mae," we all said in unison, raising our own glasses in the air. I sipped the Scotch, letting the familiar burn ease down my throat.

"Our trip didn't go so smoothly," Magnus said, starting to tell us about their journey after we left. "That ship left with a thousand people, and we lost a hundred on the way from an illness we couldn't cure. Now it's nothing more than a common cold to us, but at the start, before we understood the way alien viruses worked, it was deadly. That was the least of it, but I won't bore you with the details. The fact was, we arrived a month late, and our morale was low when we lowered to the surface."

"My sister Isabelle?" I asked, fearful at what the answer would be.

Natalia's face softened. "She's fine, Dean. She lives out in Terran Five."

I relaxed, nervous and excited to see the sister I hardly knew any longer. "What happened then?"

"They knew the layout of the planet from their first trip, but we didn't know everything. The weather patterns surprised us, and the wildlife was so unique," Magnus said, pausing for a drink, "but it was paradise to us. Free from the bull of Earth politics, we did what needed to be done. We started at ground zero here and built everything you've seen."

"How did you end up being farmers?" Mary asked, a hint of laughter in her voice.

"I still work for the colony, obviously, but we wanted more. When Dean was born, we left the house we'd built in the city and gave it to a younger couple just starting out. We wanted to be away from the noise and people for once." Magnus set his hand on Nat's, squeezing it lightly. "She deserves a quiet place to raise a family."

"You both deserve it," I said.

We sat in the living room for hours, talking about all the stuff between their landing and now. We drank to old times, we picked away at a light dinner, and before we knew it, we were all tipsy and exhausted. I asked Magnus to pass word to the crew that we would see them in the morning, and Mary and I headed to the guest room Natalia demanded we stay in.

Mary was already breathing deeply as I pulled the blankets over my shoulders. I heard the light pitter-patter of footsteps approach our room, the door squeaked as it pushed open, and I recognized the sound of Carey jumping onto the bed. He came over to me, sniffed my face, licked it, and curled up between my legs.

I slept like I hadn't in months.

FOUR

From the helicopter, we got a much better view of the settlement. We'd been so distracted when we'd lowered in our Kraski ship that none of us had caught a good look at Terran One. Now, flying over at a low altitude, I could make out all the different farms, then neighborhoods, as we headed for the base. Fields of varying colors stretched out beyond the horizon, a grid of sustenance and prosperity.

Magnus pointed landmarks out to us. He also described how each neighborhood had all the necessary supply stores, hospitals, and schools, so the locals didn't need transportation to other areas. It reminded me of old city planning for lower-income areas. They wanted everything necessary along a bus route or within walking distance. For a colony, it made a lot of sense.

It blew my mind to see how far they'd come in just seven years. The amount of work that must have gone into creating what we were looking at had to come at a price. Magnus assured us that they owned worker robots for much of the labor.

In the distance, I spotted a large mountain, pristine lakes mottling the landscape near it, and I knew where I wanted to visit first. I wondered if there was anything resembling fish in that water.

We neared the base, a large structure by the landing

pad we were at the day before. As we settled toward the ground, I spotted my friends near a bay door. Clare, Nick, and Slate stood looking no worse for wear, and I silently thanked whoever was listening for bringing them back in one piece.

"Time to make history," Magnus said, opening the heli door. Mary got down, I ran out after her, and we jogged toward the building. The copter lifted and left us in silence after a few minutes.

We greeted our crew, Mary going for hugs with the two men we'd left in space, me following suit with what started as a manly back pat but escalated into a 'thank God you're alive' embrace. "Everyone okay?" I asked, getting assurances that they were.

Slate grinned at us. "I was having fun up there. I think someone needs to train those pilots better."

"Speak for yourself. Those guards were ready to rip my head off," Nick said. Now that we were just a few feet apart, I noticed the red lines in his eyes and a bruise on his cheek.

"Did they hurt you?" I asked, anger boiling under my skin.

He shook his head. "No worse than I'd expect. I'll be fine. I'm just glad the call came in when it did. I think they were ready to push me out an airlock."

"I heard the news but wasn't going to believe it unless I saw it," a new voice said, coming from the doorway. "If I live to be a hundred, I doubt you'll find me more surprised again."

"President Dalhousie!" I called, happy to see the woman who made all of this happen.

She fluttered my comment away with a flick of her wrist. "No more 'President' for me. Just call me Patty, please."

Patty had been a fit, healthy fifty when we'd last seen her, but the woman before us had been through a lot. She looked like she'd aged twice as much as Magnus. She was now a small gray-haired woman, but the fire in her eyes was still burning bright. Her once long hair was cut shorter, giving her a grandmotherly look.

"I've been filled in by the others, but come on in. We need to talk." Patty hugged us tightly and turned, leading us into the large base through a steel door with guards at it.

"Still need guards?" Mary asked.

"This is a colony, not Utopia. Humans will always be humans, and yes, we do still need policing, and a military for space and New Spero," Magnus answered for her.

We were led down a wide hallway, which ended eventually, and we turned left past a door that required Patty's thumbprint to open. We found ourselves in a metal corridor, and I had flashbacks to climbing the tube on the Deltra station, Bhlat clomping around trying to kill us. Mary seemed to notice a change in me, and she grabbed my hand.

The corridor went on for a couple hundred feet or so, at an ever-declining angle, before opening into a large, cavernous room. Screens were set up at numerous long desks, with a massive screen front and center, where it looked like they could air multiple feeds at once.

"What is this?" Clare whispered, stealing the words from all our mouths.

"This is New Spero Central. We have feeds from all major centers here, and we watch for anything out of the ordinary." Patty walked toward the front row of desks, where five workers sat, headsets on, screens showing various city shots and views from fence lines.

"You spy on everyone?" Slate asked. The question

was so unlike the soldier, I hoped his being around me for a few months hadn't made him question authority. Or maybe it was a good thing for the man who'd obeyed someone his whole adult life to be a free thinker.

"We don't spy on them. This is a new planet. We watch for anything that might pose a threat to the people. We've saved countless lives with our perimeter cams catching predators lurking too close to villages and cities," Magnus said, and I felt better about it all. If my old friend was behind it, then I would blindly follow his lead.

"What kind of predators?" Mary asked, stepping forward to squint at the screen's images.

"Daniel? Can you bring up the feed from 1179, please?" Patty asked, pointing at the large screen in the front of the room.

It showed a snowy landscape, the area fenced with a twenty-foot-tall barrier. Red lights blinked on the concrete fence posts. It took a minute to see them, but once I did, they were everywhere. They were white, almost blending in with the snow. I couldn't tell how tall they were, but they had to be four feet at least. The camera zoomed and paused to show us three of them in a cluster, reminding me of a cross between a lizard and a wolf. Long thick tails left lines in the snow behind them, powerful snouts sniffing the air.

"Holy crap," Slate said, unblinking as we watched the video. It started up again, and we watched as they approached the fence, trying to touch it but getting shocked by electricity. A couple of them repeated the effort and failed, but were still moving, as if the shock was nothing more than an annoyance.

One of the creatures ran over to a concrete fence post, which was at least three feet wide. Another one stepped up, and they used each other to lift themselves up, until there were three of the animals stacked on one another, the top one jumping and grabbing hold of the top.

"We lost twenty people the first night we met these guys. That's why we watch the feeds live."

My stomach sank as I watched dozens of the things get lifted and climb over the fence. They were smarter than any animal I'd ever seen. Patty showed us another video of people forming a violent riot, and how they were able to subdue it quickly. It appeared all wasn't paradise on this colony planet.

"Now, enough about us and New Spero. Tell me how you came to arrive seven years later, looking like nothing has changed, in the same ship you left Earth on," Patty said.

"Should we wait for Heart?" Slate asked, looking around the room.

Patty turned to Slate, looking at him silently for a minute before speaking again. "The general isn't with us any longer. He passed away two years ago: heart attack."

Slate deflated at that and sat down in one of the swivel chairs at the long desks.

"A lot has changed for us. I think you know the new general." Patty pointed at Magnus, who just shrugged when we looked over to him.

"Someone had to do it, and it might as well be someone I trust. Me," Magnus said, getting a tense laugh from our group.

"I'd say congratulations, but I'm sure you'd rather be sitting on your porch sipping sweet tea than worrying about invasions and space station turncoats," I said, clapping him on the arm.

"Speaking of which, where is Mr. Andrews?" Magnus asked Patty.

"He's fine. Almost good as new. He's finding a new home at Terran Three." Patty tilted her head toward the screen, showing the city covered in snow. "He claims Naidoo threatened to hurt his family back on Earth, but I call BS on that. His accounts have shown some interesting deposits over the years. Either way, I apologize for your treatment, everyone. Can we have the story now?"

We moved to the back of the room, where a guard brought in refreshments. I guzzled water as we went through the trip, and my own personal emotional rollercoaster. I was ready to put it all behind us after this telling.

When it was over, Patty mopped her face with a hand, and looked to have aged another year. "After all we've been through, she wants to cut a deal with them. That might explain something."

"What?" I asked.

"It takes a month to get a message to and from Earth. We've sent messages to them but haven't had a reply in over a month. I was hoping there was just a technical issue on Earth, but it could mean two things. Either they're choosing to not talk with us" – she paused, leaning forward in her chair – "or they aren't able to talk to us."

"Why didn't you tell me?" Magnus asked, clearly frustrated.

"We didn't want to worry you. You have enough on your plate," she replied.

"You wanted me in this position, you have to tell me everything. Would you have held this back from Heart?" he asked, receiving a blank stare from Patty.

"The Bhlat are coming for Earth, one way or another," I said. "Naidoo opened the door for them and invited them in. What do we do about it?"

"What do you mean? We need to worry about New

Spero's safety now. We gave those people a choice, and whoever's on Earth chose to stay, knowing the dangers. They were all part of the Event, just like all of us. The universe is a dangerous place," Patty said.

This wasn't the president I remembered, always worried about everybody. She was older, tired, and jaded. "It may not be your job to help Earth, but I'll be damned if we're going to sit back and wait for the Bhlat to come to us too. Let's look at it like we're going on the offensive, and saving Earth is the positive result." I thought speaking her language might help my cause. It appeared to.

"It takes two months to get back. It could be too late by then," Slate said.

"Or they chose not to transmit because they knew we were arriving and would blow up their story. It might not be too late at all. Maybe a carefully worded message would do the trick," Mary said, making a lot of sense.

"Another thing is bothering me," Patty said quietly.

"What's that?" I asked, wondering just what else could be wrong.

"The hybrids."

I couldn't believe I'd been so selfish to forget them. "The hybrids," I repeated, a flush coming over my skin. "Where are they?"

"We thought they were trouble. As far as we knew, Leslie and Terrance were terrorists, and were the reason you were lost to us. They were killers, and we couldn't trust the lot of them," Patty said.

Dread set in. "Where are they?" I asked again.

"They're in a prison in Russia. Half the world's leaders wanted to ship them into the sun, but we compromised on prison. Forever."

She looked terrible, the guilt of their anguish evident on her face.

"We have to do something!" I said, remembering the friendly faces we'd met in Long Island. Seven years in prison, and I doubted I'd get the same reaction from them. "I know where they're welcome. I'll send them there to have new lives."

She nodded, but it seemed a distant, noncommittal action. "If we get through this, you have my word that you can do just that. I'm sorry about Mae too, for what it's worth."

An alarm chimed from the front of the room, and Daniel, the officer on the computer, called back to us. "General, you're going to want to see this. Trouble in Terran Five again." The screen showed us the white lizard-wolves stalking toward the city, this time in a different area. It looked like they were crossing a frozen lake.

"Wait, they aren't coming for the fence," Daniel said as we watched them change direction. It was snowing, wind blowing fiercely, causing a white-out. He zoomed in a mile or so, and we spotted a blurry barn. A group of people were outside, surrounded by horses.

"What are they doing outside like that in a storm?" Magnus yelled. He jumped on to a computer and tried for a few minutes to contact Terran Five. "No luck. The storm must have killed the transmission tower. All this technology, and we still use waves to communicate with each other. Come on, Dean. We have to go help them." He tapped the face-to-face calling program, trying for any contacts under the Terran Five: Operations listing. They all failed.

If those creatures were that close, I knew there was no way we'd make it in time, but we had to try. "Are the other Terrans closer?"

"Good call. Dan, send a request for assistance to Terran Four. We're taking a cruiser. Anyone else?" Magnus asked.

Mary and Slate ran after us, heading toward the landing pad.

★ ★

The ship was smaller than any we'd ever been on, more the size of a helicopter than anything I'd seen, but it acted much the same as the larger Kraski ships. Two seats up front, two in the back, and as much room as a cube van in the back for storage. The walls were lined with climbing gear, medi-kits, and weaponry: everything we needed for a rescue mission.

We'd tossed on suits before getting on board, and they reminded me of the modified space suits from our recent adventure. These didn't have the helmet attached, and though they were thin, their primary function was to fend off the cold, with an extremely high puncture rating. That would help prevent one of those lizard-wolves from biting our extremities off.

"How far is Terran Five, exactly?" Mary asked, sitting up front with Magnus, who was acting pilot on the vessel. Slate sat in the back with me, his large frame tight against the undersized suit he wore.

"Eleven hundred miles as the crow flies," Magnus said, the landscape of the planet zooming by as we flew near top speed toward the Arctic-like city. "That makes our trip a quick twenty minutes. Those monsters can go fast, but they were skulking along that snow, the storm probably slowing them some."

"Why have a colony city in the snow?" Slate asked, breaking his contemplative silence.

Magnus shrugged. "Why do people live in northern

New World

Canada or Alaska?" He waited for a reply. "No, seriously, if you know, tell me." He barked a laugh, and when no one else followed suit, he continued. "They have resources up there. A stone much like diamond, that sparkles like a geologist's dreams and conducts electricity better than anything we've ever seen. And it isn't always snow-covered. Just three-quarters of the year." This made him laugh again, and I joined in this time, for his sake.

"Of course," Slate said, his question satisfactorily answered. "Did those colonists lose a bet?"

"You're a funny guy, Slate. I think I'm going to like hanging out with you. We asked for volunteers, and after all everyone had been through, living in a safe place with everything you could need to survive, we didn't have to do a lottery. We had all the positions filled in a week. We were as surprised as you are." Magnus tapped some icons, and the ETA appeared on the viewscreen. Ten minutes to destination.

"Did we get through to Terran Four?" I asked, and Mary sent a message to Dan back at the home base.

"Dan says they left just after us," Mary answered.

"It'll be close. Everyone ready? Shoot to kill. I know we're the aliens here, and believe me, we do have animal rights activists on our asses here too, but lives are at stake. Stick together, and hopefully, we can extract the group before too much damage is done." Magnus lowered us below the clouds, and instantly, we couldn't see beyond the viewscreen. Snow enveloped the small vessel, but he had no problem flying it using the computer navigation system.

The plan was to land a hundred yards from the structure in the video, and get between the oncoming creatures and the humans, if we weren't too late. It took another minute for Magnus to lock in on the coordinates, and

41

when he did, we lowered quickly to the ground, still unable to see much more than blowing white flakes as we bumped the surface softly.

The doors hissed open, hinging toward the sky, and we got out, pulse rifles in hands. My heart pounded and sweat covered my back, a contradiction to the freezing temperatures outside. Why had we come with Magnus? Shouldn't we have left this type of thing to the trained soldiers? Then it hit me: I was the only non-military among our group of four, and probably still had more experience in the field than half the actual soldiers now filling that role on New Spero. My confidence increased, my steps becoming firmer and my grip a little lighter on the rifle as I followed Magnus toward the barn we could just make out through the snowstorm.

"You two go right," Magnus called through our earpieces.

Slate and I obeyed, cutting right to flank the people on the other side. Only when we arrived, there were no people standing up.

The familiar hum of a transport vessel came at us from our other side, and soon another ship landed near us, armed men emerging from the doors, much like we had only moments ago.

Magnus shook his head. "Damn it! We're too late."

That was when I saw it. The half-eaten horse lay blanketed by a thin layer of snow, a pool of blood staining the white ground. The closer I looked, the more I saw signs of a struggle, footprints from both humans and animals mixing, but quickly being covered by the ever-falling snow.

"They might still be alive," one of the newcomers said to us. "These things will feed" – he pointed at the horse – "and drag anything else back to their nests. We have

New World

some at Four, but they're smaller and fewer. Seen it a few times."

"Let's go after them," Magnus said matter-of-factly.

"In this storm, we'll be lucky to make it a mile without giving up," the new guy said, the three other soldiers with him keeping quiet.

"Look…" Magnus started to argue, but we all stopped short as we heard a small voice.

"Help! Daddy!" it called from the barn.

I ran toward the sound, gun raised just in case. "Where are you?" I asked, voice rising above the wind.

A small figure emerged into the doorway, wearing a snow suit and a pink hat. It was a little girl, no more than seven years old.

"I'm Dean. What's your name?" I asked, knowing she would be terrified.

"Monica. They took my daddy," she said, fat tears arriving at the corners of her eyes.

"Who did? The animals?" I asked.

She nodded.

"Which way did they take them?"

She pointed to the west. "He told me to hide in here, under the hay pile. I miss him. We were out for a horse ride, and Queenie hurt her leg. The horse doctor lady came with some help. Then *they* came."

I didn't have to ask who *they* were.

"I like her." The tears were starting to fall. "Isabelle, the horse doctor. She makes me laugh. Can you find my daddy?"

I felt like I'd been punched in the stomach. Isabelle. My sister was a veterinarian, and Magnus had told me she lived in Terran Five. It had to be her.

"Guys, we're going after them." One of the men from Terran Four came over and gave Monica a heated blanket, ushering her toward their transport vessel. My friends nodded grimly. "I think my sister was among the ones attacked."

Mary's eyes widened. "How's that possible?"

"I don't know. The girl said her horse got hurt, and they were stuck out here from the storm, and a horse doctor named Isabelle came to help. That has to be her." I was shaking with adrenaline and the need to stop talking and go rescue them.

"Let's go. These little bastards are cave dwellers, so we either attempt to follow the tracks being covered by more snow every minute, or we assume they're going to the mountain three miles west of here and fly there," Magnus said.

"I'll follow the tracks and meet you there." Slate took off on foot. His pace was fast and efficient.

"You heard the man, let's get on the ship or he might beat us there," Mary said, moving for it already.

"You guys will never find them, and if you do, how do you know they aren't already dead?" one of the guys from Terran Four asked.

"We don't know, and that's why we're going. Get that girl back inside the gates, and tell them what's happening right under their noses," I said before rushing toward the transport.

Moments later, we were taking off, and if possible, it seemed the snow was falling even more heavily. As we neared the mountain, I felt a tugging I couldn't explain. It was like nothing I'd ever experienced. I sat in the back of the transport, my blood starting to burn. I wanted to cry out, but I couldn't.

"Ma…ry," I squeaked out through the pain. Her face turning to me was the last thing I saw before all went black.

FIVE

When my eyes came open, I was alone in the small ship. My body still ached, but the searing pain was gone.

I felt for injuries and scanned myself for blood, but everything seemed normal, except for a throbbing headache. I moved to the medi-kit and shot myself with a small dose of painkiller, instantly feeling the thumping subside.

"Mary, Magnus, come in," I said into my comm, but no reply came. They must have known I was breathing, and had gone for the people first, hoping whatever happened to me wasn't fatal. Seeing me passed out, but having to leave my side, must have been difficult on Mary.

I threw on an insulated cap and grabbed any weapons I could fit on myself, along with a few rations of food and an emergency kit. One thing I remembered from those outdoor TV shows was you never went into a situation without being prepared. Especially heading into a mountain full of alien monsters, on a planet you'd just set foot on the day before.

Satisfied I was ready, I lifted the door, exiting the ship. The cold hit me like a brick wall, and I ran through the blowing snow toward the mountains. The footprints were fresh enough that they were still easy to follow.

"Dean!" a voice called thinly through the wind. "Dean!"

Gun ready, I spun, only to see Slate running toward me. "You okay?" he asked. When I nodded, he asked where the others were. I told him what had happened, and he stepped closer, looking me straight in the eyes. "You look fine," he said, and with that, we were off together after Mary and Magnus.

"Did you see anything out there?" I asked, assuming he saw nothing but snow and ice.

"Yeah. They dragged them along this path. There must have been some fight left in the people, because one of the creatures was limping along, left behind. It was hurt pretty badly, so I put it out of its misery."

The way he could casually talk about killing something always struck me as cold, but I think a part of me was only annoyed that he could turn it off when I held on to it so tightly.

The signs of the creatures and their prey were everywhere as we neared an entrance to the hillside. The mountain was tall, reminding me of visiting the Rocky Mountains as a teenager. Foreign trees lined the countryside, and I tried to focus on the task at hand, knowing I would have time to study this new world once we got our people back. The wind bit at my face, but the suit kept the majority of me warm as we followed the footsteps and drops of blood into an opening in the rock wall. The stark contrast of red human blood against the snow reminded me we probably didn't have much time.

I tried the other two through the comm system, but either the storm or the rock was causing a disruption, and no one replied. The cavern opened up wide, and we turned our suits' lights on, allowing us to see in the dimly-lit space. It looked like a huge bear cave, the kind you wouldn't be stupid enough to run blindly into. We did just that, guns raised, ready for anything, but we saw and

New World

heard nothing.

The large room got smaller, the ceiling coming down rapidly as we went, and soon we were stuck with a choice of left or right. The cave separated into two tunnels, and we didn't know which one to take.

"What do you think?" I asked.

Slate looked angry at having to decide. He was better at shooting first and thinking later, so this wasn't his forte. "We could split up," he suggested.

"With no radio communication, that adds to our risk. Let's go left." I went with my gut, and Slate seemed happy with it. He took the lead, gun up and lights shining forward as he bulldozed down the ever-tightening hallway. When I started to worry we would get stuck, it widened again and opened into another cavern.

"Where the hell did they go? Should we go back and try the other option?" I asked.

Slate started to answer, but I thought I could hear someone calling my name, and I didn't make out his words. An alien sensation ran through my body, akin to the racking pain from inside the transport vessel, but more subdued: clearer now. My feet were moving, but I didn't recall telling them to. It was as if an outside force was pulling strings, and I was a puppet. The rational part of my mind told me to be afraid and wanted to panic, but I didn't. I went along with it, taking comfort in the new control.

"Dean?" Slate said my name, but he sounded miles away. I felt a tapping on my arm, but I didn't stop and turn to him. I kept moving, flowing down the floor toward my goal. I wasn't sure what that was, but it was close. So close.

"Dean! Stop walking; you're freaking me out!" Slate was in front of me now, his large frame preventing me

47

from continuing. I bumped against him, getting angry that he'd try to stop me from getting to wherever it was I needed to be. My pulse rifle raised, pointing at his chest.

"What the hell is wrong with you?" he yelled, moving away from my aim, which didn't follow him.

"I must get there," I said, the words not my own, but from some part deep inside me. I could feel the blood pumping in me then, each beat of my heart pushing the life-force around my veins.

"Get where?" he asked, but I was walking faster, leaving him in the cavernous room as I exited through another hallway. This one wasn't as tight as before, and for the first time, I noticed carvings on them. The part of me that was being pushed down tried to force itself out, to warn me something was wrong, but I didn't let it. The hieroglyphics became denser on the walls as I went, and I could make out the sound of footsteps following at a safe distance behind me. Slate wasn't a threat, so I didn't worry about him.

The hall went on for a couple minutes before I reached my destination, which I knew the moment I crossed into the room. The energy was palpable, and my blood sang, thrumming in my ears like an airplane taking off. The LEDs on my suit flickered, and a small part of me wanted to scream. The other part was excited, ready for what was coming.

"Dear God," Slate said from behind me.

A light illuminated thirty or so yards inside the room, starting out small: a clear gemstone, glowing blue suddenly. I stepped toward it and the light expanded, the drawings on the walls of the cavern burning hot blue as well.

"Dean, I think you should stop," Slate said, but he didn't come anywhere near me.

The room was at least one hundred yards wide, and I

New World

could see it all now, basking in the cool blue light. In each corner, manufactured pillars were erected, fitting from floor to ceiling. In the center of the pillars, which were spread out the full distance of the room, stood a table of sorts, made of the same material as the columns. The gemstone hummed a near-silent but constant song, and the blue rays pulsed in it, seemingly in time with my own heartbeat.

I neared the gemstone, squinting against the bright light, and saw the table had small illuminated icons on it. There were at least fifty of them, each a unique image of hard lines and squiggles. My hand settled flat over them, moving of its own volition, and I heard Slate calling to me.

The words were getting louder, and I turned to see him rushing toward me. I felt my finger touch down on the table. The icon it hit grew bright and bathed the entire room in green light. Slate collided with me, but something told me he was too late.

★ ★

The light was gone, along with the pounding of my heart on my eardrums. I lay on the ground, recalling walking away from Slate, and knew I wasn't in control of whatever had taken over me. It left me feeling dirty and used.

"Slate?" I asked, not able to see anything in the dark room. I fiddled with the LED controls for my suit and they flicked on, casting a white glow over the larger man beside me. He groaned, sitting up before feeling himself for injury.

"Dean, just what the hell were you doing? First you

pass out on the way over here, then that?" His voice was raised, telling me he was at his wits' end with me. Slate liked things he could understand, and what had happened didn't fall into that category.

"I have no idea. My blood was burning, pumping hot and fast, then my brain disassociated, allowing something else to move me. I'm sorry for pointing a gun at you. I swear it wasn't me."

"It sure looked like you," he muttered under his breath. Slate turned on his own suit's flashlights and stood up, taking stock of our situation. We weren't in the same room we'd just come from. The air felt stale and thin. Slate unzipped a breast pocket, unfolding a breathing mask from inside, and I followed suit. With the mask against my face and strapped to my head, my breaths took on a smooth flow once again.

"How do we get back?" he asked.

"Don't you want to know where we are?" I asked, scanning the room. It was a far cry from the rocky floor we'd left behind. This room was manufactured, the floor a solid metal alloy, the walls silver and smooth. A stone, much like the one in the cavern, sat behind a glass case; the same icons were visible on the screen. I walked away from it, seeing the drawings etched on the metal walls. Wherever we were, it was eerily similar to the place we'd just come from.

"I'd prefer to go back and help the others." Slate was touching the glass screen above the stone, but nothing illuminated or moved. It was dark.

He was right. They needed our help. My fiancée was in danger and trying to rescue my sister. If I ever needed to get somewhere to assist, it was now.

"Why did it work back there?" I asked under my breath. My heart rate was fine now, my mind clear. "You

New World

felt nothing? No draw to that room, or to the light?"

Slate shook his head. "I felt angry. Angry at you for walking into it blindly."

I couldn't blame him. "Let's look around, and maybe we can figure out how to get back. This has to be some sort of teleportation device. I wish we knew where it sent us. Probably to the opposite side of the planet." I held my gun up, moving to the side of the room, wishing there were lights so I didn't have anything jump out at me from out of the darkness.

"This time let's stay together, okay?" Slate grumbled, moving in front of me. If he wanted to take the lead, I'd let him. I'd already shown there was a glitch in me. My back twitched, reminding me of being shot on one of the Kraski vessels during the Event. I had Mae's… Janine's blood in me still. That was it.

"I think the device picked up on my blood being alien. Maybe it recognizes the Kraski DNA and allowed me transport." I was grasping at straws, but it was the only thing that remotely came close to an explanation.

Slate looked thoughtful a moment before turning to me, grabbing me by the shoulders. "Dean, if that's true, what was it doing on New Spero? I thought this was an unspoiled planet. If there's a device that allows Kraski transport, then –" He stopped talking, letting go of me, his shoulders sagging slightly. "We aren't on the other side of New Spero now."

I didn't reply. Instead I walked to the doorway, which didn't open. The power was down here. Slate grabbed hold of a manual lever, and pulled hard, the cords of his neck straining as he did so. Eventually, the door popped, hissed, and slid open.

The hall beyond was dark, ominous. My imagination told me there were creatures out there, ones that would attack as we passed any corner. Another part told me we were on a station where the entire crew was killed in an intergalactic attack, their spirits lingering and angry, waiting for redemption. With a quick shake of my head, I tried to let my childish fantasies dissipate, leaving me calculating the facts.

"If there's no power, maybe we can find a backup system and turn it on." If we could get power to the area, the touchscreen with the icons might lead us back to the cavern. It might have worked because there was no power needed for the carvings.

Slate didn't reply; he just began moving quietly and efficiently down the hall. I tried to emulate his movements, making more noise than him, but not enough to put a target on our backs. We tried a few rooms along the way, manually opening the doors, but none of them proved helpful. It all had an unused feel to it, like it had sat empty for a very long time. I was left feeling queasy, and suddenly wished we were back at Magnus' farmhouse, sharing a meal and laughing about the rescue we'd successfully pulled off. I focused on that feeling and set it as my intention. Now I just needed to get from here to there. That was the hard part.

"This place feels wrong," Slate said, whispering the words near my ear. Our speech was muffled slightly by our oxygen masks, and I wondered at how much time we had breathing from them. We hadn't had enough time yet to have their newly advanced technology explained to us.

"It feels old." It all felt very far-future, but ancient at the same time.

We kept moving, seeing no signs of life anywhere. Eventually, we made our way to a large doorway, which opened into a massive room. Clear crystals glowed ever-so-softly in the middle of the room, casting an unwelcom-

New World

ing glimmer over the entire area. As we neared them, we could see they were encased in a tall glass cylinder that stretched from floor to ceiling, appearing to go on for at least fifty feet.

"Either this is part of a ship's engine, or this powers the facility we're in. I wish I knew more about advanced alien civilizations." I meant it as a joke to lighten the mood, but even I couldn't smile as I said it.

"I think we know enough for my liking." Slate looked intense, like he was reverting from the fun-loving soldier we'd started to see on our journey together.

I turned to him, looking him in the eyes. "Other than the obvious," I said, waving my hand, palm up, around the room, "is something bothering you?"

He seemed like he was going to slough off my question, but his mouth twitched. "I was up there, flying around space, avoiding being blown to smithereens by some inept New Spero station pilots, and I got to thinking, what if? What if I do die here? What if I've lived my whole life bent on revenge for my brother dying, before finding out there was no one to blame? The Event nearly destroyed our world, and many of us came out different people, but I was still a soldier for the same people I hated for sending us to war in the first place."

"That's in the past, Slate," I said softly.

He ran his big hands over his close-cropped hair, and I could feel the frustration emanating from him. "What if I never find a good woman? What if I never have a family of my own? What if I die here, never getting an ending to my story, when it's been so full of anger and resentment up to this point?" His words were getting quieter as he went, and I wanted to give the guy a hug and tell him it would be all right. But truth be told, I could empathize with his story, even though it was so far removed from my own.

"Tell you what. Let's figure this out." I pointed at the crystals in the tube. "Then we can find our way home and you can retire, meet someone at one of the colonies, and live that dream out on New Spero."

"Do you think we'll actually ever be safe, no matter where we go?" he asked.

I didn't know, but the threat looming over our heads with Earth and the Bhlat clouded my thoughts. I resolved right then and there to make it my business. We'd been thrust, whether fairly or not, into the middle of the battle between the Deltra and the Kraski, and then the Bhlat over all of them, and unless we resolved it, we would never be truly safe.

"I'm going to make that happen." I felt foolish for saying it, but Slate nodded, accepting that I meant what I said.

His jaw took on a hard line, a new resolve that we'd need to figure this puzzle out. We spread out over the room, looking for anything that might have power left in it, or a manual switch to turn on. A half hour later, we'd both found nothing and were back in the same spot we'd started the search from.

"Now what?" he asked.

"We keep searching." I led the way back out of the room, upset we hadn't found anything, but sure the answers were out there, within the metallic walls of the strange structure. The weight of the bag of supplies on my back was starting to get heavy, and I knew I was about five minutes from asking Slate to carry it for a while. I was glad I'd brought provisions into the caves. It looked like we might end up needing them after all.

Once again in the hallway, we kept going, avoiding the smaller side rooms, which at this point were fewer and fewer. Maybe the exterior of the hall walls was touching outside at this point. That would explain a lot. It could either be a pedway, if we were above ground, or just a corridor to connect two structures together.

Eventually, a door appeared at the end of the walkway. A small glass window allowed us to see through the thick metallic door, and I peered into it, expecting to see more of the same.

Someone was looking back at us from the other side.

SIX

"Get out of the way," Slate said, shoving me to the side and raising his gun.

"Hold on. It didn't look armed." Whatever it was, it looked as startled as I'd been to see someone there.

Slate waited a moment, his back against the wall beside the door lever. He held his finger in front of his oxygen mask, telling me to stay quiet. We heard nothing. After staying like that for a long minute, Slate snuck over to the glass and looked through it.

"They're still there. Sitting on the ground, arms in the air. What the hell is that?" he asked, and I moved beside him, looking in. The alien was stout, a dark uniform adorned its body, and it looked like it had multiple limbs. Two were in the air, another two fidgeting nervously in front of it. It was dark in the hall, but when I shone my light through, large eyes looked back, reminding me of a baby seal. Underneath the eyes, a protuberance emerged, not unlike an anteater's snout, but only about five inches long. The whole effect was non-threatening, but things in nature often appeared that way to lull their prey. I wasn't going to be fooled.

"What do you think?" I asked.

He shrugged. "Maybe it can help us get back home." He said the word *home*, and for a second, I thought of my house in upstate New York. That wasn't my home anymore. We didn't have one.

I agreed, and we decided to open the door, but cautiously, and with rifles pointed at the defenseless-looking creature.

The door popped, then hissed as Slate slid it, and I kept my rifle pointed at the alien, who scrambled back, all four of its arms now raised and waving around. It let out a series of squeaks and squawks in the process.

"Hello," I said, lowering my rifle. Slate kept his pointed in the alien's direction, but I took the lead. "I'm Dean, and this is Slate. We're lost and need help getting out of here."

It clearly didn't understand me and kept chittering away, the noises a mix of bird and dolphin. "We don't know what you're saying." I pointed down the hall from where we came, hoping it would know we'd emerged from the room with the solitary gemstone and hieroglyphics. I drew one of the symbols in the air with my right index finger and repeated it a few times before the alien seemed to acknowledge it comprehended.

"You coom from fer away." It spoke in squeaks, and a speaker on its suit repeated in near-English. Once again, I was amazed by the universe's ability to translate language. The more I spoke, the sooner we could speak fluently together.

"We do come from far away. Very good. As I said, I'm Dean," I paused, putting a hand on my chest, "and this big man with a gun is Slate. We mean you no harm." Slate lowered the gun beside me and tried to smile, but it looked forced and a little scarier than the gun. I glowered at him and he stopped, giving me a real smirk.

A few more squawks: "I am Suma. I mean you no harm."

"That's good. I was getting worried," Slate said, noticeably relaxed in front of the short alien.

"Stay on guard. We don't know anything about Suma here." I whispered the words, but the alien got onto its wide feet, and I saw it was even shorter than I'd initially thought, no more than four feet tall.

"I stuck here. Want father."

I clued in. This was a child. "How did you get here, Suma?"

It pointed the way we'd come. "Same way you did. Through the *Shandra*. The Stones."

My blood turned cold at hearing the name. *Shandra*. It was as if part of me understood the word: an ominous portent of things to come.

"Slate. That name. The puppeteer guiding me through the caves. I think my Kraski blood led me there, and now I feel as though I know the name. *Shandra*."

Suma's eyes went wide when I said *Kraski*. "You not Kraski," it said matter-of-factly.

"No, I'm not. But have some of their blood pumping through my veins." Suma took a step back at that, like I was some sort of freak, hell-bent on stealing alien blood. "It's a long story, and it was given to me freely to save my life. If we can travel through the Stones, let's go. You can show us how it works."

It squeaked a couple times, the translator not picking up what Suma said. "I cannot show you."

"Why?" Slate asked, his jaw muscles flexing.

"Because we are stuck here."

The thought of being stranded on this alien world turned my blood to ice. I needed to get back, to help my sister, but that outcome was probably already decided. I could only hope it ended with Mary and Magnus leading those people out of the cave, and back to their homes.

"How did you get here?" I asked Suma, who looked

New World

like an admonished child as it spoke.

"My father is the Gatekeeper on my world. I was playing with my brother, and I hid inside the *Shandra*. I somehow turned it on, and I came here by accident," Suma said, and I was ninety percent sure Suma was a female of her species. I couldn't bring myself to ask, in case I was wrong, or in case they didn't have different sexes.

"Why won't this one work?" Slate asked.

"The stone needs to be charged, and this one is too weak." The translator was working almost perfectly.

"That means we need to find the juice to light this building up," I said. "Do you know where we are? Are we still in Proxima?"

Suma looked at me, head cocked to the side, like she was trying to comprehend the name I'd just said. "I think this is one of the outer cities: a civilization that vanished thousands of years ago. My people haven't studied all of the planets thoroughly yet, but I believe this is one of those abandoned."

Thousands of years. I looked around at the hall we were in. To think a race of aliens walked them centuries upon centuries ago was mind-boggling. I couldn't help but wonder what had happened to them. "You're saying the stone can transport us to any number of planets, and they all have a similar room where you appear and can travel from?"

"Yes. Some are buried deep on worlds that have no idea the Stone exists. Others have been destroyed over the millennia. My world is one of those in charge of keeping them active where possible." The squeaks and squawks became softer. "I'm going to be in so much trouble."

"Do the different drawings on the table represent different worlds?" I asked, excitement at the possibilities causing my hand to start shaking.

"Yes."

I glanced over at Slate, whose gun hand was at ease. He leaned against the hallway, deep in thought.

"How do we power up the stone?" I asked.

"I don't know. There has to be a backup system somewhere, because my people have been here and returned before. I'm not permitted to see the logs yet."

"Why's that?"

"Because... I'm still a child in their eyes." She looked down, her snout wiggling in discomfort.

"Suma, we'll find the power and get you home safe. Right, Slate?" I asked.

"Right, boss," he said, giving me a determined look.

"How long have you been here?" I asked the smaller alien.

"Two cycles of *Saaranla*."

"Is that long?" Slate asked.

"I've had to sleep once."

I slung the pack from my back, getting a bottle of water out. I opened it and passed it over. She looked at me dubiously, big black eyes glistening in the dim light. "It's water. Take it. We have more." I did have more, but only enough for a couple days, tops. When she found a way to stick her snout into the bottle top and slurp some liquid up, I passed her an energy bar, which she told me tasted like *Laaran*. I took that to mean something bad, judging by her reaction, but she ate most of it before tucking the last few bites into a pocket.

"Thank you, Dean," she said through the translator.

"How far have you gone?" Slate asked her.

"Not very. I was afraid I'd get lost, or that my father would track me. But that's foolish. The Stones don't keep track of destinations. He wouldn't know where I'd traveled to."

"Boss, let's keep moving the way we're heading. It has to lead somewhere, and if we aren't expecting any baddies hiding out in the shadows, we can move quickly and not worry about noise," Slate said.

I looked at Suma, hoping we could trust her story. Every instinct was telling me we could, but I'd been wrong before.

"Let's move." Slate grabbed my pack, taking the burden from me, and I was grateful for the respite. We'd only left the complex that morning a few hours ago, but it already felt like days.

We moved as quickly as we could. Suma's short legs carried her quite well, and she had no problem keeping up with us. We kept going, checking doorways as we went along. Half of the rooms were empty; the other half didn't seem to have a purpose we understood. If the race had vanished a long time ago, maybe they'd packed up and left the world in search of somewhere else.

Eventually, we came to a large door, with nowhere to go but back or through it. Beside it a smaller slab stood, probably a maintenance closet. The large door had a viewscreen on it, but with the power out, it was blank, so we couldn't see what was on the other side.

"This has to lead somewhere important. It's the first entry with a viewscreen, and it's much larger than all the others," I said. "Suma, what do you know about these people?"

"Not much. We study the worlds in school, but I didn't see what diagram I touched. It was all an accident. If it's one of the outer worlds, it's rumored they ran from something, abandoning whole worlds, traveling far away, never to be seen again." She shifted on her large flat feet.

"Adds up. It looks like these guys left of their own

volition, but why?" Slate asked, reaching for the manual lever. "Do it?"

I nodded. "Do it."

The door opened, and we were hit with a gust of wind, sour air pouring in from outside. I walked over, trying to comprehend what I was seeing. We had to be a couple thousand feet up. Huge buildings were erected into the clouds, with intricate pedway systems between them. The city went on for miles in all the directions I could see from my vantage point. I felt nausea creep upward from my toes to my head, before settling back in my stomach. It looked like something from a nightmare. The sky was dark, electricity shifting from cloud to cloud before shooting lightning bolts down toward the ground.

Slate closed the door to shield us from the blowing wind. "What now?" he asked.

Suma's back was against the wall, and I remembered she didn't have an oxygen mask like us. "Suma, can you breathe?"

Her eyes were wide, and her snout frantically flailed. I slipped the mask off my face and hoped giving her oxygen wouldn't do more harm than good. She breathed deeply through what passed as her nose but was still struggling to get enough air without a proper seal.

Slate opened the small door beside the entry. "It's a closet. Bingo." Slate rifled through piles of junk before he pulled out a mask, passing one to me.

"How does it work?" I asked, but Suma was already grabbing it and placing it on her face, twisting a cap on the bottom. It hissed and her panic subsided.

After twenty or so seconds, she removed the mask. "If we go outside, we will need these. The planet's atmosphere is not stable."

"There's no tank on this thing. How does it work?"

New World

Slate asked.

She moved her lower arms in a gesture I took to be a shrug. "Look at your mask. Does it have a tank? Same principle."

I hadn't given it much thought, but it appeared a filter mask worked with a science that was beyond me. Or it was magic. Either way, I was okay not understanding it.

Slate, on the other hand, was playing with one, trying to comprehend the process.

"It's the end of the line. Let's mask up and go out there. The power source may be underneath us, a mile or so from the base of the building," he said, looking at me for confirmation. When I nodded, he passed me one of the masks. "These look superior to the flimsy airline ones we have attached to us. Let's use them."

"What makes you think the power is under us?" I asked.

He pointed inside the closet door, where a paper blueprint hung above a shelf. It showed a few buildings, with blue lines coming from a source below that looked similar to the stones in the room we'd found earlier. It appeared to power a few square miles, each building having lines connecting to it. The image was detailed, and I ripped it off the wall, folding it up and shoving it into a pocket.

"Might come in handy. And here I thought you had some insight into alien technology," I said, smirking at him. "How do we get down there?"

Slate started for the door. "Let's find out."

"Suma, do you want to stay here?" I asked the small alien female, who was already putting the mask back on. Her snout bent to the side inside the glass-encased mask, but she could still speak through her translator, though the squeaks were muffled.

"I will come. I may be of help," she said.

The last thing I wanted to do was put her in danger, but if we didn't power up this dead building, we'd all die here, so I didn't argue with her.

Slate opened the door, the cool stale wind blowing against us again as we moved from the relative safety of the structure to outside. The lightning crackled, startling Suma, who grasped my arm; I patted her hand, letting her know it was okay. Even in the wind and eerily black sky, it was near silent out there, and that added to the strange feeling in my gut.

We were on a balcony that wrapped around the rectangular building. I walked around it, getting much more of the same vantage: miles of similar skyscrapers, all dark and dead, pedways connecting each of them. I pointed to a building next to us. "That has to be where we came from." I ran a finger in the air, tracing our steps from the room we arrived in, across the pedway, and toward the door we'd met Suma at only a half hour ago. Out here, it looked like our journey so far had been nothing but a quick jaunt across a couple of city blocks. The sheer distance the city went on for, and the fact it was supposed to be abandoned, made me feel uneasy.

Closing my eyes, I took a deep breath of filtered air, calming myself. The only way to get back to New Spero was to power this grid up. I only hoped there was a way to do that below.

Slate was already walking in the other direction, his stride full of purpose. Suma walked along behind him, all four arms firmly at her sides.

"Dean," Slate called, "I think I found the elevator."

I hurried to catch up, focusing on them the whole time to forget I was so high up from the ground. I was worried vertigo would kick in and I'd be left clutching a

New World

wall, unable to help. I neared and saw the device he was talking about. It was a lift with four sides, but no visible cables. "What do we do with this?"

Suma stepped forward, pulling a small tablet from a pocket on the back of her uniform. "There is an energy reading still. Sometimes these civilizations ensured they wouldn't get stuck, so they had backup systems in place."

Slate looked at her dubiously. "They don't consider the *Shandra* worthy of backup power?"

Suma just did her lower arm shrug again and continued. "I don't begin to suggest I understand their reasoning. The lift appears to be controlled by these foot pedals." She pointed with her top left hand to a spot where two metal squares were etched with different symbols on each.

We were all standing on the lift, looking closely at the floor, when Suma crawled over and pressed one of them. We didn't have time to react as we started to move very quickly. I fell, pressure keeping me down on my knees as we lifted higher and higher. "Stop it," Slate croaked.

Suma hit the same lever again, and we came to a stop at the next level. I stood up, this time getting a full view of the city. We were even higher, twice as high as we were, and even in the darkness, I could make out an ocean of lava in the deep distance. To the other side, mountains, as black as midnight, loomed like a bad omen. No wonder these people had left their home.

"I'm going to guess the other lever takes us down?" I hadn't finished the question when Suma hit the lever, and we were quickly descending. This time, knowing it was happening, we were able to stay on our feet. I grasped the railing on the side of the lift, as did the other two, and I wondered if a harness system would have been safer.

As we lowered, I kept my eyes out for a structure

we'd seen on the blueprint. There it was, a few standard blocks away, maybe half a mile in total. I only hoped we'd find a way to turn the power source on once we got there. I pointed toward it, and Slate nodded as the lift slowed and stopped at ground level.

We exited the lift, my legs and stomach both glad to be off the thing. The ground was made of a concrete-like substance, and considering how long it had sat at rest, there were very few breaks in it. Every twenty or so feet, I could see signs of something trying to come up through it. Nature always took over, unless you were on an abandoned alien planet. Maybe the lava and lightning were what constituted nature on this world. I didn't intend to be here long enough to find out.

Slate moved with efficiency, Suma and I following along, me with my gun at ready, though I could see no sign of any threats. It never hurt to be prepared.

Suma began to slow, and I slowed alongside her. "Are you going to be okay?"

Her snout twitched under the clear face-plate of the filter mask. She squeaked a reply. "I'll be fine. We don't move this much at home." I kept with her slower pace, Slate eventually noticing we weren't right behind him. He slowed as well but kept fifty yards ahead.

There wasn't much of interest down on this level: mostly just the bases of the skyscrapers, and some maintenance sheds. The living appeared to all happen above ground on this planet, or at least in this city. It wasn't long before we made it to our target. The building, a squat, square brick-walled complex, looked out of place among the thin, cloud-high structures around it.

I ran a gloved hand along the smooth stone walls as we looked for a door. It all worked together: the traveling stones, the gemstones in the clear cylinder up top, and now this. My mind flashed to the stones we'd worn to stay on Earth while everyone else was lashed into the ships. It all worked together on a scale as large as our universe. One day, I suspected we'd understand it all. Today, I just wanted to find a door, get some power, and leave.

"Over here," Slate said from around the corner. It was still quiet down on the ground, but the wind was blowing small debris around. Pebbles and small metal sheets clattered down the streets, reminding me the planet wasn't so much different from our own.

Suma and I rounded the side of the building. Slate was there, pulling on the door. It wouldn't move. I grabbed hold of what had to be the handle, and we both tugged on it, even putting our legs on the wall for leverage. Nothing.

"Keep looking for another way in?" I asked, but Slate was shaking his head.

"I'm growing tired of this place." He lightly shoved me back and unslung his pulse rifle, red beam blowing a hole in the rocks. He did this a few times, until the opening was large enough to get through.

Suma had jumped and hid behind me. "You're safe, Suma."

She shook until Slate put the gun away. "What is that?" she asked.

"It's a gun; a weapon."

She tested the word, a strange sound through her small snout. "Weapon."

"You don't have guns where you come from?" I asked, curious that a race might be non-violent. No wonder she hadn't seemed too afraid of our guns when we'd encountered her. She was just afraid of seeing pasty near-hairless aliens.

"We don't have guns." She didn't elaborate.

"Boss, can we do this later?" Slate was getting into Rambo mode, and I was good with that. I closed my eyes for a split second, seeing Slate standing over Mae's bleeding body. *Target down.* I shook it off and patted Slate on the shoulder.

"We can do this later. Let's get some power."

SEVEN

The inside of the power plant, for lack of a better term, was black. Our LEDs lit the way as we entered, guns raised against the off chance we were about to be ambushed. We stood at rest, listening for any sounds. All we heard was the wind dancing around outside the hole in the wall.

Slate motioned us forward, and Suma stayed behind me. I couldn't tell if she was more afraid of the unknown or of Slate. Either way, I would try to keep her feeling safe. We were in a small room with lockers along the wall and a table in the middle of the room. I searched through the cubbies, finding uniforms and heavy boots. The material was thick on everything, but clearly made for something other than a human. I held one of the one-piece uniforms up, and imagined thin legs and a tail, with arms down to their knees. I guessed I'd never know for sure.

In the middle of the room, Slate searched under the table, and found an assortment of tools. Some looked much like ones you'd find in any house's garage, and others were far more complex. "I hope we don't need to use one of these to turn the power on." Slate held up a device with ten prongs sticking out of it, and what looked like thousand-year-old grease piled on each tip.

Suma walked over to him, sorting the tools on the table, not saying anything. I smiled and headed for a doorway that would lead us further inside.

"Are you ready?" I asked, more for the sake of saying it than needing to.

Slate was always ready. He nodded, raising his gun as I turned the handle, feeling the years of neglect fight me as I pressed the lever. It eventually moved, and I pulled, opening us up into the next room. It was the right door, which was good, because it was the only door.

"This is it," Slate whispered as we walked inside the large open bay room. Machinery sat in clumps along the edges of the room, but the center was what drew our eyes. A massive clear crystal the size of a dump truck sat glimmering as our lights reflected off it. The thousands of edges on it each angled the light out in a beautiful pattern around the room's wall and ceiling. "Isn't that something."

It was. Where the crystals in the "boiler room" we'd seen up top had been glowing a tiny bit, this one was dead. It was just a crystal down here. The largest single crystal I'd ever seen, but it was here.

"Does the rock power things, or does it just act as a transmitter?" Slate asked, and I shrugged, having no idea.

Suma came behind us, her black eyes even wider than normal. She walked around the room, and just as I was about to tell her to be careful, I noticed she wasn't just out for a stroll; she was figuring it out. She found an input into the crystal and traced it back to the machines sitting idly around the edges of the room.

Five minutes later, she was standing at a large machine that looked like a combination of a commercial furnace, an icemaker, and an oil derrick. It was just ten feet wide and twelve or so high, but she stood at the hunk of junk like it was going to be our savior.

"What do you have there, Suma?" I asked, breaking

New World

her from her analysis.

"This is the start. We fire this up, the rest will follow. In ideal scenarios." The small alien continued to astound me. Clare would love this one. Mary would too. I'd been trying to forget about my friends and loved ones since we'd traveled, just wanting to focus on the task at hand. Thinking about Mary and getting back to her gave me a well-needed boost of energy.

"What do we do?" Slate asked, hands ready to work.

"We have to get each operational again. Mostly cleaning and lubricating."

A few minutes later, we started moving from machine to machine, of which there were about seven, leading up to the initial power generator. Slate held the ten-headed lubricator tool and stuck it out, trying to get me to take it.

"No way. You made the joke earlier, you deal with it. It's only fair." I spoke too soon, because that meant I was crawling under the machines to make sure the wiring was in place and intact. They looked different than the cables I was used to, but I imagined the principle held the same. They were thick, round, and clear. Instead of metal as the conductor, it looked like a fiber-optic material, possibly the same as the crystal. I wasn't sure.

An hour later, we were covered in dirt, grease, and sweat, but Suma thought they just might be operational.

"Let's move back, just in case something goes terribly wrong," I suggested, moving from the center of the room to the side, beside the first machine, from where we could also make a quick exit.

"It has a hard start," Suma said, moving to a panel on the machine. It had a touchscreen on the outside, but it was dark.

"How do you know all this?" I asked her.

"My father is the Gatekeeper, and my mother studies

how other races tick. She's a technology expert of many solar systems. She wants me to take after her, so I've learned how to understand machines."

"Is that what you want to do?" I asked.

Her lower arms raised up into her version of a shrug. "I suppose. I really want to take after my father, but after today, I suspect I'll never be allowed in the *Shandra* again."

Her honesty was refreshing, and I hoped we could get her home to hash it all out. Whatever she did, she'd do it well. Her hands found what looked like a large primer and pushed it, while turning a knob to the left and holding it. Soon my feet vibrated, along with the floor.

"You did it!" Slate exclaimed. Suma beamed, her snout twitching inside her filter mask.

Lights appeared on the first machine's touchscreen, and symbols I didn't recognize glowed on a white background. Suma peered at them thoughtfully before hitting a series of icons. The vibrations increased as each machine began to spring to life, one at a time, ten or so seconds between them.

Recessed wall lighting glowed white as the power made its way around the room, and soon our suit lights were unnecessary. Mine turned off automatically, and I saw Slate's do the same. My friend was grinning ear to ear, and he stuck his fist out for a bump. I happily obliged.

"You're amazing, Suma. How long before…" I stopped asking the question as the huge crystal began to glow from the center out. It was like watching the sunrise from a high vantage point. One moment it's dark, the next a soft glow, and in a while, you're covered in all the sun's glory. We stared at the stone for five minutes, feeling the energy vibrate off of it. A series of cords glowed from underneath it, snaking out toward the city, the clear fiber optics blue with energy. It was a brilliant sight. Eventually, we had to avert our eyes to avoid damaging them.

"Time to see if our building is up," I said, making for the exit. "Great work, Suma. Your parents will be proud of you." Her pace slowed at this, and I put an arm around her short shoulders.

"Thank you, Dean," her translator said after a small squawk.

We headed outside and could already see the effect of the power being on. Buildings started to light up floor by floor, until we were covered in the soft glow of a long-dead city block. Street lights I hadn't even seen before were on, lighting our way back to the tower.

"That's better," Slate said, casually walking with his rifle slung over his shoulder. "We should be able to get back up and to the room in twenty minutes."

I was happy with that timeline. I wasn't sure how long we'd been gone, but it hadn't been more than a couple of hours yet. Given the circumstances, that was a win.

The sounds of the city had changed when the power turned on. There was a constant hum as things turned on for the first time in centuries. In a few lower buildings, which appeared to be stores of some sort, I spotted screens playing advertisements.

"Hold on," I said, walking over to one. A thin alien, with a tail as large as its legs, talked to the audience, his language silent through the glass window. His face was long, with no visible nose and a slit of a mouth. His eyes were deep-set and marble-sized, black as the night was now. He pointed up, long arms extended to a sky that was still partly blue but in the middle of a lightning storm. "I think this was before they left. Before things got too bad here." The video was short, ending and repeating on a loop.

The constant hum we'd been hearing accelerated, and the ground shook violently, almost enough to send us sprawling. I grabbed the wall, and Slate caught Suma, steadying her.

"That can't be good," Slate said, looking around for a sign of trouble.

"Who knows what happened when we fired it up? Maybe we caused an explosion in a building's power system." I was going to say more, but a loud screech cried through the air, causing us all to cover our ears.

When I looked up, five small drone-like ships were hovering near us. They were each only about a foot across, but the red lights flashing on them made me think they weren't there to guide us home.

A series of robotic commands came through the front one's speakers, and Suma's translator automatically relayed the message. "You are trespassing. Drop any weapons. Place hands on your heads."

The message repeated twice before we caught it all. "What happens if we don't?" I asked quietly, hoping Slate was on the same page as me. Our eyes locked, and his finger twitched, ready for a trigger. I spun, pushing Suma behind me, and fired my rifle in quick succession, hearing Slate do the same thing. The unsuspecting drones didn't even move as we blew four of them out of the air, scrap metal falling to the ground in a clank. That left one, which flew away spewing out commands Suma's translator didn't pick up.

"Run!" I said, keeping Suma in front of me. The drone was following us, and we were only half a block from the lift to bring us back to the platform where we'd started this city walk. Small blasts hit the ground between us as we zigged and zagged down the road, Slate firing back over his shoulder as we ran.

Just as we neared the lift, Slate turned, stood firmly, and took aim just as a red beam fired at him. He let off a volley of shots, being rewarded with a small explosion. He jumped to the side to avoid the red beam, which ended up hitting the ground at my feet. "Yeah!" he cheered.

"Let's get out of here." I moved to the lift and we all got on, Suma hitting the pedal again. The sooner we got back, the sooner we'd get the hell out of this abandoned nightmare. The lightning seemed to be flashing more often now, and after having been below, walking the city streets, I could see why a race would want to leave this place. It was unnerving.

The lift carried us upward, my knees holding firm against the sudden change in trajectory.

"What's that noise?" Suma asked, moving to the side of the lift.

I hadn't heard anything, but when I concentrated, there was a constant hum again, this one getting louder by the second.

Suma pointed, and Slate and my gazes followed along to see a cloud moving to intercept us.

"What the hell is it?" Slate asked, his voice panicked, but it only took us a few more seconds to answer that. It was a horde of drones.

EIGHT

"We have to get inside!" I yelled as the lift stopped short of the platform we needed to get to. "Suma?"

"It's stuck." She pressed the pedals, but nothing happened. "Maybe they jammed it."

We were only five feet from the ledge, and Slate jumped, pulling himself up with a grunt. I saw the cloud of drones coming in fast, and at this distance, I could make out individual units, rather than a clump of them. We were running out of time.

Slate's hand reached down, and Suma grabbed it. He pulled her up with ease as I jumped, grabbing the ledge myself. I worked at pulling myself up, the months of training having done wonders for my upper body strength. The first laser fire hit as I rolled to my side on the platform, Slate and Suma already running for the doorway. I chased after them, smoking holes appearing on the walkway around me as the hundred or so drones fired away at us.

The door was there, and Slate got it open, ushering Suma in first. When he turned to let me in, I felt the shot hit. It burned into my leg, nearly causing me to fall, but Slate grabbed hold of my collar and threw me inside like a bouncer tossing a drunk onto the street. He slammed the door shut behind us, pulse fire hitting the outside of the building like rain on a tin roof on a hot summer day.

New World

"Will it hold?" I asked no one in particular. My leg was bleeding, but it looked more like a graze than serious damage.

Suma was moving down the hall to a touchscreen on the wall, which was lit up in glowing green light.

"If I can…" Her mask was off her face, and her snout was straight forward, the ends of it mechanically moving back and forth. The gesture seemed a mixture of concentration and nerves. Her thick hands fluttered across the screen deftly, and in a minute, the firing ceased.

Slate was activating the window screen on the access, which had been black before we had the power on. It now showed us what was on the other side. The hundred or so drones had stopped attacking and were slowly moving back the way they'd come.

"Great work, Suma. How did you do that?" I asked.

"I knew they would be linked to the network somewhere. I just had to break through their clearance settings. It was basic. We've had this technology for centuries." She made it seem so easy, and I stumbled toward her, throwing my arms around the small alien girl.

She didn't seem to understand the gesture at first, but soon I felt her four arms wrap around me, and Slate was there, picking both of us up.

"Quite the team. You did well, little buddy." He patted the girl on the shoulder, and she beamed, her big black eyes wide. "You too, boss." As if I needed the motivation. My calf was burning up, but I knew we could get back soon if the device would work. Slate slipped some water out of my bag, and we all drank, relishing the refreshment. I realized just how tired I was; the exhaustion of the day started to take its toll.

I found a bandage inside the pack, and after rolling up my pant leg and painfully washing the wound with a liberal amount of water, I placed the cloth over my calf. It stung but already felt better. They evidently had improved the bandage, because if I didn't know better, it was healing me on contact.

"Time to go home, Suma." I got up, and we started to walk back the way we'd come. The place was lit now that the power was on, making it much easier to see our surroundings. I could see the signs of centuries of vacancy, even in the sealed corridors. Our footprints were still on the floor, evidence we'd been the first people to tread on the floors in a long time. When I closed my eyes, I could feel the echo of a race that had once lived vibrantly in a technologically advanced society. I prayed they still lived and thrived on a new world, much like we would on New Spero.

The trip was fast, and soon we were walking past the room I thought of as the boiler room, the stones glowing blue, energy thrumming out into the halls and rooms of the high-rise. We kept moving, arriving at the *Shandra*, the room we'd started our adventure in.

"Here goes nothing," I said, approaching the door. My heart pounded in my chest, my face getting flushed as I worried the room would be dark, dead. We'd be stuck forever on this horrible empty world.

The door slid to the side with a hiss, and Suma let out a tweet her translator didn't relay. The room was dim, but as we entered it, the hieroglyphs came to life along the walls. So many places to see, so many worlds out there. I couldn't let my brain think about it, because it made everything I knew seem so small and insignificant. If there were hundreds of known worlds with rooms just like this, that meant the universe was so much larger than even the corner we'd seen, travelling faster than light and traversing wormholes.

New World

Suma led us to the center of the room, where the table stood.

"Which world do you need to go to?" she asked.

Slate and I looked at each other. The sickening feeling that had finally started to subside was back.

"Proxima. We call it New Spero." My own voice sounded distant to my ears.

She looked at the icon options. "Which one?"

"We don't know. Until a couple of hours ago, we had no idea what a *Shandra* was, or that we could use them to travel between worlds," I said, trying to keep calm, but failing.

"I'm sorry, but I don't know where your home is." The squeaks came out softly, and I could tell that Suma was upset she couldn't help us.

"Your father is a Gatekeeper?" Slate asked, showing more common sense than me.

"Yes. My world's finest, and we come from an ancient lineage of gatekeepers."

"Then he'll know how to get us home." Slate slid his pack and rifle off his shoulders and nodded to the table. "Take us there."

"I can't. If I bring strangers through, he'll be very upset. I wasn't supposed to be using it. I'll never be allowed through again." Her squawks rose in pitch.

"Suma, he'll understand. I'll take the blame," I said, hoping the rest of her race were as sensible and kind as she'd been.

"Okay. I do want you to make it home. I like you both."

I smiled at this, and Slate's face stayed intense and impassive. I wondered to what lengths the big man would have gone to twist her arm into helping us. I pushed it away, since we weren't going to have to find out.

"Are you ready?" she asked. We held our belongings and said that we were.

She used the console on the table, tapping an icon with four arrows crossing over each other like a compass. A mountain range stood behind the symbol. Soon the rock lit up, and the room went so brilliant I had to close my eyes. This trip was far less startling, since we hadn't been moving and were expecting it, but I still felt nauseous as the light dimmed, and we found ourselves in a totally different place.

A siren emanated from beyond the door at the far side of the space. This room was massive, at least twenty times the size of the last one, and the pillars stood a great distance apart. The floor was white, like pristine marble, not a speck of dirt evident to my gaze. The walls were adorned with pictures on screens, reminding me of my favorite section of the Metropolitan Museum of Art. New York suddenly felt like a lifetime ago. I looked up, but the light coming from the ceiling was too bright for me to see how high the room went up.

"Tell me this is your home," I whispered to Suma, who gave a lift of her snout, which I was starting to associate as a smile.

"It is home."

The doors opened, and a dozen beings entered, their thick legs and torsos looking a lot like Suma's, but they were at least twice her size, dwarfing even Slate. "Oh boy," I said under my breath as Suma stepped between us and the quickly advancing entourage of her people.

"Stop," she said, twitching at how loud her own voice came out. She fiddled with something on her sleeve, and when she spoke again, the translator was turned off. It was a private conversation, and she didn't want us to be part of it.

New World

A man at the front of the group knelt as he arrived at Suma, wrapping his four arms around the smaller alien. He squawked at her, his voice much deeper and more threatening than hers. She visibly shrank at his admonishing, and I instantly knew the sight of a daughter being disciplined by her father. A minute later, he rose, lightly pushing Suma behind him, and he stepped forward until he was only two yards from us. I saw Slate tense beside me, so I reached a hand out, setting it on his arm. "It's okay," I said, hearing my words translate through Suma's father's suit.

"It is not okay. You should not be here, hoomans." The last word came out wrong, and it felt all the more ominous for the misnomer.

"We agree. We just want to get home," I said, adding a hint of supplication to my voice. "Suma is an amazing child, and we can't thank her enough for helping us get out of that city."

"From the sounds of it, she wouldn't have been able to get back without you two either. I suppose I owe you some gratitude," his deep bird-like words translated.

"We really just want to get back. We don't want to waste any of your time, sir."

He motioned for the rest of his crew to relax, and a few of them left the room, their heavy steps echoing in the large open chamber.

"You now know of the *Shandra*, and I cannot allow you to leave," he said, pausing, and Slate reached for his gun, "without being trained how to use it properly." Slate lowered it, giving me a side glance. At least I knew he was always ready to survive. I needed a guy like that at my side.

"Come, we will take refreshment." He turned, leading us away.

"You sure this is a good idea, boss?" Slate asked when we were a good ten yards behind Suma's father.

"If we're going to win a war against the Bhlat, I have a feeling we'll need every trick in the book."

Slate's eyes lit up, and I could see him already beginning to calculate how we could use the *Shandra* to our advantage. I had an inkling and hoped the training we received would be enough to implement it and change the tides of the inevitable war that was coming.

NINE

"Goodbye, Suma," I said, hugging the small Shimmali girl. We'd learned a lot about their people in the short couple of hours on her world. I promised we'd be back, and she was excited to meet my mate, as she called Mary. "Thank you, Sarlun." I stuck a hand out to Suma's father, who, once you got to know him, was a strong and intelligent man. It made a lot of sense to have this man guarding their portal to other worlds. Shimmal was a small tropical world, with lush green trees rising hundreds of yards in the air as far as the eye could see. They lived on a fruit-like diet, and though they had an abundance of amazing technology, they elected to stay grounded and close to nature. It was a prime example of an elevated society.

Suma and Sarlun left us at the table, now having confidence we could get back home. I slid the tablet into my pack. It contained the star charts for every *Shandra* planet out there, and with it, we could go anywhere. There were also notes on each civilization from each planet they had on record. There were some that remained unknown, and Sarlun urged me to avoid many more. When he handed me the tablet, I swore I would.

I waved as the door closed, and Slate and I were left alone in the bright white room.

"What do you think, boss?" Slate asked.

"I think knowledge is power, and we're a lot smarter after today. I also think I need to go back and make sure my fiancée and Magnus made it out safely." If they or my sister were hurt based on our disappearance, I wouldn't be able to live with myself. Sarlun assured me some beings were drawn to the stones like a *Slil* to a flame, which I assumed was something akin to a moth. When I'd told him about my near out-of-body experience when I first found New Spero's portal, he just gave what could only be a knowing smile.

I tapped the table, like I'd been taught, and found the symbol we determined to be that of New Spero.

"Ready?" I asked, and Slate nodded his assent. The icon glowed as I touched it, and the room went bright once again.

When I opened my eyes, we were inside the cavern, the etched hieroglyphics glowing softly. I now found myself recognizing some of the symbols and felt the power this new tool at our disposal had.

"Quick, let's see if we can find any signs of our friends." I ran for the doorway, Slate following behind, his rifle at the ready. We hurried through the caves, back the way we'd come, and at the entrance, elected to go the other direction, deep into the mountainside. Cold air filled the halls, the smell of decaying meat mixing with the stale breeze.

"This way," Slate said, taking the lead. We emerged in a large room, where the signs of a battle were evident. I saw dozens of dead animals and a lot of blood. Scraps of human clothing lay in tatters across the floor, and I knew there was no way everyone had made it out alive. The urge to cry out for Mary was strong, but I didn't want to draw attention to the deadly animals if they were still lingering around a corner.

New World

"Let's go. I think they got out. Look," he said, pointing to footprints in the pools of blood. They were heading the way out. I saw signs of those same footprints as we went back for the exit, and soon we were back outside, freezing cold air filling my lungs as I ached to scream Mary's name.

The snow was still falling heavily, any signs of footprints long gone. We'd been away all day, at least eight hours, and when we reached the spot where the transport vessel had been sitting, there was no evidence one had ever been there.

"Damn," I said quietly.

"Come in, Terran Five," Slate said into his headset. He repeated it a few times, but he just got static in return. "Looks like we're walking. You up for it?" He glanced at my injured leg.

"I think I can make it. I'm more worried about freezing to death."

"The sooner we get moving, the sooner we're warm." Slate started to walk, taking my pack again.

Terran Five was only a couple of miles away, and even though the snow was piling around us, making each step a difficult one, I knew I'd find Mary at the other end, and that was enough to keep me moving at a fast pace.

★ ★

Mary and I sat side by side on a couch, hot coffee on the table in front of us. I felt like I'd never be warm again, even though I'd been inside for an hour already. Her arm was bandaged; otherwise, she looked no worse for wear.

Her hand slid over to me, intertwining her fingers with mine. We left the rest unspoken. We'd both thought there was a chance we'd lost the other today, and the relief was great as Slate and I showed up at the gates. They'd told us Magnus and Mary had returned with the missing people. I'd fallen to my knees as they said the words, half from the pain in my calf, half from happiness that they were all right, no thanks to me.

Magnus walked into the room, smiling wide at the sight of us on a couch. "You guys make this all seem so normal." The hospital waiting room was cramped, and with Magnus in it, the space we had shrank in half.

"I just want to see my sister," I said, butterflies dancing in my stomach as we waited. Mary assured me she was going to be fine. Isabelle had been bitten by one of the creatures and had lost a lot of blood, but she was in good hands.

We gabbed, me finishing my story about the *Shandra* while drinking coffee. An hour or so later, a nurse approached us and told me I could come in.

"Are you coming?" I asked Mary.

She shook her head. "You go alone. She needs her brother."

I understood but still wanted her by my side. Setting my cup down, I got up on a sore leg and realized just how exhausted my body was. I'd end up in a hospital bed myself if I didn't get some rest soon. I took tentative steps while following the nurse down the short corridor, and after a few doors, she led me into a room with beeping machines and blinking lights. My sister lay on the bed; bags were hooked up to her, and her eyes were closed.

I went to the bedside, reaching out to grab her hand. She looked so small and pale. Someone moved in the corner of the room, and I noticed we weren't alone.

"Hey, are you a doctor?" a familiar voice asked.

The day had been rough, so when I saw the man's

New World

face, I nearly dropped to the ground. I hadn't seen him in a long time, not since a few months after the Event.

"Dean?"

It was James.

My old friend came toward me, a questioning look on his face.

"James! What are you doing here?" I asked.

"What am I doing here? What are you doing here is the better question!" Both of our voices had risen, and I saw Isabelle stirring from her slumber. "You're supposed to be dead." He lowered his voice; the word *dead* was nearly an inaudible whisper.

I grabbed the man, hugging him fiercely. Seeing someone from my pre-Event life brought it all back, and I stood there holding James, tears flowing freely from my eyes. When we pulled apart, his eyes were red and puffy, probably a match for my own. "I'm not dead," was all I could bring myself to say.

"Am I?" a small voice asked from the bed.

"No, Issy. You're not dead." I turned to her, really seeing my little sister for the first time. She looked so much older than the last time I'd seen her. Seven years was a long time. Seven years with interstellar travel, and life on a harsh colony planet, could be a lifetime.

"But... how?" she asked.

James pulled up two chairs, and we sat there, each telling our stories of how we ended up together on this night. Theirs was far longer than mine, but luckily with much less danger. Until today, when Isabelle had gone out to help a lame horse in the snowstorm.

"And you two?" I asked, looking from face to face.

James nodded. "We heard you were dead. Magnus held a ceremony for you all, one that Dalhousie wouldn't sanction. He said she never believed you were lost. Issy and I were among the few that knew you, and the only people there that knew you before everything. From our old lives. We'd both been through a lot, just like everyone, and our connection drew us together. She saved my life, Dean." He said the simple words, used over and over by people over the ages, but in this case, I believed him. His face was full of lines, his hair gray and receding, but there was a sparkle in his eyes that only the love of another human could provide.

"I couldn't be happier for you two. I'll come back later with Mary. We can go on a double date." I laughed at how silly it sounded, but maybe something so normal would be good for all of us. "You sure you're okay?"

Isabelle slowly nodded, her eyes sagging closed. "Dean. I'm so glad you're here. I love you."

"I love you too, sis." I patted the back of her hand lightly, and her eyes fully closed.

"She needs some sleep. Coffee?" James asked, and we stood, leaving the room to its beeping machines and blinking lights.

★ ★

*T*erran Five was quite the complex. I could hardly consider it a normal city, since most of the buildings were connected via corridors and pedways. It reminded me of the alien bases and cities I'd seen. Were we heading in the same direction as those other races? They did it here because of the long cold months, where being outside for more than a minute could result in frostbite, or worse.

Our rooms were in a visitor apartment, not far from the landing pad and military base, and we were grateful for the private suite.

New World

Light crept in through the windows, the midday sun occasionally peeking past the thick cloud cover that T-5 never seemed to get rid of. Mary was still sleeping soundly beside me, her chest rising up and down slowly in a mesmerising flow, lulling me into a semi-conscious state. I'd slept for a solid eleven hours, and I still felt like I needed more.

Mary and Magnus had left me in the transport, worried I was dying of some unknown cause, and I let them know they were right to do so. The lives of the colony people were more important at that moment. They followed the tracks into the cavern and were ambushed by a few of the creatures as they entered the room where I'd seen the blood. All in all, they killed twenty or so of the wild animals before the rest scampered away, but they got their say in, biting Mary in the arm and Magnus in the thigh.

One of the colonists had been dead on arrival, but the other three had made it back, Isabelle being the worst off. As I watched Mary sleeping, I wished I could have been there to help, but knew the resource I'd found was more important. I'd told Magnus and Mary about it, and we decided to keep it under our hats for the time being. If we passed the details on, we had no idea what kind of abuse the *Shandra* would suffer, or for whose cause. No, we would keep the information to ourselves, and make that decision when the time came.

"Dean?" Mary asked as she rolled over and rested her head on my chest. It was familiar and comforting.

"I'm awake. Just thinking."

"I was dreaming that we took a vacation. I don't know where we were, but there was a beach, and some drinks." Her warm breath was lulling my eyes closed.

"We should go on a vacation. Or find somewhere on

New Spero to relax for a while."

"We should. Let's talk to Magnus about helping us set it up," Mary said before her breathing deepened again, and I decided to close my eyes. Today could wait; I needed more rest.

Sleep came, and I rolled fitfully as I dreamed of the *Shandra*, the star map, and the palm-sized Deltra device I still had stashed away.

TEN

"I can't tell you how good it was to spend some time with you. With both of you," I said, looking across the table at my sister and James. "You look great, sis."

"I feel about a million times better. You didn't have to stay all week, you know. James was here for me." Isabelle glanced over at her husband. I'd learned they'd been married last year. It brought a dichotomy of feelings to me. On one hand, I was so happy they'd both found love, but on the other, I was upset I hadn't been there for either of them, and I'd missed my little sister's wedding.

"It's been great to see you too." Mary had met them each once after the Event, but both occasions had been a whirlwind of rushing, interviews, and politics. For us to be able to spend a week with them, just talking and playing games, was priceless.

It still felt strange to see everyone around us seven years older. It was as if we'd blinked and missed out on such a huge important chunk of everyone's lives.

"Mom would love seeing us like this. She always wanted us to spend more time together. I'm sorry I was such a spoiled brat when I was younger. I don't blame you for not coming to the coast with us. You had your own life, even though I didn't know it back then," Isabelle said. "I'm sorry about Janine too." She looked sideways at Mary and gave a small smile that said, "Sorry for bringing her up."

"Thanks. It *is* all pretty unbelievable." I'd told her about Mae, and how it was really Janine, the woman I'd met those long years ago in Central Park. To Issy, that was fifteen years ago. Hearing my sister talk about our mother and father over the past few days brought up a lot of pushed-down emotions. It was easy to forget all the things and people who made you what you were when you didn't have anyone reminding you of them.

"You guys are off?" James asked, stating the obvious. We were at the Terran Five landing pad, inside the hangar to keep the cold blowing snow off of us while we waited for the rest of our crew.

"Back to Terran One, and then we don't know. We'll be in touch, one way or another," I said, spotting Slate coming through the doors and heading our way. Magnus had left the day after the mountain. He needed to get back to his family, but Slate wouldn't leave until we did. His loyalty was to a fault, and I really appreciated it. We'd been through a lot together.

We took turns doing the hug goodbye dance, Isabelle and I locking eyes for a moment, and my heart longed to go back to those days in the country. Dad would be tinkering in the garage, and Mom's nose would be stuck in a book, sitting at the front door, letting the sun cast its glorious rays on her for the afternoon. It made me miss them both so much.

Mary must have seen the misting of my eyes, because she kissed my cheek and led me away.

"Keep in touch, buddy," James said, waving when I looked back.

"You know I will." These were the people I needed to protect. They all needed protecting, and deep down, I knew we had to go on the offensive. There would be no

New World

beach vacations for Mary and me. Not until the Bhlat were dealt with.

The transport vessel that was earmarked for us sat fueled and ready to go, the doors already open. Mary would pilot it, and Slate took the back seat so he could stretch out.

Soon we were lifting off, my tablet full of downloaded images from my sister and best friend's wedding, my heart full yet heavy at the same time.

★ ★

"You're telling me there's still no word from them?" I asked Patty. She looked like any other woman of sixty in our living room, wearing jeans and a sweater. Some things never went out of style, even on a colony planet.

"None." She sipped her tea and leaned back on the couch.

"And you still think it's Naidoo cutting off communication with us?" Clare asked from beside the former Earth president.

Patty nodded. "I do."

We were in our new house's living room, which was spacious when it was just Mary and me there, but the space was getting tight with our whole crew and extras hanging out. Magnus and Nat were there, with little Dean in tow. I was positive the kid was far better behaved than I'd been at his age.

Slate stood behind us, listening thoughtfully but not saying much. I'd grill him on his thoughts later, maybe over a Scotch in the backyard after dinner.

The back door closed and Nick sauntered into the room, a beer in hand, wearing an apron that said "Kiss the Cook." They'd really gone all out, bringing supplies from Earth. "Burgers are almost done. Grab your buns and get 'em while they're hot."

I couldn't believe we were having a barbecue in a house on New Spero. Not just any house, but one that Patty said they'd built for us years ago. It had stood empty and was only a few miles from Magnus and Natalia, which suited us just fine.

Carey nudged my leg as he came in from outside, leaving his perch beside the barbecue that any red-blooded dog would be happy to drool by. The younger pups came along with him, following his lead, and Maggie plopped down on my right foot. I scratched behind her ear, and Carey looked up at me before moving over to Natalia. He hopped up and lay his head on her lap. I caught Nat looking over at me, to make sure I was okay. I loved my time with Carey, and when they left later than day, I would give anything for Carey to stay behind, but I knew he couldn't. It had been too long. He had a new family now.

"Dean?" Mary elbowed me lightly. The room was looking at me, waiting for a response.

"Sorry, what was the question?" I had been so lost in thought, I hadn't heard them.

"Do you think we should send someone to Earth?" Patty asked. I didn't like the way she was looking at me, like there was a secret being passed between us.

"I think it might be a good idea. Maybe it could be resolved by having a face-to-face with them. I'm sure she was pissed after her little puppet man from the station was apprehended, trying to keep our arrival quiet." Or the Bhlat had already shown up, destroying Earth and stripping it of all its minerals and water. I closed my eyes and pictured people around the world, chained to each other, faces dark with dirt and backs slumped in exhaustion. I wasn't going to tell the rest of them what I really thought might be happening.

"Food's ready," Mary said, changing the subject. I knew she was tired of speculating. "Patty, if you want to send someone to Earth to check on things, I say do it, but know that Dean and I won't be on that ship. We just got here and can't leave it all behind again." Mary's words poured out hot and fast, her back turned to us in the living room.

I noticed Patty's eyes widening just slightly before settling back to normal. "I wouldn't dare, Mary. I was thinking of asking for volunteers."

Magnus grunted, and I caught the tail end of Nat's elbow hitting his stomach. That was her way of telling him there was no way he could stick his hand up. Magnus made eye contact with me and winked.

For a minute, no one spoke, everyone seeming to ignore Patty's comment.

"I'll do it," Slate said, speaking for what felt like the first time that evening.

Patty brightened. Slate and I had discussed a plan, should the need arise, but I wasn't sold that the need was there quite yet.

"Good. I need a strong young man like you beside me." Patty stood up, moving toward the kitchen, where the food was laid out on our table.

"Wait. What do you mean, *beside you*?" I asked, following her. Maggie slipped off my foot and trudged along behind me, sitting between my feet when I stopped.

"I'm going," she said matter-of-factly. "If it's just the new woman being spiteful, then I'll talk to her and explain the truth. If it's the worst, and the Bhlat are there, we need to know."

"Your people need you here," Mary said, coming to my side.

She shook her head slowly. "These aren't *my* people. I'm not their leader anymore. I'm just Patty. They have leaders at each Terran site, and we have people like Magnus in place to care for us. And now you." She looked side to side from Mary to me, a sad smile on her face.

"It's too dangerous." I didn't know what else to say. She made a good point. She might be the only one who could talk sense into Naidoo.

"What you all have done for our people hasn't been dangerous? I've sent you across the galaxy only for you to have to kill again, and then come back to see your lives turned upside down. Let me have this. I need it." Patty grabbed a plate, putting potato salad on it, and prepared a bun for her hamburger.

Doing something as normal as having a barbecue while talking about sending our former president on a ship to a potentially hostile Earth wasn't the strangest thing I'd seen in the last few weeks.

Should I tell her about the *Shandra*? I wanted to, but I also didn't want the details to leak out. If she went to Earth and was taken by the Bhlat, they would have ways to make her talk. I needed to keep the stone portal in our tight little circle.

"I can't argue with that," I said. "What do you have to say, General?"

Magnus shifted uncomfortably on his feet. "Believe me, we've had this discussion a few times. I never win. I support her at this point."

Patty walked by him to the pile of burgers Nick had set down. "Damn right you support me."

"I'll go," Clare said, surprising me.

"You will?" Patty asked.

"Me too." This from Nick. "I have nothing here but some distant family I don't even know. I'd rather be useful than static."

"Quite the team I'm amassing. Thank you, everyone." Patty moved back to the living room, her plate full.

Mary and I stood flabbergasted in the kitchen. Guilt coursed through me, but I wasn't going to leave so soon after coming. We had a new life here. "Then good luck to you all." I raised my glass of beer in the air, and we drank to their venture.

Magnus put some music on, trying to break the dark mood that was settling over the room. We chatted, ate until we were stuffed, and drank more than we should have, a group of old and new friends in our house.

It was close to midnight when people started to file out of the door, a friend of Patty's arriving to usher everyone back to their own places.

"When will you be leaving?" Mary asked Patty as we stood by the door, the night fighting to get inside our house.

"In three days," Patty said before turning and walking in an unstable line toward the passenger van waiting for her. Magnus and Nat were left with the dogs as the van drove away, a cloud of dust lifting as it moved down the gravel road. It was a lone sound in an otherwise silent night. The only other noise was a humming sound that echoed down the countryside every night as the sun went down, and Natalia explained it was a bug akin to our grasshopper.

"Good party." Magnus slid his free arm around Natalia's waist. His other arm was propping up his son Dean, who was sound asleep with his face tucked into his dad's neck.

"It was nice to have you all over," Mary said. I hardly

heard them. The journey my new crew was about to take worried me too much. "Dean?"

I was at the edge of the front porch, my toes hanging over the first step, staring up at the sky. I saw thousands of points of light in the dark space above. Could I travel near some of them with the *Shandra*, or were most of those stars dead a long time ago? The chaos of the universe threatened to overtake me. So many worlds, each with their own climates, animals, plants, and insects. So many other races of beings. So much love and hate, peace and violence.

"Dean?" Natalia asked this time, and I could make out her soft footsteps on the wooden porch. "It's okay, you know? It isn't your responsibility." Her hand moved to my shoulder. She was right, but I couldn't shake the feeling that it was my calling.

I remembered working for a big accounting firm in New York when I first started out. They'd seen something in me: the way I worked overtime, how I was extremely affable with the clients, and how I always got the job done before the deadline. I was promoted a couple times and felt the weight of the company on my young shoulders.

One day, I couldn't take it anymore. I was working too much, and too hard for someone in his twenties, and I ended up quitting, taking the plunge to become my own boss. I'd thought they would fall apart. There was no way they could survive without me. The thing was, they didn't just survive; they flourished. A new guy came in, attracted some huge corporate clients, and they were on top of the world. Lesson learned: you're always replaceable, just like I'd replaced that muscle-bound army guy in the Boathouse that night I'd met Janine.

I blinked, and the stars zoomed back out, just pin-

New World

points of light again. "Thanks, Nat. You're right. My place is here with my friends. We deserve a break, don't we, babe?" I called back to Mary, who stood in the dim glow of the porch light smiling at me.

"We sure do. Maybe we can make our own little mini-Dean." I winked at her, and we all laughed.

"If you're getting started on that, we're going to get going. Thanks again, buddy. See you tomorrow?" Magnus asked.

"You bet. I need someone to show me how to use that backhoe so we can get this garden planted," I answered.

We took turns at the goodbye hugs, and when they walked down to their vehicle, Carey stopped, saying goodbye, jumping up, front paws on my thighs. I leaned down and whispered something to him. He gave me a lick and bounded off after his family. Something was still sitting on my foot after they were all down at the SUV.

"Dean, it looks like someone wants a sleepover. Do you mind?" Magnus called from the driver's seat.

Maggie looked up at me, her pink nose glistening, head cocked to the side.

"We'd be happy to." I wasn't ready for a dog quite yet, but having this little girl stay over for a night seemed harmless enough. For some reason, she seemed to like me.

Soon they were down the road, leaving Mary and me in the silence of the night, outside Terran One, on New Spero. Our new home.

"We made the right decision," she said quietly.

"I hope so."

We sat on the porch, sipping our drinks, looking up at the strange night sky, while Maggie slept between us.

ELEVEN

"You have everything you need? Did you bring enough of that egg mixture? It wouldn't be a trip without Nick's omelettes." I made the joke to cover the tension I was feeling. Seeing them loading a ship for the journey back to Earth made it all the more real. They were leaving, and Mary and I were staying behind. It felt wrong.

"Of course we have the mixture. I even managed to pry a couple dozen real eggs from the market downtown." Nick smiled widely, but I sensed part of him was wishing he could stay. If Clare hadn't volunteered, I doubted he would have stuck his hand up.

Magnus exited the ship, Slate right behind him. They chatted quietly for a minute, out of earshot of the rest of us, and the younger man nodded along to the advice Magnus was giving him. Slate got a clap on the shoulder, and they walked down the ramp toward the rest of us.

"Slate, take care of everyone, would you?" I asked. "And yourself." I added the last bit, and he gave me a hard stare.

"I wish you were coming, boss," he said. "Don't worry about anything. They're in good hands with this crew. We'll make sure Patty gets where she needs to and talks some sense into them. If it's the alternative, we'll do what

New World

you said. Gather as much information as we can and relay it back."

"Perfect."

The trip would take them two months, with another month for any message to get back to us. Waiting that long was going to be next to impossible. My pulse quickened as I thought about the *Shandra*. Should I try to go to Earth? Sarlun had identified the icon for our home planet, but he did warn me they hadn't tested it. It could be damaged, making it a one-way trip – or worse. Where would it open up? The unknown made it not only dangerous, but potentially deadly.

Patty arrived wearing a black uniform. The New Spero colony logo of a red sun behind a series of buildings was on a patch sewn onto the breast of the garment. It looked sharp.

"We'll be in touch along the way," Patty said to Magnus. "Take care of this place for me."

I had the urge to disclose the *Shandra* then but kept it to myself. Slate knew about it, but he wasn't going to break under pressure, no matter what they did to him. I tried to stop thinking about the worst-case scenario, but lately, that was all I seemed to find myself in.

A half hour later, we watched the ship lift up, then head away; the trip to Earth was under way.

"Godspeed," Mary said under her breath, and I followed suit, wishing them a safe and uneventful journey.

"They'll be okay. I have a feeling we'll hear good news in a couple months." This from Magnus. I was feeling the opposite but kept it to myself.

"How about we go into town and get some supplies for our garden?" Mary asked, anxious to get working on our little house and yard.

"Deal. See you later, Magnus? We still on for dinner?"

I asked.

"As long as you guys are bringing cash for the poker game after." Magnus and Natalia had invited a few couples from the area over, and since there was no currency on New Spero yet, I had no idea what we were buying into the game with. I had the clothes on my back, and not much more for possessions. "The dogs will be happy to see you both. Maybe Maggie can stay over again?"

Maggie had spent the other night over at our place, hogging the bottom of the bed and waking me up in the middle of the night to go outside. She was really sweet, and having an animal around felt right.

On the other hand, she belonged with her family too. "I know what you're trying to do. Mag, I really am okay with Carey being with you guys."

"It just must be so hard. You blinked and seven years went by. He still loves you."

"I know he does. That's why I'm happy he's been able to grow old with people that love him too. I don't think we're ready to have another dog yet, but I'll let Maggie stay over any time she wants."

Magnus' suit's comm beeped, and he tapped his ear. "Good. Thanks for the update," he said to whoever was on the other side of the conversation. "Our ship just passed the station. I have some work to do. See you two later."

"Bye," Mary said, leading the way off the landing pad and toward the SUV we'd been given. Having our own wheels and house was a strange feeling, especially since it was just ours. There were no payments, mortgages, or leases. We were just given the keys, and our names were on the database as owners of them. The rest of the colony participated in the bartering utopia of ideal socialism. I knew it had been tried before on Earth, and while the thought was good, it never worked out as hoped. Patty and the other leaders had high expectations about their colony world.

As we drove into town, the buildings got larger. The roads were paved, and traffic picked up heading into the core of Terran One. It was a couple hours after sunrise, and people were on their way to get supplies for their daily tasks or to work in one of the countless manufacturing plants or stores.

We stopped at an octagonal stop sign: some things were universal, even on another world. My window was down, letting the early morning air creep into the vehicle. The sounds of a six-story apartment complex being erected carried to us, and Mary commented on how lucky we were to have a house in the country.

"I think our days of city living are over," I said, but as we drove on, we passed some quaint shops, coffee shops, and restaurants, and the idea of leaving your home to walk down the street for dinner did have a certain appeal. It was one of the things I'd always missed about being young and living in Manhattan.

"How have they accomplished this in just a few years?" Mary asked, staring at the impressive inner core of the city.

"I have no clue. I was expecting some metal buildings, cots set up with curtains to separate sleeping chambers, like a field hospital. Maybe not that bad, but you get where I'm going. It must have taken a lot of minds, a lot of work, to come up with plans for five cities."

"Nat tells me they're all on the same footprint."

I thought about Terran Five and inwardly scolded myself for not noticing that. I blamed the exhaustion and the snow-covered streets. "That makes sense. Still…they've done something quite amazing." I followed a white van and turned where it turned. It had *Garden Supply* painted on the back and sides, and that was where we were headed.

I parked, turning the engine off. "Babe, are you sure this is what you want?" I asked, looking at Mary in the passenger seat. She was in capris and a red tank top, her brown hair pulled into a loose ponytail. I was the luckiest man on New Spero.

I was already starting to sweat, finding we were in the middle of what passed for summer in our region.

"I want a garden, if that's what you're asking." She pulled out her tablet, and she thumbed to the supply list she'd sent the store yesterday. "Should be ready to pick up."

I set my hand on her left arm as her right reached for the door handle. "That's not what I mean."

She stopped, turning to meet my gaze. "Then what?"

"This. Do you want to live in a country house on a strange colony, living out our days tilling the soil and chopping wood?"

She didn't speak for a minute. "Dean, I just want to be with you. I want the fear of an alien race coming to steal us, or kill us, or enslave us, gone first, though. Then I'm happy to sit on our porch, sipping sweet tea and watching you chop wood, while Mary Jr. plays with dolls beside me."

I smiled. "Me too. If things go south with our friends at Earth, we have to do something." I didn't ask this time; I just said it matter-of-factly.

She nodded. "We will. I'll be by your side."

"Mary Jr.?" I laughed, and we got out of the car. "That sounds like a good life to me. Let's get there and start by loading up a trailer with your garden supplies."

"*My* garden supplies? Don't think you're going to put

all of this on me."

We walked through the large building's front doors, which slid to the side as we stepped near them. It reminded me of the large orange box store I had in my hometown, and the comforting smell of wood and soil reached my nose.

There was a pick-up counter to the left, and we approached, waiting in line behind a large man talking to an employee.

"What do you mean, you don't have any more four-by-eight cedar left? I need twenty to finish my job," the burly man said, his voice rising.

"Sir, if you've noticed, we're on New Spero, and our tree farms aren't at full maturation yet. We'll be happy to substitute oak in place. We still have oak." The woman was keeping her cool but looked like she'd had about enough of the man berating her.

"Fine, but I'll be talking to the council about this. Gave away all the damned cedar, even though I'd requisitioned it last month." He turned from her and looked in our direction. "Can you believe this?"

So much for a utopia. I just shrugged, and we made our way to the woman. "I'd ask how your day's going, but I think we know," Mary said to the lady. "We sent our list in yesterday and are here to pick it up."

"It's true. You *are* here." The forty-something-year-old woman's eyes grew twice their size, and she nearly squealed. Her name was Tammy, according to the nametag. "Mary Lafontaine and Dean Parker. I heard from Sally that you were here, but I didn't believe it. I thought it might be some propaganda to keep the people hopeful. But by golly, you're here in the flesh. You both look so…amazing. Are the rumors true? You got married at an alien court and had to offer your firstborn to their leader to escape?"

I barked out a laugh, and Mary nudged me, suppressing her own laughter. "I have no idea where you're getting that from, but I assure you…we only have to 'lend' our baby to the king for a year."

Tammy's eyes grew even larger, and I thought for a moment that they would pop out of her head. "Oh my God!"

"Tammy, relax. She was just kidding," I assured the frantic woman. "Where did you hear that crazy story?"

She pulled out a stack of what looked like magazines. "From these," she said, sliding them out like a deck of cards. They weren't magazines; they were comics.

I grabbed one and read the title. "The Survivors of Earth" was scrawled across the top of the cover in black lettering. A silver ship chasing a dozen smaller, clearly made-up vessels across space, with a gray planet underneath, was the cover image. Red beams fired from the silver ship.

I thumbed it open and saw the artist's rendition of Mary in a tight body suit. Her figure was modified to the ideals of a teenage boy, and now she did laugh when she saw it. The artist's Dean looked older than I was; silver streaked the edges of his dark hair. The artwork was good, if not a little exaggerated.

"Can I take these? I'll bring them back." I asked, getting a nod from Tammy.

"Only if you sign them after," she said.

"Sure. Oh, and who makes them?" I asked, looking for a name.

"Leonard. He works at the permits office. He started making these before we came here. Now he has tens of thousands of downloads a month for each new issue. He only prints a few, since paper has become harder to come by."

"Thanks, Tammy. Now, where can we get our supplies?"

TWELVE

"You guys knew about these?" I asked, waving one of the comics in front of Nat and Magnus. Little Dean made a grab for it, his sticky boy hands trying to reach the paper, but I managed to pull it up in time.

"We did. I've had more important things on my mind to talk to you about than comics." Magnus twisted the cap off a beer and passed me one. "Have you seen issue seven? That's where we meet. They got it all wrong, but I'm amazed there's even a passing reference to the reality. Leonard must have had a source on the inside who knew some of our real story."

"The one where Slate blows up an entire planet was good. How dare that virus try to spread to humans." Mary grabbed the bottle of red wine and poured herself and Nat a glass.

"Quite the imagination. The stuff happening on Earth, was that true?" I asked.

"Some of it. It was getting bad. The forced treaties and weapons agreements…things got out of hand. We needed to separate ourselves from it. Earth will never be home to us any longer." Magnus put his arm around Natalia, who gave him a loving gaze.

"Mag, they may still need our help," she said, ever the caring woman. She inspired me to be better.

"What are we going to do if the Bhlat are there? Fight

them? Our fleet isn't ready for that. If what Dean said is true, and they've mined all those worlds, enslaving and killing entire races, then we may be doomed. I'm going to enjoy the food tonight, have a few beers, spend time with my loved ones, and do it all again tomorrow, until we can't anymore."

Natalia took a step back, putting herself between her son on his chair and her husband. "You listen to me. If they need our help, we'll help them. All of this around us isn't real if the Bhlat are out there threatening it. I will not stand by while my son's life is in question. And neither will you." Her pointer finger pushed into his large chest.

He raised his hands in supplication. "I hear you. Okay. I'm with you, but if it comes to it, you're staying here, and Dean and I will go kick their asses. We've done it before and will do it again."

"Don't you dare leave me out of this ass-kicking. I've been thinking about it since the first time they chased me on that space station, almost killing me. I'm in too." Mary stuck her glass in the air, and I hesitantly clinked it, along with Magnus and Nat.

The last thing I wanted was to fight the Bhlat, especially with Mary by my side. I wondered if there was a way I could stow her away with Suma, somewhere safe and protected. The *Shandra*. My mind clicked, and a piece of the puzzle fell into place.

"I have an idea."

The doorbell rang as the first guests arrived. My friends looked at me, waiting, and when the bell rang again, Magnus stuck a finger in the air. "This conversation isn't over. Dean, I love it when you have big ideas. It usually means a win for our side."

★ ★

*T*he sun beat down on us, and Maggie barked as I threw the ball down the yard. Mary beckoned me from beside the garden, her sun hat covering her face from this angle. I could tell she was excited by her posture.

Maggie ran to my feet, dropping the ball with another bark. I tossed the ball toward Mary, jogging after it while Maggie ran full throttle, ears flopping in the air.

"Look how well it's coming along," I said, standing beside Mary, who was beaming at the large assortment of sprouted greens coming from the twenty-by-forty-foot patch of garden. Some food like lettuce was already being used on a daily basis, and others were just growing, their cycle a lot longer from germination to harvest. The last few weeks had been a lot of work but had gone quickly.

"We should be able to feed our wedding guests with our own food," Mary said.

Maggie dropped the ball at my feet, and I threw it as far as I could; the excited cocker raced after it. The ball bounced off the ground and she hopped, trying to catch it in her mouth but failing. She lay down with it in the cool shade of a New Spero tree, panting heavily.

The sound of a vehicle racing down the road carried to us, dust kicking up as it drove up our driveway.

"Are you expecting anyone?" I asked Mary, who shook her head in return.

We walked around the back deck, toward the front of the house. The instant I saw Magnus, I knew something was wrong. His face was dark, a scowl shoving deep lines in his forehead.

"We heard from them. You need to come with me," he said. Maggie barked at him and rolled at his feet, but he was too upset and focused to notice her.

Patty and the crew had made it to Earth. It had been three months. My hand shook slightly and I took a deep breath, knowing suddenly that we were going to need to move ahead with my plan. I had hoped it wouldn't be needed.

I picked Maggie up, putting her in the car, and we jumped in. "Let's go."

He raced down the roads, which rarely had other cars on them out here. He took the gravel streets around the city, and in ten silent minutes, we arrived at the base. I knew better than to even ask what happened. Magnus would talk when he wanted to. I saw sweat dripping down the big guy's brow as he pulled into a parking spot.

"You two are going to help, right?" he asked tensely.

"You know we are," Mary said, and some of the pressure eased in Magnus, like she'd hit a relief valve on his tank.

"Good. We need you." Magnus opened the door and we all got out, Maggie following along and looking around timidly.

The base wasn't large. It was made up of a handful of buildings that lined the landing pad. The largest structure was the hangar, where a couple dozen ships sat idly. People moved around now, more than I'd ever seen there before. They all wore uniforms.

Magnus led us into the two-story building beside the hangar, where he and Patty had offices. We walked past their offices and into an elevator that took Magnus' fingerprint to access. We lowered, and the doors opened to the room where Patty had shown us the footage from Terran Five.

"We've had a lot of messages from our ship since they left. Once every couple of their days, to be exact.

The farther they get from us, the longer the messages take. Two months to arrive, and one month for that last message to arrive to us. Technically, it's been eighty-seven days. Today, we received this message. Daniel, play it, please," Magnus said to the white-uniformed officer at the screen controls.

A message started, sound waves dancing on the screen. A throat cleared. *"We're about to arrive and should be able to see the station around Earth in a couple of hours. Our sensors are showing activity, but..."* Patty's voice went quiet, the sound bar falling to the bottom of the screen. *"God help us...they're here...If you get..."* The message ended.

"That's it?" I asked, a cold shiver racing through my spine. *God help us. They're here.*

"That's it. We're waiting for another transmission, but we know that message is close to a month old. Anything could have happened by now. We need to discuss options. The other Terran military bases' leaders are coming here for a briefing in a half hour. Do we tell them about your plan?" he asked me, putting the pressure on me now.

"No. The less they know, the better."

"Dean, I mentioned some war vessels being built. I may have left a few details out. They're ready."

"Ready? I thought they were just a concept. Where are they?" Mary asked, expressing the same angry tone I was feeling.

"They were in-system but far enough away, should the testing go wrong. They're operational." Magnus had a grim look across his tired face.

"Then send them toward Earth. We may need the backup," Mary said. "Are they capable of FTL like our smaller ships?"

"Same drives, just scaled up for size. If anything, we

New World

can go out fighting if things go south. I suppose it's a good thing I sent them a month after Patty and the others left," Magnus said, his grimness transforming with a smile.

"You sly old dog!" Mary shouted happily.

"They needed to be tested anyway. What better way than in defense of Earth?" Magnus asked. "The other Terran leaders will be here soon. I'll tell them you're off on a mission to help our cause."

"Are you sure we need to even mention Mary and me?" I asked.

"It'll give them hope. We named this world New Spero. Spero means *I hope*, and they need it. Earth needs it. Will you stick around?" Magnus asked.

I looked over at Mary, wondering if she was ready to do our part. "Dean and I will go now. Sarlun swore he would help us if we needed it. We need it."

"Do you have the supplies I requested ready?" I asked.

"Daniel will show you to the lockers. I got them together the minute we started this plan. Take the transport to the mountains and do what you have to do. We need to know where the Bhlat homeworld is for this to work." Magnus sat down, playing the message again.

They're here.

We left, making assurances we'd be back as soon as possible. I was glad Magnus was staying behind for the time being. New Spero needed him to take charge, and Nat would be furious if we took him away without her saying goodbye. I could tell from his eyes he wished he was coming with us. He'd feel more useful out in the field on a mission than behind a desk with a bunch of suits, as he'd call them.

"I wish Slate were coming with us," Mary said. With

113

the rest of our crew gone on the trip to Earth, it was just the two of us.

We were at the lockers, just outside the hangar, standing in our underwear. I went to the door and made sure it was locked. "Mary, I'm sorry we got sucked into this again. I wish things were different. I wish we could just have a normal life."

She walked over to me, placing a cool hand on my stubble-covered cheek. "We'll never have a normal life. It's not ours anymore. We were chosen to help the Kraski get our planet, and we foiled both sides. It's up to us to protect the people we saved." Her lips touched mine warmly. "Let's end this. Then, and only then, can we say the word *normal* again."

"You're right. Let's suit up." I slid my uniform on, noticing how nicely it fit now that they'd taken measurements. I slung a pack over my shoulder and felt my breast pocket, where I found the Deltra portable shield Kareem had given me. It still had Bhlat DNA in it, and I expected I'd need to use it again, though a strong part of me wanted to throw it on the ground and stomp it to pieces.

"We'll do what we need to do, together," Mary said, reading my mind.

I just nodded, grabbed the other pack, and moved for the door.

Soon we were in the lander, Mary piloting us toward the ice-cold part of our planet, heading for a portal to multiple worlds.

THIRTEEN

The caves were just as we'd left them. We used an air horn to startle away any of the dangerous creatures hiding in the area or tunnels. Terran Five dispatch told us they hadn't had any altercations with the animals since Magnus and Mary had rescued my sister and the others, and I hoped that meant they'd moved on in search of other food sources.

The sky was clear, and the whole area was far more beautiful to look at now than it had been while I was sick. Snow piled down in sheets from the dark sky. It reminded me of the Rockies from my ski trips, and Mary said something along the same lines.

"Last time, you left here with a wild animal bite, and I left after spending the day on a deserted alien world. What will today bring us?" I asked, adding a chuckle.

"Hopefully, right back here in an hour, with the Bhlat planet icon for your portal."

"My portal? I don't think it's mine."

"Then why did you get drawn to it?"

"I think it has to do with Mae's blood inside me. It's changed me...made me part Kraski...I don't really know."

We left the supplies we didn't need to bring, and we each carried a pack on our backs, with our rifles held firmly in our hands.

"This way." We entered the caves and took the path down the tunnels Slate and I had walked a short few months ago. It was all familiar, but in the way a dream was familiar. I knew the path, but if you'd asked me which directions to go before heading in, I wouldn't have known. My feet led us to the doorway where the *Shandra* stood. "Here we are." I unslung the pack and headed for the middle of the room. The large gemstone in the center of the room began to shine; the hieroglyphs on the walls shone to life in their blue luminescence.

"It's beautiful," Mary said, spinning to catch all the different icons on the walls. "The spacing seems off. Are some missing?" she asked. I just shrugged and walked to the table.

My blood wasn't singing or burning this time, and my body movements were of my own volition, so I hoped I could make the stone work. The room was bathed in blue light as I touched the table. I slid my tablet out of my pack and found the data from Sarlun. A series of icons appeared on my handheld screen, and I picked the one labeled for their world.

After finding the corresponding icon on the table, I took Mary's shaky hand and tapped the icon, which glowed bright green. Instantly, we were covered in green light.

A flurry of deep squawks came at us as the light dimmed.

"Is this it?" Mary asked me quietly.

"Yes. Turn your translator on." I used the pad on my sleeve to turn the recently upgraded translator on. We had earpieces in and small mics at our suits' necks that would take our words and relay them aloud in the appropriate language. After a few more squawks came to us, the translator clicked, telling me it was ready.

New World

"Greetings. We're here to see the Gatekeeper," I said in English, then heard the Shimmali language emanate from my suit.

The voice had been coming from a speaker, and after a few minutes of silence, the main far doors slid open. Something was running toward us. Mary looked ready to hold her rifle up, but I set a hand on her arm.

"Suma!" I called. The short, stout alien girl ran on thick legs, approaching quickly, then stopping suddenly as she saw Mary.

"Who's this?" she asked, her black eyes staring at Mary.

"I'm Mary Lafontaine."

"You look funny," the small alien said.

"This is my mate. Mary's a human female," I said.

Mary just smiled at this.

"What are you doing here, Dean?" she asked, her snout lifting in the air.

The deep noises of Sarlun carried down the open room. "Dean Parker. To what do we owe the pleasure?"

"We need your help."

★ ★

Outside, music played in the garden, where amazing flowers and plants of all colors and sizes grew. Shimmal's two stars burned at opposite ends of the sky, and I was sweating the instant we stepped from the cool building into the humid tropical outdoors.

The melody was soft and instrumental. Our races really weren't that much different from each other. Other Shimmalians walked around, some wearing robes, others in uniforms. Some were in what I could only guess was loungewear, the equivalent of shorts and a tank top on Earth.

"You want to find the Bhlat homeworld? We don't like to speak of them here. Though they are far away, the tales of their power have reached even our distant world." Sarlun gestured with his four arms as he spoke.

"So you don't know where they are?" I asked, feeling my hopes crumbling quickly.

"They are not on our *Shandra* table."

"Does that mean they don't have a portal?" If they didn't have a portal, our plan was going to be almost impossible with the time crunch we were under.

"Not necessarily. The *Shandra* were created ages ago by the Theos, long before any races of beings lived on the worlds on which the portals existed."

My fingers were going numb. Sweat beads ran down my back, and not just from the humidity. He was telling us a race of gods had created the portals before any of us existed. Was that possible? "How do you know this?"

"We've studied with dozens of other beings, compiling and contemplating religion, history, and science. This is the truth we have come to know." Sarlun sounded sure of himself.

"Could there be worlds with portals that aren't on the table?" Mary asked, and I chided myself for not thinking of it. It was nice to have her analytical mind around.

"Yes. We believe some have been shut off. Whether they were removed as a safety precaution, or for other reasons, stands to be seen. We believe the Deltra had something to do with it. They were always trying to get ahead of their time: a young race with highly skilled scientific minds. Last we heard, they were under the thumb of the Kraski, but if your tale is to be understood, they are gone now."

New World

Guilt at his casual discussion of our destruction of the Deltra aboard the Kraski mothership echoed through my body.

He continued. "If there was any hope of opening the hidden worlds from the *Shandra*, they would be the last resort now." Sarlun's black eyes stared hard into mine. He knew we'd killed the Kraski off, and most of the Deltra with them. I judged his people to be a peaceful one, but I wondered what he would do if his world was threatened. He seemed to have an understanding with me.

"The Deltra may not all be gone," I said, watching his expression change and his snout twitch.

"Is that so?" he asked, his usual deep squawk now lighter, airier.

"Can you help me find a world on the table? I have the coordinates in here." I pulled out my tablet with the location of the hideout planet Kareem was on.

"Come with me."

An hour later, we were in Sarlun's private office, which was substantially cooler than outside. Everything on this world was so cold and sterile on the surface; then you would see a splash of color and understand how much they appreciated the arts. *Less is more* might have been their mantra. His office was no exception: cool white walls, with one small bright piece of art in the center of each.

We stared at the star chart: a wonderful 3D hologram of the system in question appeared. The planet was highlighted, and the icon for its portal was showing on the wall screen.

"That's it. We haven't been there for over a century. Last time we arrived, there was nothing but flora and some wildlife. Dangerous creatures." Suma sat beside her dad, staring up at him as he spoke.

"Dean, where's Slate?" Suma asked, sipping green liquid from a glass.

"He's in danger. That's why we're here. All of our people are in danger." I hoped we'd find the answers we were looking for with Kareem.

"Dad, is there anything else we can do?" she asked.

"Where was their town?" Sarlun asked.

Mary took over and directed him to the spot where we'd landed and walked to their village.

"The *Shandra* is not close. We'll supply you with a few things to assist you along the way." Sarlun hit a comm-button and started squeaking out orders, turning off his translator. "The supplies will be ready. I have something else to share with you." He reached down, pulling out four small devices, and handed them to Mary.

"What are these?" Mary asked, carefully looking at them.

"They will allow you to communicate instantly with anyone, no matter their distance in space," Sarlun said.

"Thank you. These will come in handy." Mary passed one over to me, and I noticed it looked much like a cell phone, but with a clear crystal casing.

"Thank Suma. She wanted to be able to reach you."

Suma sat in her chair, her legs hanging down, and her snout lifted slightly. "I'll show you how it works."

Ten minutes later, she considered us able to communicate between the devices. Once we were able to lock in her frequency so she could talk to us, she was happy we understood how to work them.

"With these, you might have an advantage against your enemy. Or they might have the same knowledge, but at least you'll be on an even playing field." Sarlun stood up, his large frame making the office feel small. "Whatever happens, do not utter our names to the Bhlat. We haven't had dealings with them and would appreciate staying out of their way. We do these favors as friends, but that friendship only goes so far. We are a peaceful world."

I stood up and stretched a hand out. He took it with his lower right arm, and I shook. "Gatekeeper Sarlun, you've been more than helpful. I look forward to sharing stories with you when this is all done with."

"I as well. Come, we'll escort you to the *Shandra*."

Mary chatted with Sarlun on the way down, and Suma sidled up to me in the hallway. "Dean, please make sure you save Slate. I like him."

"I like him too."

"And be sure to contact me whenever you like. I need to get updates."

"Suma, thank you so much for everything. You've been a godsend." The squeaks and squawks that came from my translator sounded excited.

She looked up at me with her big seal-black eyes. "Who would have thought that being abandoned on that world would have turned into the most fun day of my life?"

Fun? I wished I could look back at it and feel the same way. "It was meant to happen."

We walked the corridors, passing numerous white-uniformed Shimmalians. Some spoke greetings; others kept to themselves. It wasn't long before we were at the *Shandra* room, where two guards were stationed at the doors. They saw Sarlun, bowed, and let us through without hesitation.

Inside the large white room, I spotted supplies by the gemstone and table. It had me thinking that we could transport larger items than just people from planet to planet, depending on how large a room the *Shandra* at the other end was housed in. New Spero's room wasn't that large, but a room like this could take a transport vessel or a large group of people.

"This should be enough to get you there. These will allow you to move quickly." Sarlun pointed at two vehicles that looked a lot like motorized scooters. You sat on them, but there were no wheels. "The tutorial is on it, and we loaded your path into the mapping system already."

"Thank you," Mary said, running a hand over the cool metal of the machine. She loved motorbikes, so taking a rip through an alien planet on a hovering scooter would be just up her alley.

"We also have provided cooling tents. From what you said, the temperatures are similar to our planet, and if you're stuck outdoors at night, you'll get eaten alive outside or sweat too much inside. Our tents will keep you safe from both."

I was eternally grateful for their assistance and hoped the combination of their supplies and ours would be enough to get us to Kareem, and home again quickly. We didn't have time to spare.

Suma ran to me, giving me a hug, and hesitantly gave Mary one too.

The pair started to walk away, and Sarlun stopped, turning to us. "Be careful. May the Theos guide your path." With that, they left.

His words rang in my mind, sending goosebumps over my body.

"Mary, are you ready for this?" I asked, knowing her answer.

She nodded, and we found the icon for the planet Kareem, Leslie, and Terrance were on. At least we hoped they were still there. Mary took the honors and tapped the table. Blinding light enveloped us, and then it was gone.

FOURTEEN

When I opened my eyes, the room was black. I hit the LEDs on my suit, and so did Mary on hers. We found ourselves in a room, four posts in the corners, and it couldn't have been more than forty feet by forty feet in size.

"You good?" Mary asked.

"Just looking at the room. If the Theos made each of these rooms, why do they look so different from each other?" I asked.

"Some of the races may have updated or adjusted the aesthetics. Do you think Suma's people found theirs like that? I'd say they moved and upgraded it to suit their Gatekeeper needs. See the walls here? Wood supports with dried vines. They used the local plants and supplies to build the room, and it appears we're underground too. So they dig it up, support it, install their columns, carve their hieroglyphs, and voila; we have a *Shandra*." Mary waved her arm in a flourish.

"Sounds plausible. Let's see if we can get out of here." The hover scooters sat on the ground, propped up on their bases. Mary tapped the screen and we watched a quick tutorial, using our earpiece translators to decipher the message. In a matter of minutes, they were up and running, blue light softly glowing underneath as the scooters lifted off the ground.

We slung our supplies over the seats and moved for the doorway, which wasn't mechanical like the others we'd seen. It was a large wooden door, ancient-looking, on thick black metal hinges. It squealed as I pushed it open, and I wondered when it had last been used. Maybe Kareem had come to the planet using it, contrary to his previous story. I wouldn't blame him for trying to keep the portals a secret. I'd done the same, even with my own people.

With the scooters hovering along with our hands controlling them, we wound our way down the dark soil-walled corridor. At times, it was too narrow to walk side by side, and I took the lead, rifle ready for anything coming at us. Nothing did. It was silent and sealed off. The incline told me we were underground, and that an exit would appear soon.

The end came abruptly, and only a short distance from the portal room. We used the door, both of us having to use all our weight to pry it open, and soon the humid night air hit us. We were outside. When we closed the door, we noticed it was well hidden away in the face of the hill, a wooden handle almost invisible among the shrubs and rocks placed beside it.

Mary tapped her screen. "I'll mark our location."

"Good idea. I'm all out of bread crumbs." The joke didn't stick, and I let it go. I was nervous. Anxious about traveling a couple hundred miles at night on a floating Vespa, and not knowing whether Kareem would cooperate. That was *if* they were still on this out-of-the-way world.

"Terrance and Leslie aren't going to be happy," Mary said as she straddled her hover scooter's seat.

New World

"We'll make the promise again." I had already told them I'd try to get the other hybrids on a ship to unite them here. I'd failed to do that. It weighed on me alongside everything else I'd done and would have to do.

Mary didn't reply. She just donned her EVA suit's mask, which would give us night vision and better oxygen supply as we raced into the night. I copied her and felt the rumble of the hover device as I sat on it.

I'd never been one for riding motorbikes or all-terrain vehicles, so the concept was a little foreign. The tutorial had made it seem so easy, and when Mary sped away, I hit the map function, showing the terrain and a line leading to our destination. This unit was all hand-controlled, and I hit the thruster. It started me forward too fast at first, and I almost flew off the thing. In a couple of minutes, I caught up to Mary, who was clearly waiting for me.

"Do you have the hang of it?" she asked through my helmet's earpiece.

I gave her a thumbs-up and nearly bucked myself again. I needed both hands.

Once I was going at a decent speed, and not worried about falling off or hitting a cliffside, I started to look at my surroundings. A large moon hung in the sky, light from the close star showcasing the lines and craters of the celestial body. The area looked much the same as I remembered the planet: mossy, warm, and lined with the large trees we'd seen before.

The map showed us making good time, and though it was on a different time system than we understood, I estimated another two hours before we arrived. An hour in, and the scenery was getting repetitive; I already wished the journey was over. My mind wandered to the task at hand. A lot of pieces needed to come into place in order for us to defeat the Bhlat, but did we need to defeat them? I set the goal in my head to work with them, to show them we were strong and not someone to be walked over, but that we also had compassion. Would a malevolent race understand the concept of compassion and empathy, or was war so engrained in them from birth that they were well past negotiation?

The base we'd arrived at almost a year ago had shown me a different side of the Bhlat. We didn't know much about them, and the details we'd downloaded from their base were mostly military. But there were children, women, and scientists on the base, telling me not everyone was a warrior. That was a good sign. The downside to that whole scenario was…I'd killed them all. I could still see them when I closed my eyes some nights, mixing together with the image of the Kraski puking out green bile, and the Deltra becoming all but extinct as we blew up the Kraski mothership.

Every one of them wanted to take our world, so I had to let it go. It still hung over my head like a dark cloud most days. As if on cue, real clouds rolled in as the wind picked up.

"Hang on," Mary said.

The wind blew from the west, pushing us to the right as we generally headed north. The speed was picking up, and rain began to fall on us: light drops at first, then fat heavy drops that made our visibility near nothing.

"What should we do?" I asked, fighting to stay upright.

From a few yards away, Mary fiddled with her map. "When I zoom, I see hills a couple miles to the east. Let's head there and hunt for some reprieve from the storm. If this is anything like a tropical storm, it may only last a short time."

I agreed and followed her lead, the wind pushing hard

at our backs now.

The ground changed from swampy moss to something a little firmer-looking as it became unlevel, small hills protruding from the surface. Moments later, we stopped on the far side of a large hill, with a flat cliff on the east side. We were protected from the wind and most of the rain as we stepped off the scooters and leaned our backs on the soft wall of the knoll.

"I guess we wait it out," I said, wiping my face mask with a gloved hand. The night vision was on, and it gave me a basic view of the dark swamp that stood before us. It went on as far as my eyes could see, and I tried to step farther away from it, remembering the creature that had pulled me under the last time we were on this planet. I didn't want a duplication of that, especially at night in a storm.

Mary got off her scooter and started to walk along the hillside, looking for a spot for reprieve from the onslaught of rain. I joined her, jogging to catch up.

"Doesn't look like much... wait, what's that?" She pointed to a crevice where two hills met up. They were pushed close together, but there was enough room to walk between them, and trees grew from both sides at angles, creating a makeshift canopy.

"Looks good to me. Better than standing beside this swamp."

We grabbed our supplies and brought them over to our new resting spot. My stomach rumbled as we settled along the wall of the opening, small splashes of water dripping down from the trees above, giving way to the torrential downpour.

Unclasping my helmet, I set it to the side and reached for my pack, when I heard howling. Mary was moving around, and I raised a finger to my lips. She stopped, and the howl rang through the night air again, this time closer.

"Can't we find a liveable world with no deadly animals on it? Just once?" I joked, grabbing my pulse rifle.

"Let's just hope they stay away, and the rain subsides sooner rather than later so we can keep going." She passed me an energy bar. "Here, take this. We may need it."

We sat back to back, watching each end of the opening we sat in, guns in our laps, and chewed on our bars.

"Just once, I want something to be hassle free. Remember our old lives? We used to complain about having to get up in the morning to go to work. But at the end of the day, we could just relax and watch the game on TV with a cold one. I guess those times are gone."

"I never felt that way. I was in the Air Force and loved doing it. What's that old saying? 'If you love what you do, you'll never work a day in your life'? That's how I felt," Mary said.

"I was an accountant, so working on small business ledgers wasn't something I could classify as loving. Though there was something calming about going through the sheets and balancing on the first try. It acted like a meditation for me at times. There were worse careers I could have chosen." I shifted closer to Mary, moving away from a drip from the rain above. "Do you miss it?"

"I do. I miss the schedule of it all. Waking up at five in the morning, working out before breakfast. But even though we're in a crazy situation, I wouldn't trade it for the world. I met you. I needed to meet you."

"Do you think our first marriages even count?" I asked.

"How do you mean?"

"The way I see it, we were duped: married to aliens.

New World

That can't really count."

Mary laughed and leaned her head on my shoulder. "I suppose you're right. I like that idea. How about you? Could you go back to pushing paper and doing someone's books?"

"No way. All of those years of practice, and now I don't need the skill."

"Every skill makes up who you are. You think a certain way because of it, and that's proven to be valuable. I won't be flying F-16s any longer, but that training allows me to succeed in our new universe. One that's rapidly expanding." Mary stretched her legs out.

"At least you can still fly ships. That's one skill that's transferable." The wind was decreasing; the pools of water outside rippled less and less as we talked. "I think the storm's dying down."

We sat there chatting, waiting to hear another howl, but we didn't. It was a half hour before we got up, seeing the rain was nothing more than a light patter now. Mary made for her scooter, her rifle on her back, her pack in her hand. As she strapped it to her seat, I walked out, looking at the sky to see if the clouds were still moving on. To the west, I saw amnesty coming in the still-dark night.

Mary was almost done and had fired up her ride when something jumped into my view.

"Dean, look out!" Mary called, but it was too late. The thick creature hurled itself off the canopy above the hillside and landed with a squishing sound right in front of me. It sank a couple feet into the soft ground, giving me just enough time to roll out of the way before its large paw wiped my face from my head. I felt the swing just clip me as I rolled to the wet ground, my rifle all but forgotten as I scrambled to evade the second swipe.

The thing reminded me of a bear, but its face was smaller, more human, making the whole attack that much more terrifying. It released a long howl as it came at me. I fought to back away from it, but my hands sank into the mossy ground, handcuffing any movement. This was it for me. There would be no saving Earth from the Bhlat, and after everything that had happened in the past two years, I was going to die by the paw of a monster on a planet I didn't even know the name of.

The creature stood on two legs, an angry scowl on its tortured face, and it growled as its right arm came flying toward me.

"Dean, get your head down!" Mary's voice yelled, and the smell of burned fur and blood hit me like a brick. I ducked and got a hand out, rolling to the side as the huge thing fell beside me, surprise crossing its face before it smacked into the swamp, water splashing a yard high.

The whole attack had only been a few seconds, but I was out of breath. My hand shook so hard, I had a hard time taking Mary's when she offered it to me. She pumped a couple more blasts from her pulse rifle into the hide of the dead monster for good measure.

"We need to go. If there's one, there are probably more. I don't want to be around when they show up."

"Why do I get all the terrible attacks on this planet? Good thing I have people to help me, or I'd be dead twice already." I made the joke to cover my dread. I'd thought I was going to die, and it wasn't a feeling that shook off in a minute.

Howls came at us from every direction as we got onto our hover scooters. "Which way?" I asked.

"No idea." Mary put her helmet on, and I did likewise, turning the night vision back on. "I'd suggest keeping your rifle at ready." She started to move north, and I joined her getting around the hills. More creatures cried out in the night as we raced away, hoping to not come across any of them.

FIFTEEN

The two-hour trip took its toll on my body. The wind was still blowing, and we passed through a couple more areas with inclement weather, reluctant to stop either time. We plowed through, ending up near the spot where we'd first landed on the planet all those months ago. We rode by the swamp where I'd been pulled under, and I recalled Mae saving my life. I shook it off as we rode, until coming to the town. It had expanded since we'd been there. More log cabins were erected, but few beings lingered on the streets as the sun started to rise, pushing through the thin clouds. Mist rose from the damp ground as we shut the scooters off.

"I hope they ask questions before shooting," Mary said, holding her rifle.

"They did last time."

We were in a large clearing, just past the tree line separating the village from the forest and swamps. A few ships were nearby, quietly sitting on the ground. I recognized one of them as the insectoid ship we'd seen last time. Another wasn't familiar.

A Deltra sentry could be seen a hundred yards away, walking the other direction. Worried they might think we were sneaking in, I stuck my pinky and thumb into my mouth and whistled sharply. That got his attention. He spun around, gun raised, and I was impressed at his reac-

New World

tion time. I suspected the sentries didn't have much action here, unless those smooth-faced bears were a problem in town.

He said something in Deltran and I threw my hands in the air. Mary lowered her rifle and did the same.

"This better work," she whispered.

"Who goes there?" my translator said in my ear.

"Dean Parker and Mary Lafontaine," I said loudly. He was only thirty yards away now, and I saw his expression change.

"Keep them up," he said, gun still raised as he approached us. "How did you get here?"

Mary nodded toward the trees. "Hover scooter," she said, and he looked confused, the translation likely not clear.

"What do you want?" he asked.

"We're here to see Kareem. It's urgent." I was getting tired of holding my arms up, and I started to lower them. When he didn't object, I let them drop to my sides.

"Come with me," he said, letting us walk in front of him. He didn't ask to take our weapons, but when I glanced back at him, his grip on his gun looked tight, and he eyed me with suspicion.

We neared the same building Kareem had been in before. When we got to the door, the sentry knocked and was let in. Another guard came out, watching us as the first sentry disappeared into the big structure.

"Nice morning," I said to the newcomer, getting a grunt in return. "Not a big talker? Sorry for waking you guys up. We didn't have a choice." I swear the guy cut me a smile, and if I wasn't mistaken, that was the first smile I'd seen from their race. It was nice to see the commonality.

"You're Dean, right?" he asked, his voice quiet.

"My reputation precedes me."

"Terrance and Leslie have been waiting for their friends."

Guilt washed over me. Just a second ago, I'd been making jokes; meanwhile, the hybrids were probably dying in the Russian prison on Earth.

"I'm sorry. I failed them," I said somberly. Mary set her hand on my forearm.

"They won't be happy. I hope you have better news for them and Kareem," the pale hairless guard said, his smile wiped away.

The door swung open, the first sentry waving us inside. "He'll see you now."

We followed them into the large space we'd first been in when Mae had escaped in Leslie's ship. They took us farther, through a doorway at the far end of the room. It smelled sterile in there, reminding me of a hospital. I'd spent enough time in one of those with Janine to recall it vividly.

The door opened into a hallway. Wooden floors led us to a series of rooms; some doors were ajar, with Deltra and other races milling around, getting an early start to their days. No one stopped us, but all of them stared curiously as we passed their bedrooms. I wanted to stop and look at the different aliens, to talk to them and learn about their people. There would be time for that eventually. Other things were more pressing now.

"In here," the first guard said, ushering us through the doors. The room was dimly lit but was a good size, with a bed on the side. Machines beeped softly, and I wondered why they'd brought us there. Then I saw the bed wasn't empty. Kareem was in it. His skin was even paler, if that was possible, and as I walked to the edge of the bed, I knew something was wrong.

New World

"Kareem?" I asked.

His eyes opened, and he looked from Mary to me. "We meet again. I wasn't expecting this. Have a seat."

The guards slid a couple chairs over, and the lights in the room brightened by a few watts.

"Are you okay?" Mary asked the sickly-looking Deltra leader. I could just make out his tattoos peeking out from under the thick blankets.

"No. I'm dying."

"I'm sorry." I couldn't think of anything else to say to his calm statement.

"Tell me why you're here," he said.

Where did I start? "We need your help. We think the Bhlat have invaded our planet."

"You think they have? What does that mean?"

"Many of us have moved on to a new planet, at Proxima. But our communications with Earth take two months to relay, and our leader went back when the messages ceased to come." I explained to him what had happened after we'd last met. How we thought Mae had died crashing into an asteroid, and how we found the device he'd described to us. He seemed pleased it still existed but was surprised the Bhlat knew of it and were waiting there.

Mary took over and talked about us chasing Mae to the Bhlat outpost. She skipped over the intimate details of who Mae was to me and cut the murderous part I had in killing all of their innocents on the base.

Kareem listened, asking few questions. When the tale was over, he asked one simple but important question. "How did you get here? We had no signs of a ship arriving, or they would have told me."

"The *Shandra*." I used the Shimmalian word for the portal to see if this had any meaning to him. His otherwise calm demeanor changed drastically. One of the electronic monitors beeped loudly, causing a small Deltra to enter the room, pushing us out of the way. Kareem shooed him away with a flick of his wrist. "I'm fine," he said in Deltran before switching back to English. "Where did you hear that word?"

"From Sarlun, the Gatekeeper of the *Shandra* on Shimmal." I didn't flinch. This seemed to flummox him even more.

"Then it's out." He sank back in the pillow, almost disappearing into the bed.

"Is that such a bad thing?" Mary asked.

"We spent a lot of hard work to isolate the portals. We blocked off all that we could. The Theos were short-sighted creating these back-door accesses into so many worlds. It was like giving the Kremlons a key to the barn," Kareem said, his reference not hitting home, but I imagined it was something like giving a fox a key to the hen house.

"We need the portal to the Bhlat homeworld." I leaned forward as I spoke. I said the words just loud enough for Kareem to hear them.

"Preposterous!" he yelled, sending his frail body into a coughing fit. When it finished, he wiped his thin lips with a slender arm. "What would that accomplish?"

I told him our plan, and he didn't interrupt once. A few times, he looked like he would interject, but each time he changed his mind, and sat back. When it was over, he looked at Mary. "You agree with this plan?" he asked her.

She nodded, but I noticed a hesitation to it. "What choice do we have?"

"There's always a choice. There's always..." He coughed a few more times. "A choice."

"I think it's our best bet. Unless we can rally enough

New World

support from your allies out there." Magnus, Mary, and I had discussed this, but ultimately, we didn't have the contacts or time to attempt such an endeavor.

"Their portal was blocked off centuries ago. The Theos Collective fought us on the decision, but the long-running religion ended up dissipating as the years went on, and eventually, they forgot about it, just like everyone else. Now there are only a handful of races that even know of their existence. Your friend Sarlun is one of the last remaining Gatekeepers in the universe."

"Something's been bothering me. If there was a portal on Earth, why didn't you use it to help your cause with the *Kalentrek*?" I asked.

"How do you think we got it there? Through the portal. We were a captured race, so few of us were left outside the Kraskis' clutches. All we could do was wait for the right time." His face took on a look of heavy loss. He noticed my reaction and spoke to me softly. "Dean Parker, you are an honorable man. I don't blame you for the destruction of my people. The plan was to rid ourselves of the Kraski with your help, not destroy you all and take your world. We deserved our fate."

"You'll help us?" Mary asked.

"I will. But you have to do something for me first." Kareem's words gave me pause. We didn't have time for favors.

"What? We'll do anything," Mary answered before I could counter.

"You told Leslie and Terrance that you'd get their people here." He looked me in the eyes. "Your people now by blood." He sniffed the air, and I wondered if he could smell the hybrid blood running quickly through my veins. "Go get them. Use the portal and bring them here, to their new home."

"We don't have time for this!" I stood up, knocking my chair over. A guard came in, gun pointed at me.

"It's okay. We're fine. Just having a discussion," Kareem said to the guard. "Aren't we, Dean?"

I righted the chair and sat back down, getting a glower from Mary.

"We'll do it," she said firmly.

"Wait." I started to speak, but she set a hand on my knee.

"I said we'll do it. We owe them that much. We left them there when we took off, and it's weighed on us long enough. They need our help too," Mary said. Instantly, I knew she was right.

"Sarlun showed me Earth's icon but didn't know if it was still functional. Is it?" I asked, sweat forming under my arms.

"It is."

"Where is it?" Mary asked.

"You call it Egypt. Under a large pyramid. The Theos planted it there before humans wandered the dust, and when it was discovered by your people many years ago, they built a tower to protect it. They didn't know what it was, only that it was clearly ancient, and alien," Kareem said. "Do you have your…?" He left the question unanswered, his eyes glancing at the pin on my uniform's lapel.

I almost barked out a laugh. For so long, we'd imagined the pyramids had a link to aliens, and they did. Machu Picchu was rumored to involve aliens, and it did. I wondered what other rumors were true. Area 51?

"From the pyramids to a Russian war camp. We're going to need help," I said.

"Patty told me to contact Jeff Dinkle if we ever make it to Earth and need someone on her side. Magnus knows how to reach him." Mary looked ready to leave.

New World

I turned to the door as I heard a familiar voice demanding to be let in. Terrance came pushing past the guard, toward us.

"Not in here!" Kareem called, stopping the angry hybrid in his footsteps.

"Where are they?" he asked, his face dark red.

"Earth," I said, ashamed I didn't have better news for the man. "We're going to get them now."

"I'm coming with you," he said.

"I don't think that's a good idea," I said, but Kareem spoke up.

"Take him. He'll be helpful. Bring them back, and I'll expose the secrets my people worked so hard to hide. I want the secret to be yours, and yours alone. It will die with you, do you understand?" he asked, a grave look over his gaunt face.

I did understand and told him as much. He nodded and closed his eyes. He didn't speak again, and we stood up to face Leslie and Terrance. Leslie had shorn her hair short, but otherwise was the spitting image of my now dead wife, and of Mae. My heart ached for a second as I looked her in the eyes. "Let's go. If you're coming, can you fly us back to the portal?"

"What portal?" Leslie asked.

"Come on, we have a lot to talk about."

SIXTEEN

"Are you sure you can make this trip with us? What about Natalia and your boy?" I asked Magnus.

"She wants me to go. She said if she can't be there to protect you guys, I'd better be." Magnus opened the transport's door, and the cool air rushed inside. It was still cold by Terran Five standards, but it was in their spring season. Snow was melting, leaving a sloppy mess near the cavern entrance that would lead us to the portal.

Leslie and Terrance were suited up and hadn't spoken much on the cramped ride from Terran One to the mountainside. They were anxious to help their friends, and I could completely understand the feeling. We all got out, bringing a vast array of supplies. The small *Kalentrek* device was in my breast pocket, though I didn't expect to have to use it yet. Mary was the last to get out, from the pilot's seat, and I gave her a kiss as she stepped onto the slushy ground.

"One thing at a time. We can do this, get the Bhlat world icon, and finish this once and for all. What do you say? Another ass-kicking mission for old time's sake?" I asked.

Magnus gave a *hoorah* and stuck his hand out. I settled mine on his, flat-palmed, and Mary followed suit. Ter-

New World

rance rolled his eyes but joined in, followed by Leslie. "Let's go kick some ass!" Magnus said. We all repeated "kick some ass!" and raised our hands. It felt good to be part of a team, even a desperate stitched-together one, off doing someone else's mission. I reprimanded myself for thinking that. I had promised to help the hybrids, and I was about to follow through on that. Their lives were just as important as the people of Earth's.

Magnus went first, blowing the air horn. Terrance did the same at the rear of our line as we entered the cavern. I took over the lead, taking us down the tunnels I was becoming very familiar with. Magnus hadn't been there before, and he gave a low whistle as we entered the room. The hieroglyphs lit up, and Leslie and Terrance looked a little less sickly than they had at their new planet's portal. Apparently, it had affected them like it had affected me the first time I'd been led here, but because they weren't fighting the urge, they didn't have the same out-of-body reaction.

The symbols on the walls glowed as we approached the gemstone in the table. We all gathered around, knowing what to expect, as I scrolled to find the icon for Earth on the screen. It was there: two horizontal slashes, one large circle, and one small circle, which I now attributed to Earth's sun and moon.

"Everyone ready?" I asked, and when no one commented, I hit the icon and closed my eyes.

When I opened them, we were in a different room. This one appeared twice as large as New Spero's portal room, with the same etchings on the walls, which dimmed within seconds of arriving. I noticed their placement on the walls was different than they had been in New Spero, and different yet from Shimmal.

"I'm not sure I want to get used to this," Magnus

said, already exploring the dark space. We all had our suits' LEDs on, lighting up the room. It looked basic – ancient, even – untouched by anyone in a long time.

We were still wearing our helmets, just in case the room was sealed off or some deadly gas had seeped through the ground, ready to kill us on arrival. The sensors showed there was air, oxygen levels normal. I unclasped the mask, the hiss loud in the quiet area.

The air was stale. It was like walking into the back of my grandfather's barn when I was a kid. Layers of dust had covered countless items he'd stored away from the turn of the century. The only living things to even go into that room were the spiders, who made happy homes of their own on the old oak furniture.

I assumed spiders would be prevalent here as well, but when I looked for them, I saw nothing but dirt walls and dust particles floating around as we disturbed the portal room.

"The door's over here," Leslie said, in her more than familiar voice. "It looks like stone."

We didn't know just which pyramid we were under, or if we were going to be stuck trying to get out. I'd had nightmares the night before that we arrived, only to have the doorway inside covered by fallen rocks. It had been a few centuries since the portal had been used, so we had no idea what the condition was on the other side of the door. I pushed my fear of the unknown down, not letting myself worry.

"Open it," I said, and walked to them as Terrance used his weight to push on the large stone wall.

"It won't move!" Terrance grunted.

Magnus moved beside him and started to push. After a minute of exertion, they gave up.

"Wait. It wouldn't be on hinges. It's probably round.

New World

We need to roll it away," Mary said, and I pictured a large stone circle on the other side. I lowered to the ground and saw slight openings at the corners of the doorway.

"She's right. We need to roll it."

"Which way?" Leslie asked. We had no way of knowing.

"Look up here. I think these are handles." Magnus ran his hand over the stone slab and showed us where a couple of handholds were recessed. "Not much room, but I bet we can get enough leverage, as long as there isn't something jammed on the side of the circle out there." I went beside him and jammed my fingers into the second opening. We pulled to the left, and after ten seconds of hard yanking, it started to roll. We kept pulling, and it rolled open.

My heart hammered from effort and joy at our success. It was short-lived when I thought about how much further we needed to go before we could come back to this room to leave. It wasn't going to be easy.

We all ushered out of the portal room. "Should we close it up?" Mary asked me.

"Good idea. I doubt anyone's coming down here, but better safe than sorry. Mary, can you pin our location on your GPS?" I asked as Magnus and Leslie rolled the door back closed. The hallway we'd emerged into was shallow and went beyond the room in both directions.

All we knew was we were underground, a pyramid on top of us. We just needed to get to higher ground, and then we could find our way out.

"Look for elevation changes in the pitch of the ground," Mary said, and we chose to go left from the room, because it seemed to rise slightly as you walked along it.

The ceilings were low, and Magnus had to duck a few

times to avoid hitting his head on jutting rocks. The halls were primarily dug from dirt, but rock was stuck into both the walls and ceiling, probably to help support the opening. We walked along the path for ten minutes, slowly moving and breathing in stale air. Mary had elected to put her mask back on her helmet, and Terrance joined her. If we didn't get out of the basement here soon, I'd need the fresh air as well.

"I'll be damned," Magnus said, stopping so suddenly that I walked right into his broad back.

"What is it?" I asked, stepping around him to see for myself.

The hall opened to a room, this one with more hieroglyphs. These looked different from the *Shandra* ones and were most likely done by ancient Egyptians. It showed small figures bowing on the ground to large people in animal masks, presumably their representations of the Theos they wouldn't have ever seen.

"At least they were smart enough to seal the portal and build a pyramid overtop it," Mary said, running a gloved hand over the stone walls.

"Do you think…?" I started to ask and let the question fall quiet.

"I know what you're thinking, and I bet some sad soul was lost on the other side a few times before they assumed their friends were just being killed." Magnus was filming the room with his suit's surveillance.

I pictured an ancient Egyptian child playing with his sister, chasing her down a tunnel they'd found in the desert. She made it to the room first, awestruck by the glowing gemstone. She stood still, the game all but forgotten. The walls began to glow as she neared the table, and the pretty drawings put her into a trance. Her brother called to her from the doorway, older, more aware of danger.

New World

She ignored him, her heart pounding so loud she could hardly hear his words. She touched an image on the screen. The room shone brightly, and when it subsided, the boy was left alone.

I opened my eyes and wondered if that had happened, or if my imagination was just filling in the blanks.

"This way. I see stairs," Leslie called from the far corner.

Each step kicked up a puff of dust as we climbed them. They were made of stone now, not carved out of dirt like most of what we'd seen so far. I guessed this section was newer than the other one, added on when they were about to build the pyramid, or built afterward to connect the two.

We found another door at the top, a stone circle we had to roll out of the way. Once out, we followed a hall in the dark, our suits lighting the way. I spotted old torch holders on the walls, some of the torches still mounted, the majority of their shapes gone to dust.

"Anyone else feel like lighting one of those just to see what happens?" Magnus asked, and I could almost hear his grin.

"I imagine they'd burn for a minute, then be ashes in your hand. They don't just look a couple hundred years old, they look a couple thousand years old. I don't need a carbon dating test to know that," I said, trying to remember anything from the documentaries I'd seen as a kid in school. "If I recall, the pyramids housed the tombs of a queen and king, each in separate chambers. I'm sure there's more to it, but if we follow the path that leads us up, we should be able to either get out or go to the ancient Egyptian mummified royalty."

"That sounds right to me too," Mary confirmed. "I don't know which pyramid we're in, but they all took an insane amount of effort. I can't believe there's been a hidden portal down inside, and no one's found it."

That got me thinking. "These days, they have all sorts of ultrasonic sensors that tell them what density of soil and rock are under things. How did they not learn there was an opening down here?" I asked, perplexed.

"No idea. I'll chalk it up to ancient alien gods," Magnus said.

I looked back at the hybrids, who had remained very quiet to this point. "Are you guys okay?"

"The sooner we get out of this dusty tomb, the better. I'm not a fan of tight underground spaces," Leslie said.

Terrance slid his hand into Leslie's. "Me neither."

The walkway kept going slightly uphill, but eventually, it came to an end. Magnus was ahead; he and Mary were feeling the walls.

"There's no exit," Magnus said, and I instantly felt the walls closing in on me.

"What do you mean, there's no exit?" Leslie's voice lifted, on the edge of panic.

"We'll find a way out," Mary said.

I tried to get a feel for where we could be. We'd walked a short way, and at an uphill trajectory. We were probably near the ground level, where they'd plopped the pyramid on top of the portal access. If archeologists hadn't found what was below, there had to be a layer of thick rock between the levels.

We spent an hour looking for any sign of an exit, and by the time we'd given up, we were covered in dust and Leslie was crying.

"We'll be okay. We can always go back," Mary said, trying to comfort her.

"We aren't going back!" she yelled. "Our family is up there, stuffed away in a prison, tormented and dying. I've

New World

seen enough of humans to know how they'll treat us."

"Kind of like how you were trying to fly our comatose bodies into the sun, hey?" Magnus asked, egging her on. It was clear he was at his wits' end with Operation Stuck-Under-a-Pyramid too.

"I don't have to justify it. You all know our story. We repented and asked forgiveness. Some of you gave it, some of you couldn't." Terrance took over for his sobbing counterpart.

"The last time anyone from Earth knew what was happening, you two escaped a secret military base and snuck around the Long Island camp, having midnight clandestine meetings. Remember the bodies? Who do you think they blamed for that?" Magnus added fuel to the fire.

"We did it for them!" Terrance said, pushing himself chest to chest with Magnus, though he stood a good six inches shorter than the Scandinavian.

"Lot of good it did them. You two were living easy on planet log-cabin, and they were blamed for everything!" Magnus yelled back, spittle flying from his mouth as he shouted.

"It was your goddamn friend Mae that killed those guards! We aren't to blame!" Leslie screeched from the ground, her hands on top of her head in a frantic gesture.

"Enough!" I called, standing between the two men, pushing Magnus back. For a second, he looked like a Rottweiler who'd had a bone taken from its mouth; I was worried he was going to snap at me. But his common sense took over, and he turned, walking away. "Neither of you are right, and neither are wrong. Both sides are to blame. We may not be able to fix it, but we can change the outcome now. We won't be able to do that and set an example if we can't even work together without fighting."

Terrance leaned against the wall and slid down until his butt was touching the dirt floor beside Leslie.

The hall had gotten pin-drop quiet, and Leslie broke the silence. "You're right. We're with you. No more bad blood. I'm sorry for all the trouble we caused. If we hadn't escaped, you wouldn't be here right now. Maybe humans would eventually have seen us as friends. Instead, we ran away, which was exactly what Mae wanted. The Bhlat are now knocking on your door, and it could be our fault, and we made you lose seven years of your loved ones' lives."

We hadn't told them all of this, so clearly, they'd been listening as we talked to Kareem. Something struck me at that moment. Something Kareem had asked, or almost asked.

"Guys, Kareem started to ask if we had our...something...then cut himself short before he looked at the pin on the uniform. What if someone added a lift on the other side of the ground? Anyone with this technology could press their pin, glow green, and lift toward the target embedded above by the Deltra or some other ancient race after the pyramid was built."

I walked around the halls again, this time with a renewed vigor. Magnus and Mary were near the end, and I moved them out of the way as I searched, this time not for a handle or a secret door or hatch in the ceiling, but a sign on the floor. I used my boots to brush away dirt from the ground near the end wall and found that section was really a slab of stone with dirt covering it. Mary got down on her knees, and I joined her, wiping the stone surface with our gloved hands, clearing the dirt off, until we could see it.

Laughing, tired, and covered in dust, we hugged; the image of Earth's icon was emblazoned on the rock.

New World

"You did it again," Magnus said, clapping me on the shoulder after he helped Mary up off the dirt.

"I'll go first." I looked up at the ceiling, wondering how thick the space between us and the well-trodden paths of the pyramid above was.

"Are you sure?" Mary said, worry thick in her voice.

I nodded, ready to get out of the sealed-off trap we were in. "There have to be openings here too; otherwise, we wouldn't be breathing in this stale air. If anything happens to me and my plan fails, look for a spot with air flow. It may be your way out. And if that doesn't work, go back and convince Kareem to give us what we asked for. We'll bring your friends back after we deal with the Bhlat." The last bit was for Leslie and Terrance. I caught his gaze and held it there for a moment. He nodded solemnly.

Mary took my face in her hands. "Do it. Communicate back to us, and we'll be right up." I felt the press of her lips against mine. They were dry and covered in old sediment, but I didn't care. Not caring who was watching, I kissed her back.

"Enough already. Tell you what. You get us out of here, and you two can have seven minutes in heaven at the Queen's chamber up above," Magnus said.

I stopped the kiss short and smiled at Mary. She was so beautiful; so wonderful. The few months we'd had on New Spero just being a couple was the best time of my life. We walked Maggie, tended the garden, chopped wood… that was the life I wanted for us, at least part-time. She seemed to be reading my mind, because she just gave me a slow, soft nod, her eyes just on the brink of tearing up.

"See you on the other side." I clasped my helmet tight, hearing the familiar hiss as it pressurized, then hit the pin on my uniform. The familiar weightless feeling engulfed me, and I floated upward.

SEVENTEEN

I forced myself to open my eyes, only after a count to five. I instantly regretted it. I was still inside the rock, and even though I couldn't feel it, I thought it was going to crush me. Just as I calmed myself out of the sudden shock, I emerged from the stone.

The green light around me dissipated, leaving me on shaky knees in the pyramid passageway. My lights were on, and they showed me two directions to go. One careened at a downward angle, the other elevated at an acute pitch. That was the way we needed to go.

"Dean, are you there?" Mary's voice carried into my ear. I'd been so distracted, I'd forgotten to tell them I made it.

"I'm here and the path is clear." I stood out of the way, making room for my counterparts to float their way to the main section of the pyramid with me.

"Gotcha," came the reply.

Soon four figures covered in green breached the hard floor, and I noticed the link in the ceiling above. There was another symbol on the ceiling, which was at least ten feet high here, too high for most people to reach unaided. The Deltra must have planted the beaming magnet above the symbol.

"Let's move. We wasted enough time down there." Magnus moved past me, taking charge. I was happy for him to do it. "Shouldn't we run into tourists or something?"

"After everything that's happened, and is currently happening to Earth, I think the travel business to ancient structures is a thing of the past," I said, hoping I was right. We wanted to get in and out as stealthily as possible.

The pyramid paths were much cleaner up here, the walls cut out of large stone blocks. We came to a set of stairs leading up, and knew they'd been added in the past century. Long wooden rails lined the sides, with manufactured steps to keep tourists from falling or suing someone. The sudden jolt of modern in the ancient pyramid was jarring.

"Looks like we're on the right path," Terrance said from behind us.

We kept moving up the stairs, taking two at a time in a jog. It didn't take us long to get to a fork where there was an option to turn a one-eighty and go up again. Signs pointed with images of a tomb for the Queen's chamber and the King's chamber above, with pictures in the backdrop of the Great Pyramid of Giza, one of the seven wonders of the world.

"Now we know where we are, at least," Mary muttered.

It felt far from Russia, and we just hoped that when we got outside, we weren't too late.

"As much as I want to go see a real mummified corpse, let's make a move," Magnus said. When no one disagreed, he moved for the exit.

I expected to be blinded by sunlight as we left, but it was night; the area's lights were shut down. Closed for business. We left, ready for anything as we did so, passing two columns at the front of the pyramid. At the same

New World

moment, we all craned our necks to the sky, looking for signs of battle or destruction.

Nothing. Just the light of a half moon, and stars shining at us from light years away.

Magnus looked at me and shrugged.

"How do we reach Dinkle?" I asked, though we'd been over it a few times.

Magnus pulled out a tablet. "We left the cell technology on our tablets for just such an emergency. As long as Jeff is still kicking, we should be able to reach him. Patty asked him to stay behind so that someone she trusted was here."

"Did he want to leave?" Mary asked.

"He was the world's most alien-obsessed man, with a talk show about it. Of course he wanted to get to a colony planet. But at the end of the day, he listened to her because she heard him out at the start and brought him onto the team. He was there when we tested our cloaking technology and dismantled the Kraski ships. It was the equivalent of you seeing the inside of the Yankees' locker room." Magnus walked some way out, and even in the dimly-lit night sky, I could make out the smaller pyramids nearby, the grounds a barren rocky plateau.

That brought me back to the day two years ago, when I'd gone to Yankee Stadium with my new little friend, Carey. Running the bases with him chasing after me had been a bright spot in an otherwise overwhelming time.

Magnus opened the facemask on his helmet, and we removed ours, stashing them in a sack from my pack, and placed them under a grouping of broken rocks where they would be almost impossible to find. We also slipped off our uniforms and did the same thing with them. We were going to be conspicuous enough walking around with rifles in our bags. Blending in was going to be key.

Magnus was fiddling with his tablet, and after he tapped the screen one last time, he crossed his other fingers and looked to the sky. "Jeff?" he asked, speaking into the earpiece mic. "Oh, thank God. It's Magnus. We need your help."

They talked for a few minutes. Magnus nodded while Jeff spoke, and I wanted to hear the other end of the conversation. "We're at the Pyramid of Giza. Yeah, that one. One hour? We can wait it out. See you then."

"Well? What the hell's going on here?" Leslie asked impatiently.

"They're here, but so far no fireworks have gone off. Naidoo has just made a statement for everyone to stay calm, but that's not going so well. As far as Jeff knows, the Bhlat have hung in space, and the connections to the station up there have been severed. He's bringing a transporter over here. I guess he was in London, or what's left of it." Magnus' mouth was set in a grim line.

"What now?" Mary asked.

"We wait for Jeff," Magnus said, sitting down on a half-sized pyramid stone jutting out of the ground.

Leslie and Terrance set their packs down and ventured off together, whispering quietly.

"I still don't trust them," Magnus said about the hybrid pair.

"What choice do we have? We can't get to the Bhlat world without them. We're committed," I said.

"All that data from the Bhlat base you downloaded and all the details on locations were encrypted, hey?" I wasn't sure if he was making a comment or asking a question.

"They aren't stupid, that's for sure. They made sure their location was hidden from anyone finding an outpost," I said.

New World

"We trust them now, but promise me this. We have each other's backs no matter what happens. You, Mary, and me. If shit goes south up there, we leave them and force the information from Kareem if we have to." Magnus' voice was a low growl, and a vein on his forehead was starting to throb.

"Deal," Mary said first.

"Deal." I knew I owed the hybrids something after they'd turned around and worked with us to get our people home, but it only went so far. My friends came first. My people too.

The hour went by slowly, and I marked the passage of the moon by its position over the Great Pyramid. I almost went back in, wanting to see the other chambers, but the risk of bumping around inside in the near dark wasn't worth it.

Being in Egypt after traveling through a portal felt like being on an abandoned alien world. No one was in sight, ancient structures pushed into the sky. It was surreal.

After some time, a light shone in the sky, moving quickly toward our location. Leslie and Terrance meandered over to us, both holding their rifles at ready. I didn't like the look in Terrance's eyes as he stared toward the incoming ship.

"This better be Dinkle," Magnus said, holding his own gun at ready.

The small transport landed, similar to the ones they had on New Spero, but it looked simpler and more worn than theirs. Probably an early model. The door opened, and a familiar face hopped out.

"I'll be damned. The rumors are true," Jeff said, a smile covering half his face. He laughed and walked over to us, arms stretched out.

He set them on Mary's shoulders and kissed each of her cheeks before coming over to me and giving me a firm hug, complete with a back slap to end the embrace. He did the same to Magnus and gave a curt nod in the hybrids' direction before speaking again. "The Heroes of Earth, back again. We thought you were dead." He said this so matter-of-factly, like it didn't bother him either way. "I'm glad you're not."

"So are we," Mary chimed in.

"Why are you so chipper? Aren't the Bhlat hovering somewhere overhead?" I asked, his demeanor bugging me.

The smile fell from his face. "I'm sorry. When I heard from you, I got so excited. If anyone was going to get us out of this mess, it's you three. I see Mae's no longer with you?" He looked at me intensely, like he was trying to say something with his eyes, maybe pass a secret message to me.

"She's dead," I said quietly.

"I see. So you got my text, then?" he asked.

Text? I hadn't had a text since... *Don't trust her.* "What the hell are you asking me? It was you?" I crossed over to him, grabbing him by the shirt collar. A uniformed man from the transporter got out, holding a gun in the air, and asked me calmly to let him go.

Magnus and Mary quickly had their weapons in the air, pointing at Jeff and his escort.

"No need to get out of hand. I was trying to help you." His voice was ragged as I clutched him firmly.

"Why did you send that text?" I was suddenly furious. Rage filled my veins as I recalled getting the message on my cell phone outside the gas station near Nashville. Mae had been with us, chasing down the two hybrids now beside us. Only now, she was gone.

"She was dangerous. I didn't have enough proof, just the word of one of them." He nodded in Terrance's direction.

I let him go. The anger was still there, but he was right. She did screw us over, even if she thought it was for the best. "What signs?" I asked, nodding to my counterparts, who let their weapons down. The air thinned as the tension lifted.

"Before we get into this, do you think we could have this discussion in the air?" Magnus asked. "We have an objective, and fighting each other isn't going to get us there."

One by one, we loaded onto the transport ship, which had barely enough room for us to sit side by side. Jeff sat in the back with us, and Magnus took a seat up front by the pilot. I was hip to hip between Mary and Leslie. Our bags and rifles leaned behind the back seats, in the small storage area just out of sight.

"Explain," I said once we were in the air, leaving the pyramids behind.

EIGHTEEN

We moved quickly through the night. Part of me wished I could watch the ground fly past us as we traveled, moving over the Middle East toward Siberia, where Jeff claimed the hybrid camp was located.

"I had a talk show for a few years on extraterrestrial beings, and the likelihood of life outside of Earth. Ever since I was a child sending letters to MUFON, I've been ridiculed for my beliefs. It didn't stop there. Even as a successful television host and blogger, I had hate mail, and naysayers putting me down. Could you imagine the thrill I had when one of the hybrids approached me a year before the Event?" Jeff's smile started to creep back onto his face.

"What?" Mary asked, as incredulous as I felt.

"Kyle came to a filming of one of my interview shows. He sat in the front row, and there was something familiar about him, like I'd seen him before. It turned out that I had, on a conspiracy blog about aliens among us. It showed images of Kyle's other lookalike hybrids. He was the Caucasian male, dark hair."

I glanced over at Mary, knowing Jeff was describing the hybrid that had looked like Bob, her husband. She just turned and gave me a forced smile.

Jeff continued. "The site had done a good job of identifying this man all over the world. There were at least ten sightings; each of the men looked very similar, though some wore their hair differently and dressed differently. The site wasn't a big one, and most people assume these things are fake or Photoshopped anyway, so it didn't make any mainstream news. When I realized this man in my audience was one of them, I couldn't wait to speak with him. I remember how nervous I was after the show was done filming. Kyle lingered in his seat, long past everyone else's departure, and once the crew was gone, I walked over to him, heart pounding, knowing this was the moment I'd been waiting for. I was right.

"He told me his name and asked if there was somewhere we could talk privately. I agreed to it, and we left the studio. We walked to an all-night café nearby where only a couple of night-shift workers were hanging out, giving us ample opportunity to talk without prying ears.

"The story he spilled was insane, even to me, a full alien believer. He claimed that a race of aliens was coming, fleeing their own system and making the trip to Earth, where they would dispose of us all, claiming the planet for themselves. I asked him how he knew this, and he said he was a hybrid alien, part Kraski, part human. He looked sickly and was coughing up a lung by the time our pie came to the table." Jeff paused briefly to look at Leslie, then Terrance, before starting again. "I asked him what I was supposed to do about it, knowing he had to be crazy. I would have left it alone if I hadn't seen him on that conspiracy website. That he was already being touted as an alien by some blogger made me listen to him. The idea that he may have been the guy behind the website crossed my mind, but this man was so into his story, I almost believed him."

The ship jumped a little bit, and my heart hammered in my chest, thinking we were being attacked. "Just turbulence," the pilot said from the front seat. I craned my neck and there was Magnus, listening to Jeff's story with interest. After a few more bumps, I clipped my seatbelt on, the rest of us following suit.

"What happened after that?" Mary prompted.

The TV host was looking forward, not meeting the gaze of anyone, just silent for a moment.

"Jeff?" I asked.

He turned to me, his eyes coming into focus. "Yes, sorry. I was lost in my story, I guess. So much has happened since that day, but it's so clear in my memory. I can tell you what color and style his shirt was, and that his white sneakers were old, with dark scuff marks along the sides of them. I'll never forget his next words."

I leaned forward, drawn in like everyone else listening.

"He said we had no chance. He hated being used like a puppet and said that the Kraski could go to hell. That's when he told me about the Deltras' plan. It sounded insane and had far too many moving pieces to work," Jeff said, his eyes shifting to meet mine. "He told me there were a few of them in the mix, but not to trust one in particular."

He paused again, and Mary leaned back, pushing out an irritated sigh. "For the love of God, just say the name already."

Jeff smiled, making me want to slap the words out of his mouth. "Mae. He told me not to trust Mae."

"What good did that do?" I asked. "You didn't tell anyone, and then sending an anonymous text to me telling me not to trust *her*. It could have meant anyone. Mary, Natalia, Patty… hell, even Leslie here. What did he say about Mae?" I was getting tired of Jeff's demeanor, and wished he'd just sent the transport and stayed in London. "What did he know about her?"

New World

Jeff shrugged. "I was trying to help you. She was with the Bhlat, wasn't she? He was right, and I was right to warn you."

"I think the part we're having a hard time wrapping our heads around is this: you could have had a conversation with us *before* we traveled off into space with Mae by our side. Maybe, just maybe, these two could have stayed on Earth, and we could've not lost seven years with our loved ones. Maybe the hybrids wouldn't be on lockdown now, wasting away in Siberia like murderers and terrorists," Mary said, keeping her voice calm. I gripped her hand, squeezing it for support.

"Yes, but… then the Bhlat wouldn't have come," he said, his grin so wide I saw all of his teeth. His comment didn't even register as I looked at him, thinking how much he looked like a wild animal with his teeth bared like that.

"What did you say?" Magnus asked from the front.

"Then the Bhlat wouldn't have come." Jeff repeated the words, and before we could react, he pulled a gun, aiming it at Terrance's head. "Anyone moves, and I blow this man's head off his shoulders. And I use the term 'man' loosely. He's more of an alien monstrosity. Part Kraski, a terrible race of cowards, mixed with another race of turncoats and self-abusers: human."

"Magnus, where are we going?" I asked, not able to see through the front window.

"We're moving up, heading into the clouds," my large friend said through a clenched jaw. If I knew Magnus, he was holding down the urge to slam the pilot's head into the dash.

"Dinkle, what's the endgame here?" I asked, feeling stupid for instantly trusting the stranger. We'd fallen right into his trap. Patty had been played by the man she thought she knew.

"The endgame is this: we already have Dalhousie and your other friends up there. Now we have the famed Heroes of Earth to bring as a sacrifice. Rumor has it they want your head on a stick, Mr. Parker. I wonder what for?"

My throat had closed, and I swallowed hard. They knew me. Naidoo had probably sold me out.

"You don't have to do this," I said, the words burning on their way out. We'd come all this way, and now it was going to end at the hands of this slick television talk show host.

"No, I don't, but humans have never interested me. Aliens? Now them, I can get behind. They're going to show me amazing things. Speaking of which, how did you get to Egypt? Inquiring minds want to know your tricks."

"You really think we're going to tell you that?" Mary asked vehemently. I set a trembling hand on her thigh.

Terrance was staying far calmer than I would have with the cold steel of a gun against my temple. I had to hand it to the guy; he was cool as a cucumber. Leslie was fidgeting. I hoped she wasn't about to lunge at Jeff, because her friend would probably end up dead if she did.

Magnus whistled up front, just a light one, but I knew what it meant. It was the same whistle I'd used to teach Carey to roll over. I scanned the seatbelts, seeing everyone was wearing one but Jeff. I got ready. We bumped into some more turbulence, and Magnus made his move. He must have snuck his hand to the steering column because we suddenly were torn to the side, the ship turning hard to starboard. Jeff went hard into the sidewall, still holding his gun. I unclasped my belt just as we came out of the barrel roll and lunged at the dazed man.

"Don't even think about it," Magnus said from the

front seat, presumably at the pilot, as I arced through the air, the training Slate engrained into me on our previous journey taking over.

Jeff's eyes went wide as he tried to swing his gun around in time to aim at me, but he was too late. Our bodies collided. My fist went into his gut and he bent over, fighting for breath. Terrance was already digging behind him to the storage area, and when I glanced over, he was passing the pulse rifles to the others.

Jeff was still gripping the gun, but I clasped his wrist while he coughed loudly. Mary came over and pried it from his fingers; soon he was slumped back in his seat, his head bleeding from the side.

"You don't know what you've done," he spat angrily. "They're expecting us. When we don't show up, they'll come looking. Do you think they'll spare the people in their search?"

"Don't put this on us. This is all on your hands," I said, surprised his perspective would allow him to see that vantage point. This type of man always reasoned with himself when he did things. He justified his terrible actions with righteous causes, but at the end of the day, he was in the wrong.

"Take us to Siberia," Magnus grumbled from the front. He was now pointing a gun at the pilot, whose shoulders took on the inevitable slump of someone caught with their hand in the cookie jar.

I went to the storage compartment and found some zip ties, which we used to tie Jeff's hands together. He protested, but soon he was sitting in the back on the floor, head on his knees.

"Should we give him something for his head?" Mary asked quietly.

I shook my head. "We'll figure it out later. For now, I

have a hard time showing the man compassion." I shifted my attention to the front of the transport. "What's our ETA?" I asked.

When the pilot didn't answer, Magnus peered over to the console. "Ten minutes. Here, look at this."

He passed me a tablet and told me to press play. It showed a snow-covered entrance to a large stone-walled prison. Guard towers were visibly manned, and a name was carved in the rock in Russian.

In the video, a stream of people emerged from a Kraski ship. Their hands were chained, and they wore orange jumpsuits. My stomach lurched when I saw who they were. Every few people, the faces were the same. Leslie clenched beside me, a low growl coming from her throat.

"This is where we're going," Magnus said. "I found it online. Maybe we should take them and let the Bhlat have this world. I'm sick of the things we put each other through."

"Just put yourself in their shoes, Magnus," Mary said. "We chased after who we thought were murderous hybrids, and never came back. They had to do something with them. When the Bhlat contacted Earth, they must have felt like they'd done the right thing. That doesn't make it right, but it makes it understandable."

The video kept playing, showing the inside of the building, the lines of cold bleak cells, and a pitiful bunch of hybrids sitting and eating in the mess hall. They were a beaten-down group, and I felt so terribly for them. We had to right it, and even though we were wasting precious time on this mission, it was an important one, no matter the outcome of the impending war.

"Arriving," the pilot said, all the fight gone out of him. He was a hired hand and most likely didn't care

New World

about causes, only a paycheck and seeing his family at night.

Snow was falling as we lowered from the cloud line, reminding me of Terran Five.

As we neared the building, something was off about it. "Shouldn't there be lights on somewhere?"

Magnus nodded and mumbled something along the same lines.

"I've got a bad feeling about this," Mary said. The feeling was mutual, and almost a constant for us over the past couple of years.

Leslie and Terrance stayed quiet, their gazes never leaving the view of the structure we were approaching. They were so close to their friends, nothing would stop them from getting to them now. I knew we had to watch our own backs. As much as I wanted to say these two were on our side, I knew they were looking out for themselves and the rest of the hybrids first, and I didn't even blame them.

The transport ship landed softly, near the entrance we'd seen on the video minutes ago.

Leslie was already half out the door, followed quickly by Terrance. Jeff was tied up in the back, and we did the same to the pilot, making sure they had no weapons.

As I followed Mary out, Leslie was standing at the large iron gates. She looked back at us and pulled. The gates swung open. We still couldn't see any lights on inside, and the towers located around the building looked to be empty.

"It's like it's abandoned," Magnus said, holding his rifle at ready.

We walked past the gates, toward the dark prison.

NINETEEN

The main doors were tall and double wide, large enough to roll through supplies. Magnus was ready to blast them open, but Leslie held up a hand and tested the handle. It depressed, and she pulled the door open.

"This is odd." Mary looked around, pointing at a camera in the corner. There was no light on it, and it didn't move with us. Was anyone watching? Wind blew around the building, pushing light snow over us. Visibility of the area was poor, but that might help us get out of there.

"I'd planned on Jeff getting us a ship. How do we move this many?" I asked, hoping someone had a better idea than I did.

"First we see how many we're talking about," Magnus whispered, getting a dirty look from Leslie. He ignored it. "A place of this importance might very well have a ship parked out back."

The entry was dim; even the backup emergency lights had expended their battery charges. There was an old bulletin board on the wall, half empty, and a depressing dirt-covered entry mat.

"Where the hell are the guards?" Magnus asked.

"If they're still here, they aren't doing a very good job of keeping anyone out. Hopefully, they did a better one of keeping them in." I got a glare from Leslie. "I didn't mean it like that. We're going to find anyone left and get them out of here."

The door closed behind us, clicking ominously. There was finality to the sound in the otherwise silent entryway. Mary jumped, smiling nervously in my direction.

The mud room, as I thought of it, had two more doors leading into a hallway we could see through the metal-lined glass. Leslie moved ahead, impatient to find her people. I expected the push lever to stop firm, keeping us from entering, but it moved, the door opening easily.

Leslie started forward, but Terrance reached an arm out to slow her. "It's not going to do us any good to run in with guns blazing and get ourselves killed. We need to scope it out first." She pulled away from him but heeded his advice, falling back and letting Magnus take the lead.

Magnus looked like he'd done this a thousand times, so we followed him, moving as a unit down the hall, keeping close to the wall as we did so. We passed a vacant reception desk; an old boxy computer monitor sat there, a reminder of the past. If I didn't know better, I would have said Jeff had been pulling our chain the whole time. He'd sent us to the wrong prison.

Our LEDs illuminated the way, beams jostling up and down on the walls as we moved, shadow figures dancing in our wake.

"I hear something," Mary said, and Magnus stopped, then held a finger in the air. We all stopped, and my heart thumped in my eardrums.

There was a faint noise coming from down the hall. It wasn't much, and I couldn't place what the sound was, but someone was inside the prison. We moved along, the tension thickening with each step. The clinking noise grew louder every ten seconds, and in a minute, we were past all of the offices at the front of the building. Doctor's office, warden's office, staff change room, lunchroom – all showing signs of recent use.

"They've abandoned it," I said.

"Someone's still here," Mary replied. The next set of doors led us to a guard station, and a large metal door stood between us and the wing of prison cells.

"Give it a try, Leslie. You have the magic touch." Magnus moved out of the way, making room for the smaller hybrid woman. She tugged at it, but it didn't budge.

"Locked," she said.

"The keys have to be around here somewhere." Magnus started to rifle through drawers.

We all set to different parts of the room, sifting through paperwork and desks. I found an assortment of poker chips, half-full flasks that sloshed as I slid them out of the way, and a couple of erotic Russian magazines that looked like they were from the eighties. No keys anywhere to be found.

Jingling metal rang from the other side of the room, and Terrance looked pleased with himself, like he'd just won a prize on a game show.

"What's behind door number one?" I whispered in a low voice.

"What?" Mary asked.

I just shook my head, waiting while Terrance inserted the metal key and turned it. With a click, it unlocked, and he pulled on the bars. They slid open, and Terrance walked through the opening.

"Stop where you are!" a panicked voice called from behind us.

I spun, pulse rifle ready to fire. Slate's training took over again, and my finger settled on the trigger ever-so-

New World

lightly as I gauged my target.

A haggard man approached us, his face red with exertion. He was holding a revolver, and an old one by the looks of it. A white beard covered most of his face and neck. I almost fired, but there was something in his eyes that made me lift my finger off the trigger.

"Don't let them out!" he yelled, panting as he came in the room.

"What happened here?" I asked, looking around the disheveled guard's room.

"They all left. When those damned aliens started arriving, everyone left. Said it wasn't their job to babysit and get killed in the process," the man said.

"So the Bhlat came, you all found out, and assumed they would come for the hybrids, killing you in their wake?" Mary asked, her voice taking on a calming tone.

He nodded. "Something like that."

"How long ago was this?" she asked.

"About three months now."

"Then why are you still here?" I asked.

"Someone had to keep the animals penned up after what they did to us. We heard the stories of them being the masterminds behind the *Event* and all. Then killing those people, Dean and Mary and whatnot. Way I figured it, if the aliens came for them, I'd be spared for keeping them safe and in one place." He shuffled on his feet. From his perspective, he was doing something honorable, and it was self-preservation at the same time.

"Just put down your gun. We'll explain everything," Mary said.

He flinched, his gaze darting from face to face, and for the first time, he saw Leslie and Terrance.

"You. How did you get out?" He raised his revolver, shakily pointing at Terrance, who had stepped in front of

Leslie.

"They're with us," I said. I glanced over at Mary. "You thought Dean and Mary were killed by the hybrids? I have news for you: you're looking at us."

He looked from my face to hers, and back again. "That's impossible. You're too young to be. You don't look a day over thirty-five."

"It's the truth. That big man..." I pointed to Magnus. "...is Magnus." I lifted my chest, putting on a bravado this man might buy in to. "You're looking at three of the Heroes of Earth. What vessel were you on?" I asked, using my old trick.

"That doesn't matter anymore. We're all doomed anyway." His shoulders slumped, and his gaze lowered to the floor for a moment. Mary went for him, racing to him with her shoulder ready to plow into his, but he spun with far more agility than I would have guessed. Mary went past him, her momentum too much to slow, and he turned with his gun pointed at her.

A red beam lashed out from behind me, striking him in the back just as his gun went off. He went down in a heap and stumbled onto Mary.

I rushed forward, rolling the man off of my fiancée, careless of his condition. She was all that mattered. My throat went dry, and I said her name in a croak, seeing blood on her uniform. Her eyes opened and she grimaced.

"Fast for a skinny old guy," she said, feeling her abdomen and chest. "It's his blood. Lucky for me, he's a poor shot."

"We didn't have to kill him," I said, helping Mary up.

"You want to let that raving lunatic walk around with a gun?" Leslie asked. She was already going for the opening in the bars. "We don't have time for this."

New World

The hybrids took the lead, Magnus close behind them. He took a quick look back at the body on the floor and shook his head. "What a waste," he muttered, and kept moving.

Another body. But given the choice, it was going to be a stranger on the ground instead of my beautiful Mary. I didn't even ask which one shot him. It wasn't important.

I grabbed his gun and tucked it away into one of the half-full desk drawers and looked to his belt for a keyring. A guy like this would always keep the keys to the cells close at hand, and from the looks of this place, automation wasn't in the budget. I found the ring in his pocket but tied to his belt on a leather strap. Pulling out a knife from my boot, I cut the hide and took the keys.

"You're sure you're okay?" I asked when no one else was in the room.

Mary looked down at the dead man and back at me. "I'll be better when we're back on New Spero, picking tomatoes and having tea on the porch." The skin at the sides of her eyes crinkled as she forced a smile at me, and I leaned in, giving her a kiss on the lips.

"Me too."

"Over here!" Magnus called from a distance, his voice carrying to us easily.

I ran to him, unsure of what to expect. What I saw was heartbreaking.

Leslie was fumbling with the locked bars, but the key she had didn't fit. She was crying, a soft sob as she struggled to open the lock. Beyond it, a dozen or so hybrids were in a mess hall. A couple were lying on tables. Others sat together, heads low to the tables, none of them speaking.

One of them looked up, saw us, and put her head

back down like we were nothing more than an apparition. Another one – who looked like Terrance, only ten years older and gaunt – looked toward us and stood up on shaky legs. "Are you real?" he asked, his voice a gravelly whisper.

"Brother!" Terrance called through the bars. "We're here to bring you to paradise." The excitement and energy in Terrance's voice was electric. I took the keys in my hand and went to the lock, trying them one by one until one inserted and turned to the side. Leslie slid it open and rushed into the room.

"Where is everyone?" she asked one of her people, who were still coming to, realizing something important was happening. They seemed like zombies, their skin gray, the flesh tight against their bones. It was horrifying, and we'd done this to them. Humans had locked them up to waste away.

The man who'd first spoken was hugging Terrance, and he broke free to answer the question. "This is all of us."

TWENTY

"What do you mean, this is everyone? When we left the compound on Long Island, there were twenty times this many." Terrance stood straight, his posture rigid and his fist cocked like he was ready to punch something.

All of them were now over beside us. Mary had already gone with Magnus to find food from the guard areas for these sad souls.

"They left us here. We heard the guards say something about the Bhlat being here, and within a week, they were all gone except some sadistic bastard. We begged him to let us go, and he said it was his duty to keep us locked up. When we realized he wasn't going anywhere and wouldn't let us go, we plead for food. We had a little bit stashed away here, and he wouldn't dare come inside with no backup, so we ate for the first couple months. Now we have nothing left. You've come at just the right time. Steve died this morning." The first one to speak to us had called himself Byron. His hair hung in his face in greasy clumps as he told us his story.

"I'm so sorry. We thought we would help by leaving."

"It *is* you two. Terrance and Leslie, our fate sealers," one of the women said, her voice so weak it came out like a whisper.

Leslie already looked a wreck, but that comment set her over the edge.

"We couldn't have known!" she cried. "We were trying to improve our future." She slid to the ground, her face in her hands.

"All you did was give us a bigger target than we already had, and we didn't think that was possible," Byron said, the others nodding along.

"This isn't all their fault. Were you all on the vessels, piloting our people to their deaths?" I waited for a response that didn't come. "Humans didn't trust you from the start. Would you have? If the Kraski had suddenly told you they had a change of heart and they wanted to be your friends, would you have listened?"

"No," the woman said, abashed.

"Then cut these two some slack. They found a world for you to go to. The only glitch was that the wormholes messed with our timelines. We're going to get you food and water, then take you to your new home. Let this be a new bridge to your future, and let your past go. Mourn for your losses and be grateful for your lives, because we're all lucky to have them at this point." The speech was a little overdone, but I meant every word of it.

"A new world?" one of the others asked. "With sunlight?" He raised his face to the dark ceiling, closing his eyes like he was feeling the rays of the sun on his pallid skin.

"Yes, my brother. With sunlight, and rivers, and food aplenty. We live there among others, the Deltra included."

"Don't forget swamp monsters," I said under my breath, getting a glare from Terrance.

"Deltra? What the hell are you doing with them?" Byron asked.

"They weren't all evil. Even those ones were only doing what they needed to keep their people alive. Even

Dean likes Kareem, right?" Terrance looked at me, raising his eyebrows in a signal saying he needed support.

"Sure. He's a stand-up guy. In an 'engineer weapons of mass destruction' sort of way."

They looked unsure, but the subject changed when Magnus and Mary came back with a duffel bag of supplies.

Magnus dumped it out on a table. Water bottles and bags of chips with Cyrillic script on them fell out. The hybrids scrambled for them, and my heart sank, feeling terrible for them. I couldn't wait to see their faces as we left the portal and walked onto their new planet.

Thinking about it made the urgency increase. "Gather anything you need, and let's leave," I said.

"How are we going to get everyone back?" Magnus asked.

"The transport isn't big, but there are only twelve of them." Mary scanned the group as she spoke. "By the looks of them, they won't take a lot of room. I think we can make it work."

"What about Dinkle and his pilot?" Magnus asked.

"I think we have a good spot for them just around the corner." I followed his gaze to a cell just beyond the mess hall. "We'll leave them a little water and food, of course. It's more than they deserve."

Soon a line of hybrids in tattered clothing, smelling like death, followed us out of the prison, their eyes wide as they walked past the guards' station and into the main halls. Byron set his hand on the whitewashed cinder blocks making up the wall, looking like he was about to pass out. I set my hand on his bony back and he turned to me, eyes glistening.

"Thank you," he said.

"You didn't deserve this. We'll make it right." I knew

we could never make it up to them, but even though I wanted that Bhlat homeworld portal location, this was important. I was glad Kareem had made us barter for it. These people needed our help.

Snow blew on us as we pushed out the entrance doors, the hybrids covering their eyes from the bright light of the Siberian morning. They weren't dressed for the cold, and we ushered them quickly to the ship. Magnus and Terrance hauled Jeff and the pilot out of the transporter.

"What are you doing?" Jeff asked, his face covered in blood from his head injury. "You can't leave me here. The Bhlat are expecting me."

"Have they seen you before?" I asked nonchalantly.

"No, when would I have met…" He seemed to catch on and hung his head.

"Tell us what you were supposed to do, and we let you live," Magnus said, standing over the tied-up man.

He looked defiant, and Magnus gave him a light kick. Jeff didn't need to speak, because the pilot did.

"He was going to take you to them, and in exchange, he was promised he would live like a king among their people. I heard the conversation. I had nothing to do with this. I'm just a hired hand." The pilot looked up with pleading eyes.

"Fine. Put Dinkle in the back, leave this guy tied in the guards' room. We'll call for someone to get him later," I said, knowing I had no one to call.

"We'll bring them," Terrance said. He and Leslie grabbed them by the arms, hauling them both to their feet.

We loaded the hybrids into the transport; I glanced back at Leslie as they entered the prison again. They came back out just as we had everyone set, Mary in the pilot's

New World

seat and Magnus and I squished beside her. From the grim look on Terrance's face, I wasn't about to ask how it went. I really didn't want to know.

With the sun behind the clouds, and a small ship full of potent-smelling hybrids, we lifted off the snow-crusted ground on our way back to Egypt and the Pyramids of Giza.

In a cramped hour, we reached our destination, my back aching from being squished into my seat. When the doors opened, we saw them: ships lowering into our atmosphere. They were bulky, reminding me of the oil rigs used to dig in the ocean.

Magnus stated the obvious. "That can't be good."

"We need to hurry," Mary whispered.

I hoped Kareem was still alive when we got back.

★ ★

Kareem slowly opened his eyes, blinking away his sleep. He looked surprised to see us, but it quickly gave way to a coughing fit. An attendant held a cloth to his mouth for him, and it came away with flecks of blood on it.

"You did it?" he asked once his breathing was back under control.

"We did," Mary answered.

"How are our friends doing now?"

I wasn't sure how he would react to the story, so I elected to keep it as simple as possible. "They've been through a lot. Only twelve came back with us."

He nodded from his lying position, his head propped up on a soft-looking pillow. "We will care for them now. Thank you for helping. Everyone deserves a chance at freedom and happiness. The sins of our past can never be wiped clean, but we can try to learn from them and better ourselves."

The comment struck home, and I thought of the bodies I'd left in my wake as we'd struggled to survive over the past couple of years. "It's time, Kareem. It's time to tell me how to access the hidden worlds with the *Shandra*."

"A bargain is a bargain. But it's for your eyes only. Do you understand?" He looked from me to Magnus, and then to Mary, lingering on her for a moment longer.

Mary and Magnus began to leave the room, but Kareem shook his head. "Stay. It is us who are leaving."

Kareem's attendant helped him sit up, and he bent over, rummaging through the small nightstand beside his bed. He pulled out a small device and smiled at me. His teeth were yellow, with small dots of blood on them. I almost pulled back, away from him, but he grabbed my arm with unexpected strength and pressed a button on the device.

A tingling energy pulsed from my toes upwards, and soon my whole body was vibrating. Mary was standing, looking at us with horror. I saw her mouth move, but no sound made it to my ears. The room around me faded, but Kareem was still there, gripping my skin, his hand hot as sauna rock against my arm. His smile was terrifying, but it told me he was enjoying his little game.

When our surroundings came back to focus, we weren't in his room any longer.

"What the hell was that?" I asked, still feeling the energy coursing over me, even though he'd let go of my forearm. Looking around, I recognized the portal on this planet we'd just come through with the hybrids earlier that day. "How did you do that?"

"The answer to both those questions is the same."

New World

Kareem's knees gave way, and I caught the tall man, finding that he weighed less than I would have guessed. Standing up, I could see how rail-thin he was; his white cloak billowed around him like an oversized sail on a small boat. "This is another one of my inventions. I'm willing to give it to you to complete your mission. I have a feeling you'll need every bit of advantage you can get." He handed it to me. "It isn't magic. You just have to set the coordinates of your target location in. Ideally, you program it in when you're first at the spot."

"You got us here by being in this exact spot before, then saving the location?" I asked, looking at the light device. It seemed obvious it was made by the same people as the smaller Shield device I'd used against the Bhlat. The look and feel was the same. He spent a few minutes going over the simple process with me, and when he was sure I understood, he moved on. I was holding him up by then; his sick body didn't have the energy to stand on its own.

"Kareem, how long do you have?" I asked.

"It won't be long now."

I half-walked, half-carried him to the portal room. He made me stop at the entrance and said a string of Deltran words: likely a prayer of his people. He regarded the room with a reverence that I hadn't, and it made me think of the portals differently. So far, they'd been a tool to help me survive, but they'd been put in place thousands of years ago by an ancient god-like race. We were standing in something older than anything we could imagine, with the power to transport us from planet to planet. The longer I thought about it, the more in awe I was of the whole scenario.

Kareem coughed a few times. "Never take it for granted."

"What?"

"Any of it. We're specks in the universe. We all think we're so much more, the centers of our own worlds. We fight each other. Even my people orchestrated the deaths of races to their own benefit. There's something different about you. Bring them together. Make them see the universe has more to offer than killing. When I look at you, I see the aura of a Theos."

My heart hammered in my chest, beads of sweat forming on my brow. What was this man talking about? "I'm just an accountant from New York who got lucky a few times. I'll leave all of that to the professionals. I just want to help us survive."

"Don't you see? It's saying things like that, that makes you special. You didn't say 'you' just want to survive. You want to help your people. Therein lies the difference between you and ninety-nine percent of intelligent life. Your instincts put them first, and you second."

I didn't know if he was right, or if by allowing myself a chance to survive, others had been saved. "I'm no god."

"That's right, because they eventually died and were forgotten. You're something new." With that, he entered the portal room unassisted, taking hesitant steps.

I walked behind him, hands ready to catch him if needed. The closer he got to the table above the large gemstone in the middle of the room, the brighter the icons and hieroglyphs glowed on the walls.

"Come. See the missing worlds," Kareem said, his voice strong once again. He tapped on the screen, accessing files no one else would have known were there. He showed me the unique string of symbols I'd need to open it again, and we spent half an hour going over it, until he was sure I'd memorized them. "You cannot write or save them anywhere but in your mind, do you understand?"

New World

I nodded.

"Do you understand?" He stood straight, towering over me, his face grim.

I stepped back from the threat and answered him properly. "Yes, sir. I do."

"This information isn't even known by modern Gatekeepers," he said, quietly locking eyes with me.

Gatekeepers. I mouthed the word, my lips sticking together as everything suddenly went dry.

The table screen showed the icons I was familiar with, but Kareem directed me to scroll to the left now. I did, and red icons appeared, each with their own unique symbol.

"If you type your code in, you can access information on each world." He had me tap it, and then the icon for the first red one. What had to be a hundred language options appeared, and he showed me how to access English.

Trellion: Class three ice planet. Life forms: Core-dwelling bipedal. Intelligent.

The details went on for pages, and under different circumstances, I could have spent days reading about other worlds and learning why some were hidden over others. I thought back to the huge drilling ships we'd seen entering Earth's atmosphere hours ago and knew I didn't have time for that now.

"Where are the Bhlat?"

"They are here." He had me scroll to the next page, pointing it out in the second row. "They live on multiple worlds now, but this is their homeworld, where their royalty lives." Kareem let out a series of coughs, doubling over on the table. I lowered him to the ground, worried when he couldn't seem to catch his breath.

"We have to get you back," I said, reaching for the device.

"No. Let me die here. It would be an honor to die among the gods." He coughed again, blood dripping from his chin. His skin was clammy, and he lay himself down on the stone floor. His breathing was ragged, and he closed his eyes between his hacking bouts. "Dean. This is your destiny. From the day you stepped foot in that restaurant in Central Park, you've been on a course. This is where you were meant to end up. Be the man I see you are. Change…the universe." His words came out slowly, between breaths, and then it was over. His chest stopped rising and falling, and I sat there holding his thin hand as the last breath left his ailing lungs.

Change the universe.

TWENTY-ONE

"Thank you for following through on your word," Leslie said, giving us each a hug. The normally cranky hybrid woman was in high spirits, having her friends back. The rescued hybrids were doing well, their ailments fixed and their body weights rising. We'd said goodbye to them before Terrance gathered us to fly us down to the portal.

"Look us up if you ever need anything." This from Terrance.

"We will. You two take care of the others," Magnus said with a wink. "And each other."

The two of them looked at one another and smiled.

We left them behind, just the three of us on our way to another impossible mission.

"After it's all said and done, I don't mind those two," Magnus said.

"You weren't the one chasing them around on a fool's errand," Mary said, mirroring my own thoughts.

Soon we were back in the portal room, where Kareem's body still lay. Some of his people had covered him with a veil, and a glowing shield surrounded him so he wouldn't be tampered with. Mary looked at him uneasily, as if he would rise from the dead and walk toward us with his white sheet covering him. We were told the shield would prevent his body traveling with the portal.

"Time to get back to New Spero," I said, scrolling to

the right icon. The walls were glowing when I tapped the symbol for our destination, and when I opened my eyes, we were back in the mountainside portal room near Terran Five. I slid out the relocating device Kareem had gifted me and added this location into it. It would be a timesaver to be able to travel right here from Terran One later.

As soon as we got out of the tunnels and into the transport ship, exhaustion took over. We'd been up for a long time and needed to sleep before we took the next step. Running around alien worlds half asleep wasn't going to do anything but get us killed.

My eyes fell closed, and as we took off for Terran One, I turned to a light sleep. Dreams of Kareem dying, of the dirty Siberian prison, and the impending trip to the Bhlat world hit me as my subconscious took over. In one of the visions, Mary ended up dying. It was a terrible glimpse into a potential future I was going to make sure didn't happen.

When I woke, Mary's head was leaned against my shoulder. Magnus was in the front piloting us safely back to the landing pad at the home base. It was dark outside, a cloud-covered night sky casting an unusual blackness to the surroundings. I woke Mary and hesitantly stepped down out of the comfort of the transport's cab.

It was nighttime on New Spero, but that didn't stop the base from being a bustle of activity.

"General, are we ever glad to see you back in one piece. Unless something happened, our fleet is due to arrive at Earth in less than two days," a breathless uniformed officer said.

"Anything else, Tucker?" Magnus asked. He looked like he was almost asleep on his feet.

"One of our transport vessels went missing this

morning," Tucker said.

"Can't you track it?"

The man shook his head. "The tracking was cut off. The culprit knew what they were doing."

"Probably some kids going for a joyride. If nothing else is urgently needed, restock our supplies and charge our weapons. We leave at first light. Mary, Dean, are we good with that?" Magnus asked us. He was using his take-charge "general" voice.

"Yes, sir." Tucker turned around and left at a brisk walk.

"You two want to go home for a few hours?" This from Magnus.

Mary nodded, and I knew Magnus was aching to see his family. I tapped the base location into the Relocator before we left. Then we were heading back down the dirt roads that had led us away from our house just a couple of days ago. So much had happened since then, and the weight of it all pressed on my temples as my head pounded.

Our house appeared, and we told Magnus we'd see him in a few hours.

"Say hi to Nat for us," Mary said. "And Magnus?"

"Yeah?"

"Get some sleep. We need to be on our toes for this to work," she finished.

He threw the Jeep in reverse and left us standing in front of our house in the dark.

Mary's hand slipped into mine, assuredly squeezing my fingers. It was her way of telling me everything was going to work out, without saying it.

In less than ten minutes, we were both showered, hair still wet as we crawled into bed. The pillow felt like heaven as my head hit it, and I only had enough time to tell

Mary I loved her before drifting off into a deep sleep.

★ ★

*D*reams riddled my sleep, and I tossed and turned as I future-projected our upcoming day. Every way I saw it, Mary ended up dead. In one of the dreams, I saw us walking fictitious streets on the Bhlat world, and I walked into a house where a thin woman lay on a bed. My old bed. The one I'd shared with Janine. Only it was Mary coughing up blood. She looked at me with sad eyes. "When the ships come…wear the necklace."

I woke in a pool of sweat, fumbling for my neck, where the chain still hung after all this time. Mary was still sleeping soundly beside me, and I leaned in, kissing her cheek lightly. I couldn't let anything happen to her, and while I knew it was my subconscious worrying, my gut told me she couldn't come to the Bhlat world with me. I needed to do this by myself.

The floor was cold to the touch as my bare feet hit it. I nearly tripped over the pants I'd left on the floor, and I snatched them up, careful to not let the belt jangle.

I fumbled in the closet, found a long-sleeved shirt of an unknown color, and walked to the hallway with the clothes. Once dressed, I made for the kitchen, where a notepad sat beside a pen. Mary's gardening notes were listed on the first few pages, and I ripped a blank page out from the middle.

Mary was going to be pissed with me, but I felt like there was no choice. Our fleet was arriving soon, and bringing in a half-dozen war machines wasn't going to end well. We needed to beat them to the punch and use the warships only as backup.

My thoughts swung to my friends: Slate, Clare, and Nick, alongside Patty. They were up there with the Bhlat. I had no idea if they were alive or dead, and the irrational part of my brain blamed myself for not going with them, for somehow not protecting them from the Bhlat when I clearly couldn't have changed the outcome.

After a brief stop in the safe under the living room floorboards, I took inventory. I had the small *Kalentrek* with the Bhlat DNA spec still loaded into it; the communicators that allowed us to talk in real time over any distance; and the Relocator Kareem had just given me. I could do this job by myself.

I scrawled out a long note on the paper, my hand cramping from the frantic writing by the end of the message. They had a big part to do, and I'd do mine. We'd reconvene when it was all over. One of the communicators sat on the counter beside the note.

When I was satisfied I had the plan relayed properly, I snuck back down the hall and gently pushed the bedroom door open. Soft light from the kitchen wound its way into the room, and I watched Mary as she slept, her chest rising and falling in even movements. I wanted nothing more than to just get back into bed, stick my head under the pillow, and let someone else deal with the second invasion of Earth, but I couldn't.

"Dean. This is your destiny." Kareem's words echoed through my head.

I made a silent promise to my fiancée that I'd be back. That we'd have the wedding we both wanted, surrounded by our friends and family. That the threat would be ended in a day's time.

With that done, I turned, leaving the door open a crack, and walked out onto the porch with my supplies.

The air was crisp as the sun began to rise over the distant horizon. Alien insects called to each other as the world around me woke for another morning. I took a deep breath in, letting my body revel in the fresh air, the freedom, and the feeling of home. Then I pressed the Relocator button.

TWENTY-TWO

I appeared at the base in a split second, the energy still tingling through me. I could get used to travelling so quickly but didn't want to know what was actually happening to my molecules as I did so. People were moving around in the early hour; a group of trainees ran laps around the landing pad near where I appeared. I ducked and took cover beside a large-wheeled vehicle.

Clare had told me about some prototype uniforms that used the cloaking technology, and I needed every advantage I could get. I headed past a couple of buildings, careful to not be spotted. I knew there would be cameras on me, but hopefully, I'd be long gone before anyone spotted me creeping around on them.

The engineering building Clare had been so excited to show me before she left was to the side; I ran to it, and a locked door greeted me. I took out the keycard Magnus had given me, hoping it had clearance for the research and development areas. The light went green as the card slid, and I breathed a sigh of relief, pushing the door open.

The room was dark, but soft lights came on as I entered. She'd shown me the cloaks at the far end of the room, and I found them hanging on the wall, right where I'd seen them before. I lined one up against my body. Too long. The next one looked a better size, and I slipped into it, finding it to be manageable. It covered my boots and hands, with built-in grips on the soles of the clothing, and gloves for the hands.

All of it was covered in the newly upgraded cloaking material. It was lighter than I'd expected, and I pulled the hood up, then faced the nearby mirror. Remembering Clare telling me the on/off control was in the glove, I tapped my thumb and pinky together, feeling a light energy cover me. When I looked into the mirror, I could see the room behind me, but only a faint glimmer of a body was visible, and only if you knew what you were looking for. I stuffed one of the large ones in a pack I'd grabbed on my way in.

With the new suit on, I left the building, heading for the transport vessel where Magnus had told Tucker to leave our supplies. If Mary woke up and saw my note, they'd be on their way, so I had to hurry. Avoiding a few officers walking from building to building, I snuck over to the landing pad where our ship was sitting, ready to carry us to the portal caves.

Beside it three bags sat, one with pulse rifles and other assorted weapons. One had food and survival supplies, and the last had the EVA suits. I took what I needed, shoved them into my bag, and ducked behind the transport, leaving it between myself and the base buildings.

Reaching into my pocket, I pulled out the Relocator and tapped it until I found the coordinates from the portal region by Terran Five. With a deep breath, I hit the icon and felt the energy spin around and then through me. When it stopped, I was outside the portal room. Before anything, I took a long drink of water and ate an energy ball from the rations. It tasted like mud but filled my stomach enough to stop the growling. I slid the cloak off and put on the thin EVA suit and clasped the helmet onto it. The oxygen from it cleared my tired head enough to make me feel temporarily rejuvenated.

I grabbed one of the hover scooters Mary and I had stowed away, then entered the portal room.

As I threw the cloak back on over the EVA, something made a noise nearby. It could have been a footstep or a rock falling from a wall. With a quick glance, I saw nothing out of the ordinary, so I moved to the middle of the room, where the once dormant gemstone began to glow.

"Here goes nothing."

I followed the instructions Kareem had given me, thankful I had been able to memorize the intricacies in a short amount of time. There was no one to ask now that he was dead. The red worlds' symbols appeared, and I found the one for the Bhlat home planet.

Before I pressed it, I took the time to read the few details they had stored into the system about the world. Not much of it was useful, but it did say the locals didn't know of the portal's existence, at least not at the time of the entry. A lot could have changed since then. There were a lot of warnings on the Bhlat. It said they were conquerors, always seeking out expansion of their colonies, often resulting in the extinction of worlds. The phrase hit me like a ton of bricks. The flying drills I'd seen coming down on Earth were what the notes spoke of. Earth was about to be eradicated. Time was running out.

I checked the seal on my EVA. When I saw the green light, I sat on my hover scooter and fastened the supply bag to it, keeping my rifle in my hand.

I pressed the icon and was bathed in light, hoping there were no long-term implications of using the portal so often over a short period of time. They were becoming an integral part of my unwanted adventures, and my tired body wished I'd give it a rest for a while.

My internal battle within my mind paused when the light ceased, and I saw someone in the room with me. How did they know I was coming? My rifle came up lightning fast, and I felt my finger brush the trigger.

"Don't shoot!" a voice called in frightened English.

I lowered the rifle just enough to get a good look at the man, and he fell to the ground, rolled into a ball. He just kept repeating "Don't shoot" over and over.

"Who the hell are you?" I asked him.

"My name's Leonard Birkhower, sir. Don't shoot."

Leonard? "Wait, the Leonard who does the Survivors comic series?"

He moved his arms from covering his helmet in a futile attempt to stop my pulse rifle from killing him. "You know of me?" He grinned from ear to ear, and I almost laughed at how silly this young man with thick black glasses looked on the ground covered in dust.

I reached down, and he gripped my outstretched hand with a sweaty palm. "What are you doing here?"

"And miss out a chance to see Dean Parker kick bad guy ass?"

"You do realize I could get killed here?"

"Not you. You're invincible."

"Kid, this isn't a comic book. I'm just a man like you."

He dusted his clothing off and looked me in the eyes with an admonished glance. "I'm nothing like you."

Who was this guy, and why was I feeling bad for him? He very well could get me killed. Of all the people I wanted to have beside me on the dangerous world full of Bhlat, Leonard the comic book artist wasn't one of them.

New World

I mentally chided myself for not searching the room better before hitting the icon.

"Regardless, how did you get here?" I asked, my patience beginning to wear thin.

"I was at the base. One of my buddies is a custodian there. We drink beer and shoot rocks in the hills sometimes."

"This *buddy* wouldn't be where you're getting top secret information about us, would it?" I thought of the issues I'd seen that touched a little too close to the truth.

He turned red and averted his eyes from my gaze. "Maybe. Your stories are too awesome to keep away from the public. We all need to know what really went down. You're heroes, and we all need to look up to you guys. You give us hope. You think it's easy moving away from Earth after seeing your family die on those vessels? Some of us have nothing else." His pitch was rising, and I had the urge to give the kid a hug, but I needed to play hardball.

"How did you get here?"

"Jeb gave me a suit and showed me how to use it." He flipped a switch; when he spoke again, a series of Deltra words echoed his speech.

"Enough of that. He knew where the portal was?"

"Is that what you call it? Of course, it makes sense. Yeah, he overheard the general talking with Tucker."

We would have to take precautions now that the location of it was out there. People traveling to other worlds would bring a lot of issues.

"You can't stay here. I have to bring you home." I started to use the console to find New Spero's portal symbol. For the first time, I looked around the room. It was much the same as the rest of them, but years of disuse showed. The ground was covered in a thick dirt layer, cobwebs hanging in all nooks and crannies. I wondered how far underground we were, and how far from a city we would be. The four corners had the columns like the other rooms had.

"I won't get in the way. Let me help," Leonard said in a small desperate voice.

My communicator vibrated lightly, and I fished it out of my pocket. I knew what this call was about.

I pressed the accept icon. "Dean here."

"Dean, I'm not going to get into it with you now, but don't think this conversation is over. I hope you understand how angry I was to wake up with you gone and a note in the kitchen." Mary's voice was angry but low.

"I'm sorry. I had to go with my gut."

"Make your gut go faster. We're on Earth now, and it's not good. Whatever they're doing is messing with our atmosphere, and fast. If we don't stop them, our people aren't going to make it." She sounded near-panicked.

"Dean, hurry the hell up. We're going up as planned. This should be interesting." Magnus had obviously grabbed the communicator. "Do what you have to do, Dean. Remember, this is about saving our people."

I would do what I had to and patted my pocket where the small killing machine from the Deltra station sat, waiting to be used one more time. I couldn't let this wide-eyed kid who looked up to me see what I was going to do with it, but I didn't have time.

"Good luck. Mary, I love you, babe."

"Holy crap. Was that...?" Leonard stared with his jaw dropped to his chest.

"Yes. Mary and Magnus. You really want to help? Promise me, whatever you see, that you won't make a comic of what's about to happen. If things go south, and they might, I have to do something I don't want to."

New World

The kid nodded.

"Promise me!" I almost yelled the words.

"I...I promise," he said hesitantly.

"Put this on," I said, tossing him the backup cloaking outfit.

He put it over his EVA, breathing heavily as he did so. I caught him once to keep him from falling over as his boot got stuck in the pant leg. When it was done, he looked down and smiled at me. "What does it do?" he asked. Instead of answering him, I showed him, and clicked the hand control. To his eyes, most of me disappeared.

"Wow. That's going to look great in the comics."

"What did I just say?" I asked, regretting my decision to let him stay. "You stay here in the portal room, sit down, and stay cloaked. No one will know you're here. I'll be back for you."

He suddenly looked terrified, as if being left alone here was far scarier than roaming a hostile alien planet. "Don't make me stay. I've always been too afraid to do anything. I didn't play sports because the other kids told me I was too slow or too fat. I've never asked a girl out, because I know they'll just reject me. If there's one thing the Event taught me, it's that I need to live. Not just survive, but thrive. Let me help you. I need to help you. I want to help them."

As I was about to tell him "no," his words soaked into me. Standing there wasn't a scared kid, but a man who was willing to risk his life to help people. "Fine, but don't do anything stupid. Listen to anything I say and do it. And when things get tough, keep going. No matter what." *And don't hold my actions against me,* I added to myself.

He beamed for a second and then paled, finally realizing he got his way.

I pushed the pack at him and he grabbed it, slinging it over his shoulder with a grunt. The hover bike came with me, and we exited the doorless room, walking into a hall leading away from the portal. Already I could feel the heat of the planet, and my suit began to cool me. I saved the coordinates in my Relocator and kept moving.

After a half hour, we came to a dead end, where a pile of small rocks barred most of the way out. We set everything down and set to methodically moving them. After another half hour, we were breathing heavily and sweating in our suits, but we had an opening large enough to fit through with the hover scooter.

I crossed through first, my rifle ready to fire if needed. My cloaked head poked out, and I let a low whistle fly. We were on a mountain, water as far as the eye could see below, a dark red star casting a devilish glow over everything.

"Welcome to hell," I said to myself.

TWENTY-THREE

"Maybe I should go back," Leonard said as the view came into his sightlines.

"It's too late for that. We have to get moving." The range of mountains we were on rose up another hundred feet or so, and I made for the peak, careful of my footing on the rocky surface. For the time being, I left the scooter behind, knowing it would be more of a burden than a help. "Stay there," I said back to Leonard, whose silence told me he was happy to do so.

The sun was still high in the sky, but the dim glow it cast was difficult for my eyes. I tripped on a few rocks on my way up, my path jagged as I made for the most acute inclines I could find. Still, I was near the top of the peak in only a few minutes. With a deep breath of my suit's oxygen, I peered over the edge, praying I wouldn't see more water. If we were on an island, my hopes of finishing my mission would be dashed.

Squinting to get a better look, I saw what I'd been wishing for: land. The mountain went down at a gradual decline toward a hard-looking surface below. Red topiary covered the distance: likely a forest on this strange world. Bright lights rose into the sky beyond, indicating a large city in the right direction.

"Leonard, I'll be right there. We have a way down," I relayed through the suit's comm, and when I looked down at him, he waved, giving me a gloved thumbs-up. The task at hand truly scared me. I only had the centuries-old details from the portal file to go by, but according to it, their closest capital city was southwest of the portal. I could only cross my fingers that it was still there, and that what I was looking for would be present.

"What's it look like?" Leonard asked as I neared him.

"Let's just say the comic won't be lacking for inspiration." I turned the hover scooter on and guided it with my hands to the peak, my tag-along's footing stumbling as we went. "You seem to be taking this well."

He grunted as he lifted a leg over a large stone. "All my life I've been afraid to do anything surprising. I was picked last for every sport in physical education, I was made fun of for having my nose stuck in the newest Star Battle books, and because of it, I stuck to myself."

We made it up top, and Leonard gasped as the Bhlat world's view came into sight. "It's beautiful," he whispered. The red color palette over everything had felt malevolent initially, but the longer I looked at it, the more I just accepted it was the nature of the planet. Was it so different than where we came from?

"You're right. It is," I agreed. "What changed?" I prompted him. The more I kept him talking, the less he'd realize how dangerous our surroundings really were.

"You."

"Me?"

"You more than the others. Magnus and Natalia were commandos. Tough as nails and went through some serious crap during their time as mercenaries. They were prepared for the Event as much as anyone could have been. Mary was Air Force, trained as well, smart and..." He paused, looking at me. "Beautiful. Not that that has anything to do with it."

New World

I held back a laugh, and now understood how Leonard had made the Mary version in his comics all the more voluptuous than any real woman.

"But you, Dean. Dean Parker, chartered accountant from a sleepy town in upstate New York. A guy who worked hard and watched the love of his life pass away so young. A man who liked to drink a pint and throw a baseball around with friends. You're the everyman who came from obscurity and saved the world. And that's why I want to be a better man."

I stopped walking and looked Leonard in the eyes. Through the helmet's visor and his glasses, his brown eyes had a red glow to them on this world, and they looked hard at me. I hadn't given much thought to my own story over the last couple years. It seemed so irrelevant with everything going on, and I was a little shocked to learn that anyone actually knew me. He'd painted a fairly accurate picture.

"Thanks, Leonard. I never thought of myself as anything special."

"That's what makes the best hero, don't you see? I'm just happy to be here with you. Can you fill me in on the plan?"

"What do you know so far?" I asked as we started down the other side of the mountain.

He looked contemplative before speaking. "The Bhlat are really there, aren't they?"

I nodded, the weight of my helmet exaggerating the gesture. "They are."

"Son of a sailor. I didn't believe Jeb when he told me the president went there and was missing."

"My other friends are with her," I said, trying to let him fill in the pieces.

"Slate, Nick, and Clare, right?" This kid knew his

stuff.

"You seem to know a lot."

"I have to pay attention to every little detail if I want my comics to be accurate."

I thought back to a couple of crazy plots from the books and asked him about the one where Mary and I had to give our firstborn to an alien race's king in exchange for our freedom.

"You were gone so long, I could only speculate on what was happening to you out there," he said. "Pretty kickass, though, right?"

"I'll be honest, I did enjoy reading them."

"Seriously?" he asked, and I noted how much farther down the slope we were. Another half hour, and we'd be able to get on the scooter. My tired body was looking forward to the break.

"Only one thing," I said.

"What?"

"You made my hair gray in the later issues. How old do you think I am?" I asked as a joke, but the truth was, I had been seeing some grays creeping into the sides of my hair, like unwanted visitors you knew would never leave once they showed up.

"You were gone for seven years. I expected you to have aged." It was a valid point. "So the Bhlat are at Earth. How are we going to save the day?"

His optimism lifted me up. Such a simple question, but important to my current mindset. But his question was one-sided. It was as if he knew we were going to save the people of Earth; he just wanted to know how I was planning on doing it.

"We're on their world. We need a bartering chip. There's no way we can fight them without losing. We have to play our one hand, and that's what we're doing

New World

here. Playing our hand." I didn't go into further details, and Leonard seemed to accept that it was need-to-know, and he'd know when I needed him to.

"Then let's do just that."

My communicator vibrated, and I tapped it through to my suit's earpiece. "Mary?"

"Dean, we're almost to their ship. They seem to have bought our story. They asked about the one we call Dean, and we told them you were dead."

Goosebumps lined my arms, like her saying that was a harbinger of things to come. "Be careful. Don't let them take the communicator. We're heading to the city now."

"We?" she asked, worry and anger mixed together in her voice.

I forgot they wouldn't have known I wasn't alone. "The comic book kid, Leonard, conveniently learned we were on a mission and beat me to the *secret* portal. We need to lock that place down when we're back." *When we're back.*

"Don't let anything slow you down. Anything." Mary had an edge to her voice, and I glanced at Leonard, who couldn't hear our conversation.

"I won't. Stay safe. It'll be over soon, one way or another."

"If this is it…"

"It won't be," I said, trying to keep the tremor from my voice.

"If it is, I want you to know how much you've meant to me. To be really loved and have a partner has meant the world to me." She laugh-sobbed in my ear. "It's meant many worlds to me. Just remember me, Dean Parker. Remember the spark we had so long ago on our trip to Peru and beyond."

I held back tears, turning from Leonard so he

couldn't see my emotions threaten to overtake me.

"I won't, babe. I never could. I'll see you soon."

"See you soon." The connection went dead.

I shoved the pain in my gut down and kept moving.

Once the ground leveled out enough for me to trust using a hover scooter with the added weight of Leonard and our gear strapped to it, we hopped onto the vehicle. There was just enough room for us, me pushed too close to the front, and Leonard complaining half of him was hanging off the back of it.

Time wasn't on my side as I hit the thruster, a little too heavily at first. Leonard's arms wrapped tightly around me to keep him from flying off the end.

"Sorry," I said into my mic, and eased up a bit. The lights of the city seemed distant as we moved from the hillside into the red-tinged forest. I had to slow to navigate the trees, and a couple times we could have walked faster as the copses got denser.

"It looks so much like home," Leonard said. "Or Earth, at least," he corrected himself. Earth was no longer this man's home.

The bark on the tall thin trees was smooth and pale, the tops of them growing high in the sky, looking to reach the dark red sun beyond. They fought to rise above the canopy of their neighbors, to reach the heavens, and grow deep in the ground to reach maximum sustenance below.

As I gawked at my surroundings, I felt a connection to the world we'd entered uninvited. If you closed your eyes and felt around, you wouldn't know you weren't on Earth. I wondered what it smelled like outside. The HUD on my suit's mask told me the air wasn't toxic to us but would be thin and hard to breathe for long. That was better than instant death, should something unplanned occur.

The ground was covered in small plants: thin grass fighting for life down below a thick overhead covering of branches and red leaves. I felt like the grass. We had to fight to stay alive, but this grass had been doing it symbiotically for years among the trees. They hadn't tried to snuff the life from the taller plants; instead, they accepted their role, and did that make them any less a part of their environment? I spotted a growth on a tree and wondered if it was invited or not. The whole ecosystem worked in harmony, a dance of life, and growth, and death.

Could we as intelligent lifeforms learn from their co-existence? Could humans be on the same side as the Deltra, the Shimmalians and the Bhlat? Would we ever find a way to cohabitate in the universe? Kareem's dying words ran through my head, and I wondered what he saw in me. The big picture was one you needed a ten-thousand-foot view to see, and I was down in the trenches, seeing it all way too closely.

"Watch out, Dean!" Leonard's voice carried into my earpiece, and he pulled tight on my abdomen. I narrowly avoided running into a large felled tree lying horizontally on the forest floor.

"Thanks. Sorry, I'm in my own head."

The forest opened up the farther along we went, and before we knew it, we were nearing the edge of it. A narrow stream ran alongside it, steam lifting from the babbling waters. Something told me it was hostile, a dangerous liquid. There were few plants near it, and those that were close angled away from it, rather than toward it for nourishment.

"Hold on to your butt," I said as I pushed the throttle forward. The scooter pushed faster, and we carried past the edge of the forest and over the small river. Once clear of the trees, the grass got thicker, still red in hue. It was like a field after a battle in the ancient days; the grass looked like it was covered in the blood of the slaughtered. I almost expected to see fallen soldiers, but it was quiet, not a tree or animal in sight.

Leonard reached over my shoulder and pointed forward. "Look."

The city crept up on us, only a few miles away now. The buildings rose high into the midday sky, some above the rose-colored clouds. The skyscrapers reminded me of the abandoned city where Slate and I had met Suma those few months ago; only this city wouldn't be abandoned. It was full of Bhlat, and at that moment, they were in possession of my loved ones, trying to take over Earth. The *Kalentrek* pressed against my chest as it sat tightly in my breast pocket. I wouldn't risk taking it off my person. The power it possessed was immense. The life it could snuff out in a heartbeat scared me.

What would Leonard think of me if I activated it among them? What would *I* think of me? I clenched my jaw, resolved to do whatever I needed to do to save my friends, but at what cost?

"Now would be a good time to tell me the plan," Leonard said when the city limits looked two miles away. I spotted roadways, and ships were flying through the sky: some were small, like floating cars, while others were large vessels, criss-crossing through a three-dimensional rush hour.

"First step, hide the scooter." I pulled over in a field lined with young trees. Crops grew from what seemed like fertile ground; loamy soil stuck to our boots as we got off the vehicle.

"Then what?"

"We activate our cloaks and walk to the palace."

"What palace?"

"The one where our target's located."

The communicator buzzed again. This time, Magnus' voice came into my ear. "Dean, we're on their ship. This'll be our last communication. Are you almost there?"

"We're at the city. Give me a couple hours."

I heard the hiss of an airlock, a string of Bhlat words, and the call cut off.

TWENTY-FOUR

I activated the translator so I could make out what any passing Bhlat were saying. I showed Leonard how to use it, and the first time he heard a Bhlat's voice, he stopped in his tracks, unable to move. It was even harder to get him to keep going once he laid eyes on one of them.

We were on the outskirts of the city, but luckily for us, most of their transportation happened in the sky. Massive pedways connected the buildings, like in the dead city I'd visited, leaving only a few to roam the streets below. This was to our advantage. Though we were wearing cloaking uniforms, they weren't infallible, and eventually, someone would notice us.

The first Bhlat civilian we encountered was once again much smaller than the initial contact I'd made on the Deltra station. That one had been an eight-foot-tall warrior, and this was a six-foot male, wearing a robe on the warm day. He moved slowly, like time meant nothing to him, causing us to slow down behind him. I mentally urged him to move along, but he just stood there, face to the red sun, sniffing in the afternoon air.

He said a string of words that translated into my ear as, "Blessed are those who are still walking today."

He said it a couple more times before opening his eyes and looking toward us. I froze, my heart pounding so hard I thought it was going to jump out and startle the

New World

Bhlat. It felt like his eyes made contact with mine; pinks and oranges swirled beside each other in his eyes, and I stared into them, petrified and mesmerized at the same time. Then he looked away, moving on to whatever chore he was set upon.

"Dean, was that a Bhlat?" Leonard asked quietly once no one was around.

"It was."

"They don't seem that scary," he said, a trembling hand still set on my shoulder.

"They won't all seem intimidating. Who are you more scared of: an old man back in your hometown or a jacked-up soldier with a gun?"

"I get it. This place just seems so normal."

"We keep moving," I said, ignoring his comment.

The surface of the sidewalk was paved with a dark asphalt-like substance. It was hard but had a slight give to it, one that wouldn't crack with season changes. Each building had doors leading into it, a couple with armed security guards. I wondered if they were banks, and just what Bhlat commerce was like on the planet. We avoided anywhere we saw Bhlat outside, and every so often, I looked up to make sure we weren't being spotted from above.

Terrance had passed some rumors on about there being a palace from which the Bhlat fleet was ruled. A king or emperor ruled them with an iron fist, killing any that opposed him. I took it all with a grain of salt, since they were just distant rumors, but now, they were all I had to go on. The farther we got into the city, the more people we passed. Our clothing made it next to impossible to see us, but we still made noise and had a physical presence. If someone bumped into us, it was over.

We came across all sorts of Bhlat as we kept close to the sides of buildings. Children kicked a ball in the alleys, dust covering their robes. Females chatted about the weather as they carried boxes from one building to another. It all seemed so *normal*.

Sweat poured down my body, and even the suit's built-in air conditioning couldn't stop me from overheating. It was getting warm out; with the layers on and the anxiety of where we were, I was flushed all over.

"How are you holding up, Leonard?"

"Terribly. Is this what being a hero is all about?"

"Pretty much."

"Then you can have all the glory from now on."

A loud Bhlat voice carried over to us from around the edge of a high-rise building, and we stopped. I motioned for Leonard to go flat against the wall. I wanted to grab my rifle, but that would expose me, so I stayed still.

"The *Tarna* will not be seeing petitioners today. Go back home," the voice called. The word *Tarna* didn't translate, and I understood that to be the name or title of someone.

Taking a peek around the corner, I saw a line of people that went on for as far as I could see, toward a section of the city to the east.

"I've read enough medieval books to know that the peasants petition the king at the palace. Follow that line, and we find the pot of gold at the end of the rainbow," Leonard said, nervously laughing.

He was probably right. A group of petitioners turned and walked past us, their heads down low. "We need water. How are we going to grow the crops? Theos bless us," a Bhlat woman said through long sharp teeth.

"Shhhh. Don't say that name," her friend hissed back. "Sometimes I wonder why I spend time with you. Shouting out blasphemy on the streets."

They kept moving, and my heart rate returned to only

slightly escalated instead of full-on panic. The woman had mentioned the Theos. The old gods' name still escaped the lips of our enemy. That was interesting, yet they didn't know about the portals, which made it even more of a mystery. Maybe there was a card I could add to this last hand I was playing.

Motioning for Leonard to follow, I turned around, heading toward the block parallel to the line of people. We'd follow the line, but from a distance. From here, I spotted what could only be the palace. It was a huge building, walls standing as tall as the skyscrapers near it. It looked a meld of glass, stone, and metal from our vantage point: as futuristic and imposing as I could have imagined.

The closer we got to our destination, the slower the travel. More and more bodies cluttered the alleys now, and it was becoming increasingly difficult to stay hidden. Leonard's deep breathing was crossing through my earpiece, and I had to tell him to calm down a few times. He didn't reply to my prodding.

A city block away from the immense towers ahead, I had to make a decision. If we kept creeping around cloaked, we were bound to be caught, and we were running out of time.

"Leonard," I said when we were out of earshot of any Bhlat on the streets, "change of plans." I told him to follow me, and we ducked and turned away from the wide entrance to the palace. Huge stone steps rose to a large open doorway, where armored guards kept a watchful eye on anyone coming or going. This wasn't going to work.

Around the corner, we found what I assumed would be there: a servants' entrance. A couple of Bhlat men were hanging outside, smoking a potent herb from something resembling a pipe. They were in the same white robes, but these were hooded. The men were taller than us by a good foot; smoke blew out one man's three nostrils.

As they entered the door, I gripped it just before it closed and followed them into the room. Boots and uniforms lined the walls, and before the two of them knew it, I decloaked, holding my pulse rifle up toward them.

"Don't shoot," the first one said, his words translating through my earpiece.

"Listen to me." I paused while the translator spat out the appropriate Bhlat words. "Do as I say, and you can go home to your families tonight."

This got the two wide gray faces to nod along. I got a good look at a Bhlat for the first time. These two had the same swirling movement in their eyes as the others I'd encountered, and mucus flew from one of the left alien's nostrils. As much as I was taught that something with teeth that sharp must be a monster, these two seemed like normal people, no different from anyone on the street back home.

"Good. Now tell me who's in charge, and where I can find them."

★ ★

"Are you sure this is going to work?" Leonard asked me from beneath his cowl. He looked like an overweight ghost in the get-up, and I doubted my plan.

"No. I'm liking the odds less and less." I pushed the cart down the hall toward the Empress' offices. The Bhlat had told us they were scheduled to do maintenance on her floor atop the towers that morning. After grilling them for an hour, we donned their clothing and made our

New World

move.

The cart held our supplies inside, and I had a pulse pistol tucked away under my too-large Bhlat uniform. I was swimming in it, worried each step would cause me to trip over it and make myself known.

The handheld *Kalentrek* was in my palm. The only solace of that was in knowing I could activate it and kill any Bhlat in the area. That might save my and Leonard's skin, but it wasn't going to help our case back at Earth.

We used a key fob on the elevator, the door opening. We entered and pressed the icon the Bhlat had advised, but instead of a lift, an energy surge raced through my body. The next thing I knew, we were on the top floor.

"Freaky," Leonard said.

I checked my pocket for the Relocator and reminded Leonard to stay close. If we needed to bolt for the portal, I had to be touching him when I activated the device.

Before we left the room, I passed the *Kalentrek* to Leonard. "Don't touch it," I warned him. I climbed on the cart, hoping no one would enter the transporter elevator, and lifted a ceiling grate. "Pass it up," I said, taking the small device and setting it there. With my tablet, I took an image of it there, turned on so the lights on it glowed softly.

"What's that for?" Leonard asked as I took the device back and replaced the grate.

"Backup plan."

TWENTY-FIVE

The doors opened, and we entered the beehive. Armed Bhlat strode down the halls, half as wide as they were tall in their armor. We kept our eyes down, our uniforms and servant cowls covering our far-too-obvious human faces.

I didn't know much about their leader, but they said she ran all things under the ever-expanding Bhlat colonies. I'd asked what kind of woman she was, and their eyes had gotten wide. They clearly feared her.

The room was open, with three halls heading in different directions from the floor's foyer. The guards seemed uninterested in us, and I doubted they'd ever been infiltrated before.

"Left," I whispered, and pushed the cart down the left hall, with Leonard following close behind.

A tall, slim female walked past us, her clothing colorful and rich: a stark contrast to the clothing we'd seen the regular ground-dwellers wearing. I heard her footsteps slow as we walked the opposite direction, and I could feel her eyes on my back as we kept going. Sweat dripped down my torso as my fears escalated and threatened to take over. I thought of Mary on their ship above Earth, and all of my friends in danger there. It was enough to keep my feet moving. The female's footsteps started up again, getting quieter the farther apart we got.

With a quick glance, I looked up and spotted two

New World

hefty guards at the end of the hall. They looked much like the warriors we'd faced on the Deltra space station, and I wasn't looking forward to fighting them again. But I didn't have a choice.

"Stay behind me," I said to Leonard, who happily slowed his pace.

The guards said something to me, but without my translator on, I couldn't make out the words. I nodded, my face still covered, and when I was ten feet in front of them, I reached under the cart I was pushing, my hand coming to rest on the butt of the pulse rifle.

They spoke again, this time louder, angrier. This was it. I had to get through the doors if my plan was going to work. My last resort was still in my pocket, and I nearly reached for it with my other hand. I could end them now, show the power at my fingertips. Show them we weren't to be trifled with. Humans weren't going to roll over for them. I had seconds to act, and I closed my eyes for a tiny moment, remembering the forest on the way down from the portal just hours ago. Kareem's last words echoed in my mind as I gripped the *Kalentrek* with my left hand, and the rifle with my right. *Make things different.*

My left hand let go and I raised the rifle, pointing it at them before they had time to react.

The guard on the left grunted, his sharp teeth bared at me. He spoke a string of hostile commands, but I didn't waver. I held the rifle straight between them, waiting for an excuse to shoot. Their armor was thick, matte black, and dangerous-looking. I had to shoot for the head, like Mary had when we'd first encountered them.

I nodded to the door, and they seemed to understand. The one on the right moved to open the door, and the other reached for a gun on his hip. I shot him in the head so quickly, it even startled me.

"Dean!" Leonard shouted behind me, but I didn't turn or reply. I just motioned for the door again, and the Bhlat guard laid his gun down to open it. Nudging the barrel of the rifle in the air, I waved for the guard to go in first. He did, hesitant to show his back to me.

"Drag him inside," I said to Leonard, my voice grim.

"Drag… drag him?"

"Do it," I said, and followed the guard inside. The room was wide, tall panoramic windows letting in red sunlight from a wide angle.

A red-robed female Bhlat sat on a couch with a small alien beside her. They talked quietly and didn't seem to notice us at all.

Behind me, Leonard groaned as he fought to pull the gargantuan Bhlat in with us. I motioned for the guard to help him, and he obeyed. Soon the door was shut, the dead guard's blood a smear across the entryway.

"Stay here," I said to Leonard, and passed him my pistol. He took it with a trembling hand.

He pointed the gun at the remaining guard, who glared at me with hate and distaste. "Don't let him get too close. If he does, shoot him in the head."

"Dean, I don't know if I can."

"You have to. Do it and let yourself grieve later."

He nodded, and I turned and walked toward the Empress and the child.

The room had a boardroom-style table in it, and it was uncanny how much their civilization mirrored our own. A holographic video played in the center of the table: images of large Bhlat ships moving around a planet. I watched it for a few seconds and realized it wasn't just any planet; it was Earth.

I almost grabbed the communicator to make contact, but waited. I stepped toward the couch, and the woman said something quietly to the child before turning to me.

For a Bhlat, she was stunning. Her wide face was framed by thick black braids, and her eyes were a light swirling red, making me think of molten lava. Her lips parted in a thin smile, sharp teeth making her look like a dangerous predator.

"I wondered when someone would make it up here. I expected it from the Kraski, if I'm being honest, but not a human." She spoke in perfect English, and I was caught off-guard. I closed my mouth, not wanting her to see my surprise.

"We're craftier than you think," I said, playing along with her banter.

"Whom am I addressing?" she asked. Beside her, the little girl's blue eyes danced as she stared at me intently.

"Dean Parker," I said, glad to get a reaction from her.

"You're a hard man to kill, it seems. Admiral Blel told me only a while ago he had your friends, and that you were dead. They seemed to want to barter but claimed they wouldn't talk yet."

"The timing just had to be right."

"Yes, so it seems." She looked over my shoulder to where Leonard was holding a gun to the guard; then she glanced to the floor, where the dead one lay in a pile. "What is it you want?"

"I want peace. I want you to leave Earth and never come back."

"It's too late for that. We've already begun the harvest. There's no going back."

I cringed inwardly. I had to pivot. "Then let us leave, and you can have it." I was literally bartering away a planet, but given the circumstance, I didn't have a choice.

She looked intrigued. "Is that so?"

"Yes. Take the planet. Use its water, use its ore, but

let us leave. Don't make contact ever again."

"Or what?" she asked.

"You don't want to find out," I said, almost bluffing, but knowing I could still end their city with the touch of a button.

She stood silent for a minute, analyzing the situation.

"We have a deal," she said, and I felt a fraction of the tension in my back ease up. She moved for the table and tapped an icon glowing on a built-in screen.

She said something in Bhlat, and I caught the name *Blel*. A gruff voice called back, and they went back and forth. I heard the name *Mary* carry over, and I gripped the rifle harder.

"What did he say?" I asked, remembering the dreams I'd had in which Mary was killed in our final confrontation with the Bhlat.

She didn't say anything for a long minute, and my eyes started to well up. "What did he say?" I yelled.

"He said there was an altercation. One of the human guests has been killed."

My gut clenched, and my vision went black. "Which *guest?*" I asked, knowing the answer.

One word escaped through her sharp teeth, her swirling eyes conveying a touch of sympathy. "Mary."

The door blew open before I had a chance to let it soak in. I almost didn't turn to the concussion blast. If she was gone, then what was the point?

Leonard's yelling voice brought me back, and I spun, firing at the incoming guards. Red pulses erupted from my rifle, and Leonard's pistol joined me as a dozen armed Bhlat raced into the room. I just needed to touch the Empress and Leonard, and we could get out of here. Only when I looked back at her, she and the child were near the window.

New World

We ducked behind the table, trading fire with the newcomers. I made a lucky shot and saw one of them drop dead. Leonard had his hand up over his head, firing backwards with his eyes closed. One of his shots hit, and footsteps started coming our way, closer to us.

The Empress called out a command, and the firing instantly stopped. She said another string of words, and the warriors lowered their weapons. I didn't do the same. For all I knew, we'd raise our hands and get killed for our efforts.

I stood up, rifle pointed at the eight or so standing guards, and crossed the room to the imposing woman at the window. The Relocator was in my other palm now, and Leonard got close.

The Empress looked at us, and to the dead guards on the floor. She held her daughter's hand as I reached to touch her and Leonard with my bare hands. I touched the Relocator.

TWENTY-SIX

"If we made a deal, why did we take their Empress?" Leonard asked, his hands still shaking. I was impressed with how well he'd handled himself and told him so.

"For insurance. I don't trust them, and right before we got rudely interrupted, we heard that... they killed someone." I wouldn't believe she was dead or let myself dwell on the implications, because I'd be a mess on the ground if I did.

"Where are we?" the Empress asked, her child finally done crying. We were in the portal cave, but I wouldn't let her see outside and let her know where the portal was located.

"Don't worry about that. Leonard, blindfold them." I ripped some fabric from the woman's robe, and Leonard gently tied the red fabric around her face, then the girl's. Neither protested.

Once they couldn't see, we led them to the portal room. The last few days' events raced through my mind. Mary's last words to me rang in my ears, and I almost stopped right there. We were close to the end, I knew it. I just didn't know what the end meant. The end of the conflict, or the end of us?

Soon we were standing behind the table in the center of the room, and I found Earth's symbol with a shaky hand.

New World

"Dean?" Leonard asked, breaking me from my daze.

Instead of answering him, I just tapped the icon, and light enveloped the four of us.

★ ★

The trip to the surface took a while, since we had to rise through the thick earth in pairs. This time, I kept my eyes closed the whole time, our counterparts not having to think about it with theirs covered. The child whimpered in my arms, but I ignored her. Their comfort meant nothing to me. All I could think about was getting up to the invading Bhlat ship where Mary was.

Once we made it outside, I nearly doubled over. Last time we'd left, the Bhlat mining machines had been lowering. Now the sky was covered in clouds, the atmosphere thin and breaking up.

The huge mining vessels didn't seem active, so maybe the Bhlat were here to barter. Looking around, I knew it was too late to salvage our world. My stomach sank, and my already morose mood took on an all-time low.

I'd lost the woman I loved and a planet in the same day.

Leonard looked around in wide-eyed wonder, his face having gone pale the instant he'd stepped outside.

With no other option, I took out my communicator. "This is Dean Parker. I have your Empress. Send a ship to me, and we end this now." I was done messing around.

A Bhlat voice spoke through the communicator, and the Empress translated for me.

"They have dispatched a ship and are willing to parley peacefully." Her voice was firm, even though her hands were tied and her eyes covered.

"Peacefully? Look at this!" I yelled, ripping the cloth from around her head. She stared upward with bright red eyes. The sky crackled, wind angrily blowing dust around the pyramids.

"I'm sorry," she said, voice smaller than I'd heard it yet.

"For what? For taking our water to expand your fleet, so you can do this to another world?" I was shouting now, tears flowing down my dusty face.

She looked down, abashed. "I heard you were barbarians. No better than a Tarkan from the outer reaches. When I gave my support, I thought we were doing the universe a favor. You killed the Kraski and most of the Deltra," she said, as if this were a good enough reason for what her people had done.

"They tried to kill us first. The damn Kraski were on the run from you! It all starts with you! You're a discredit to the universe, and the Theos would be ashamed." I wasn't sure why I said their ancient race's name, but it seemed to strike a chord.

Her tense posture loosened. "You're probably right. But all my family has done is solidify our standing in the pecking order. It's kill or be killed."

"I understand that more than you know." And I did.

Minutes ticked by in silence before a boxy ship lowered from above, blue thrusters pointing at the earth as it flew down before stopping a couple hundred yards from our position. The Empress was holding the girl now, and I pointed my rifle at them.

"Leonard, take the girl," I said firmly. He hesitated. "Take the damn girl!" He rushed over and set a hand on her small shoulder. "Get your pistol out."

He looked back at me, a grim expression on his chubby face. I hated to force his hand on this, but he

New World

wanted to be in the middle of it, so this was it.

A large Bhlat warrior stepped out, oversized gun in hand. He wore an EVA suit, the air probably nearly unbreathable for them as well. I could feel the thin air making my head light. Mix in the lack of sleep, and I worried I wouldn't be on two feet for long.

He motioned for us to come closer, and we walked toward him, the Bhlat woman and child between us and the ship.

The Empress said a few words in Bhlat and he nodded, lowering the gun. We entered the ship, but my finger didn't leave the trigger for a second.

We entered the rough-looking fifty-foot ship through a side ramp, and I got stared down by a few hulking armored soldiers, each kneeling as the Empress stepped on board. It looked to be a drop ship of some sort, and I wondered how many of these they usually used on an invasion. Or did they just steal the resources from space, defending the miners when needed? It was dimly lit, and we stayed in the bay, weapons and cold metal seats with belts lining the walls.

No one spoke until we'd been inside for five minutes or so.

"Dean Parker, we can still make our deal." The Empress turned her head and spoke softly into my ear.

"Mary," was all I said back.

"If this was your mate, then I'm truly sorry. I lost a mate once, far too young. Linna there is all I have left of him." She nodded to the little one, scared to death under Leonard's light grip.

"What do you know of the Gatekeepers?" I asked before thinking.

She stiffened. "Why do you use that name?"

"Answer the question."

"The Theos left us. Yes, we once walked worlds with them. It is said that the first Bhlat were found by them on a distant planet. One day they left, and rumors said they were seen on countless worlds sporadically over the next century or so. We never knew what they were doing, but the name *Gatekeeper* made it back to us eventually. That you ask me about it now is of extreme interest to me."

"Why?"

"Because you speak of things long lost and forbidden to our people. That you do so at such a tumultuous time for your people brings great importance to the portent it bears."

"For someone who hasn't met a human before today, you sure have a way with our words." This from Leonard. His voice was light, his hand still shaking, but not nearly as much as it had been. His gaze lifted from us to the large guards across from us.

"I can share thousands of languages with you if you so desire. It is but a simple procedure, mastered centuries ago by our scientists," the Empress said, and I wasn't sure if she was trying to impress us or distract us.

"Enough about that. That's all you know about the Gatekeepers?" I asked, anger still thick on my tongue.

"Yes. I have no reason to deceive you."

"Why is it forbidden to speak of the Theos?" I asked, curious, recalling the Bhlat on the street, worried they would be overheard using the name.

"The Theos abandoned the universe. Many beings out there think they are gods, that they created all."

"And you? What do you believe?" I asked.

She looked at me sidelong from her spot to my left, where I still aimed my gun at her. "I believe they were a wise race, far beyond our scope of understanding. They grew bored and left us all behind. The universe is a large place, one where they may still be hiding."

"Maybe they aren't hiding, just living their lives out in peace," I said.

"Peace. That is such a powerful world, but rarely one anyone takes at face value."

"Will we make this deal?" I asked, trying to read her expression. Her deep red eyes danced while staying still.

"We will."

"Will you keep doing this to other worlds?"

"We will."

"Why?" I asked, my lips sticking together as I moved my mouth.

"My world's water is contaminated. We are many, billions upon billions, and water becomes the most important resource in the universe."

I thought back to exiting the forest on the way to the Bhlat city, and how life crept away from the snaking river we'd passed.

"What about the metals?" I asked, knowing they weren't just mining water on Earth.

"If we're taking water, why not take every resource we can? It would be foolish."

Kareem's face floated to the forefront of my mind. *Change the universe.*

"Empress, what if I had a solution to your resource problem? What if I offered you coordinates to places out there that you could colonize with fresh water, and metals unheard of? Would you be willing to stop invading? Stop killing innocents for your own sake? Would you work with me, and change…" I cut myself off, not wanting to make it too cheesy. "Change the future?"

Her red eyes twitched, and a wet line streamed down her cheek. She glanced to her daughter, who looked back with wide eyes at her mother. "I would."

If she was acting, I was buying it, but I had to proceed with caution. The ship jostled and landed, presumably inside the Bhlat ship where my friends were being kept. Mary. I had to end this all and see her one more time. I felt like screaming in anguish for my lost love. It was my fault. If only I'd brought her with me to get the Empress, none of this would have happened. She'd still be at my side. I was so selfish, and I'd never live it down.

The doors whistled open, jarring me from my own thoughts. We started to walk forward; the Empress turned to me and said, "Dean Parker, we will give in to your terms. Let me speak with Blel, and you will be allowed to leave with your…" She cut herself off, remembering my mate. "You will be allowed to leave and evacuate your planet."

The guards went first, and when no one was looking, I slipped the Relocator out and saved our current location into it. A quick escape might be necessary, and I wasn't taking any chances.

Leonard went in front of me, still holding the little Bhlat girl near him. We exited the ship, and the Empress called out in her native language as a large group of Bhlat warriors lined the immense open hangar we'd landed in.

The ship must have been huge, because there were at least twenty drop ships inside the hangar, and a full hundred or so warriors stood there, suited up and ready for battle. I felt like a fool wearing an oversized Bhlat servant's robe, but at the end of the day, I didn't really care what they thought of me. I only wanted to get my friends and leave.

The group of Bhlat separated, making a path for us to walk out of the large room. The hair on the back of my neck rose as I moved forward, leaving dozens of armed soldiers at my back. I waited for the feeling of a pulse blast ripping through me, but it didn't come.

We exited through a cold metal slab of a door, the two guards from the ship still leading the way. I wanted to look around, to see the inside of a great warship from one of the universe's most deadly races, but I kept my eyes forward, watching the back of the Empress' head as we passed groups of gawking Bhlat. Here we found Bhlat in normal uniforms, men only slightly taller than humans, and women of all sizes. A ship this size wasn't housed by warriors and guns alone.

"Where's Blel?" I asked the Empress, who shrugged.

"They're taking us to him now," she said, her posture stronger and straighter than it had been since we'd first met.

We moved slowly down a couple of wide hallways. Some people shouted out to the Empress; others kneeled when whispers about who she was reached their ears. We kept moving, the Empress stoic and unresponsive to her people as we went.

My grip was tight on the pulse rifle, anxious sweat making my palm slick. I was almost there; I only needed to hold on for a little while longer. Long enough to make the deal and start moving our people.

TWENTY-SEVEN

The walk felt like an hour, but after a few more minutes, we were brought to an elevator. I didn't like the idea of entering the cramped space with the guards.

"Where does this lead? To Blel?" I asked.

The Empress asked something in Bhlat, and the guard grunted and nodded. "Yes, to the bridge."

"Then the four of us go alone," I said.

She relayed it, and one of the guards looked ready to pull a weapon. I tightened my grasp on the Empress, and she said something to them in a calming voice. He stepped back and let us enter the lift alone.

Unlike the elevator back at her palace, this one functioned like a normal one, and once inside, we lifted quickly. When the doors opened, I was ready for the fight of my life, but didn't need to be as we were greeted by two tall thin Bhlat in dark gray uniforms.

The first one spoke, her words coming through a translator. "Welcome, Dean Parker. Your Majesty." She bowed, and the other followed suit. "This way." They turned and walked toward the main bridge.

It was immense, at least ten times the size of our small ships' bridges. I spotted around twelve Bhlat officers on board. The lights were bright but not severe, and the space was spotless and shiny. This Blel was obviously a man of cleanliness and order. Almost familiar sounds emanated from the computers, once again reminding me that our races might not be as different as we seemed on the surface. I could use that.

"Mr. Parker," a thick accented voice said in English. The man rose from what could only be his captain's seat, front and center to the thirty-foot viewscreen at the far end of the bridge. He turned, and I expected to see an eight-foot-tall behemoth of a Bhlat warrior. Instead, I was greeted with a shrivelled, ancient-looking creature, shorter than myself and hunched at the back. He was bald, save for a tuft of hair that stuck out to one side from the top of his head. His eyes were black and beady; from this distance, I couldn't make out any of the swirling visage the other Bhlat had. Blel wasn't a young man. He breathed heavily, and gray hairs fluttered by his three nostrils as he did so.

"Blel," I said through clenched teeth.

"Let her go and we can talk," he said, his garbled words still translating.

I shook my head. "We talk, your forces back down, you give me my friends, and then we leave." I almost said "show me her body," but refrained.

"What do you hope to achieve here, Mr. Parker?" I hated the way he was saying my name, almost spitting it out through his dull, yellowed teeth.

"I hope to make the deal and get the hell out of here, that's what." He was giving me a bad vibe, and I felt the Empress stiffen as we had our back and forth.

"Is that so? Why should we let you live? Humans are a scourge to the universe."

"And the Bhlat aren't? I've seen the carnage in your wake."

"Is it so unlike your own, Mr. Parker?" His accent was heavy, but his words slapped me in the face regardless. "We started the destruction of the Kraskis, who were no stranger to death and slavery. Then you single-handedly destroyed them along with the Deltra, and most of their abominations while you were at it." His word for the hybrids set my blood boiling, but I let him continue. "We make quite the team, Dean. Maybe you should stay on my ship, and we can work together."

"Can we cut the crap and make the deal?" When he didn't reply, I kept talking. "You can have your Empress here, her kid, and Earth. I want my people back, and for you to vacate the area for ten Earth days while we evacuate. Then it's all yours."

He seemed to consider this, and a tall Bhlat leaned in to whisper something in their native tongue.

"No deal," he said. "You ended a whole outpost of ours. Women, children, all gone in an instant. This is unforgivable."

My pulse rifle lifted in the air, and I fought back the instinct to fire at the old unarmed Bhlat leader. "What do you mean, no deal?"

"Blel, this isn't your decision!" the Empress yelled in English for my benefit before shouting other words in her language to him.

"You sit in your palace as your mother did before you, barking orders and rewarding us for killing worlds, and now you have a heart?" His voice was loud and gravelly. "You don't get to decide any longer. I'm taking charge."

I kept my gun up and glanced to Leonard, who was sweating profusely down his brow. The officers on the bridge looked torn, deep colorful swirling eyes looking to each other for an answer on what they should do. Who did they side with?

"How dare you think to speak to me like this, Blel?

New World

I'm your Empress, and you will address me as such." The Empress started to walk forward toward him, but I held her back. If this was going to get ugly, I needed a hostage. That would only work if the crew sided with her.

A noise carried from his small mouth, and at first, I thought it might be a cough, but quickly realized it was him laughing. "Empress, I care as much about what happens to you as I do this one's mate, Mary."

He said the sentence, and I stood there blankly, body exhausted from the last couple of days, my mind taking a minute to catch up to the translation.

"Stand down, crew! Blel, you're now relieved of your duty to the Empirical Core, and are hereby declared a traitor, and you will die like one." This time, I did let her loose, while Mary's name still echoed in my head. She moved to him, her hand raised, red power glowing from her palm.

I spotted at least three armed crew coming from the edges of the room, and knew one of them would fire at her before she killed Blel.

"Stop!" I yelled, pulling my tablet from the small pack strapped to my chest. It sat beside my small *Kalentrek,* which would decimate the bridge and the ship's crew at a touch. It was a last resort, but one I'd be willing to use to save my friends.

Maybe Blel was right: we weren't so different. I left the Relocator and mini-Shield inside and flipped to the image of the powerful device sitting in the ceiling back in the palace. "Let's just say I brought more collateral." I held the tablet up for Blel and the others to see. "This is the same device I used on your outpost, and it's sitting in your capital on your homeworld now. I have a switch to activate it, and a friend on the outside has one too. If you don't leave in fifteen minutes..." I let the bluff linger without finishing it.

Some of the crew looked around nervously, clearly having family back at the capital city.

"What's it going to be, Blel?" I asked.

The Empress was still standing between us, and she was clearly ready to do some nasty business to her turncoat military leader.

"Do it. We sacrifice the old to build the new." Blel's voice was grim, and I almost panicked when he called my bluff. But the Empress didn't. Her palm glowed a fierce red, and she moved to attack him, only he pulled a small handheld gun and aimed it at her with unexpected speed.

He fired, but not before being tackled by a female officer next to him. It all happened so fast, I nearly didn't see it. The Empress dropped to the floor and I rushed to catch her, narrowly avoiding letting her head strike the hard surface. Her daughter, now free of Leonard's grasp, ran over to her.

Two groups of Bhlat were forming around the now disarmed Blel. He was being held by the woman who'd taken him down. Tension was thick as they yelled back and forth between supporters of their military leader and the Empress.

I knelt by the Empress, who was breathing. A wound in her side smoked where the ray had blasted her.

"Can you translate?" I asked.

She nodded with a grimace.

"The battles can stop. I've already made a deal with your Empress." I waited while she translated into their rough language. A few kept shouting at each other, but most stopped to listen.

She must have asked them to listen, because soon the room was silent; only Blel's labored breathing whistled across the bridge.

New World

"I have a way for your people to have water and other resources, and I've offered it to her on the condition that we're no longer enemies. That you stop the genocide of other worlds and take what I can offer you."

The words translated. Many of them looked relieved or intrigued.

"Wouldn't it be nice to be with your families, instead of fighting and mining planets with resistance?" I had them, I knew it.

Blel started to spout something off in Bhlat, but when they wouldn't listen, he spoke in English. "Mr. Parker, we are Bhlat. This will never be. We are…" His words were cut short as the sound of a pulse coursed through the bridge. Leonard stood there, pistol raised, hand trembling.

"I'm sorry," he said shakily. The young man dropped the gun and stood there, mouth open, tears falling down his face. "I'm sorry."

No one attacked him as they let Blel's dead body slip to the ground.

One crew member said a phrase in their language and came to help the Empress up. They moved her to the captain's chair and kept saying it.

"What does it mean?" I asked her.

"Long live the Empress, we bask in her eternal light." She smiled through sharp teeth, the red galaxies in her eyes twinkling as she looked at me.

Alarms sounded, and I raised my gun in defense, but they had nothing to do with what was happening on board. The wide viewscreen turned on, showing an image of Earth below, and something in the distance. One of the helmsmen ran to a console and zoomed in.

New Spero's fleet had arrived. They were going to attack this ship.

TWENTY-EIGHT

"What trickery is this?" the Empress asked. Medics ran onto the bridge and started to work on her.

"No trickery. We sent them ahead months ago, as backup. Wouldn't you have done the same?" I asked, knowing she would understand. "You have their leader, Magnus, on board here. Where are the prisoners?"

She said something to the crew member beside her, who I took to be the first officer, judging by the way the rest of the Bhlat responded to her.

"Tres will lead the way. Dean, you must prevent a war today. I can feel hope in my people. A veil has been lifted. I'll keep them from attacking your ships for as long as I can. Stop them from coming any farther."

"We will. It's best if your fleet evacuates the system. Give me a few minutes to leave the ship first." I reached and took her hand. Cool slender fingers met my sweaty palm, and she gave it a squeeze.

"Until we meet again, Dean Parker."

I smiled at her, then at her little daughter, before grabbing Leonard.

"Let's get out of here," I said, and he followed along wordlessly.

We moved closely, with Tres leading the way. No one came to stop us, but I still kept my gun close at hand.

We raced through the ship, the odd Bhlat looking

New World

confused as we moved along following their first officer. She held a lot of power, so none questioned her.

We entered an elevator and lowered into the belly of the vessel. When we got off, the surroundings were much different than they had been on the main levels. It was dingy, cold metal walls and floor, with less than ideal lighting. We were in the barracks.

My heart pounded in my chest, and I was extremely anxious to see my friends, but worried that I would find out Mary really was gone. What was I going to do without her? I'd already gone through losing someone I loved, and this time, it was even more different. Our shared trauma and situation had put us in a pressure cooker, and we'd come out together so strong and bonded.

I needed Mary and couldn't bring myself to see a future without her beside me. Each step we took down the narrow hall felt heavy, the immense weight of what we'd accomplished pressing me down like an increased gravitational pull.

If we didn't get off the ship and stop our fleet from attacking, we would be inside the enemy while a battle raged on, and no one was going to win that altercation. But a part of me didn't care anymore.

"Mary," I said through almost closed lips.

"Dean, are you okay?" Leonard asked as we walked, speaking for the first time since he'd shot Blel.

"I'm fine."

Tres turned to the right and touched a keypad; the door slid open, revealing five forms sitting or lying on the cold floor in the near dark.

I scanned and my eyes adjusted, picking out Magnus' and Slate's large forms, then Clare and Nick huddled together in the corner. Someone lay facing the wall, and I assumed it had to be Patty.

"Guys, it's me." I said the words and couldn't hold back the floodgates. I wanted to run into the room, but I didn't trust Tres not to pull a fast one and lock us away with them.

"Dean?" Slate asked, rushing over to me. He enveloped me in a big hug, his unshaven beard brushing against my forehead. He smelled like a man who'd been in a cell for months.

"We need to get out of here. Our fleet arrived, and only minutes after we struck a deal with the Bhlat. We need to stop them from attacking." I said the words, and a flood of emotions hit me. Tears fell down my face, and I wiped them away as Magnus came up to me and clasped my arm in his meaty hand.

"Brother. You did it." His eyes were wet too, and I smiled at the big man.

Clare and Nick were next, and they hugged me.

"We don't have time for this," I said, pulling the Relocator from the small pack strapped to my chest. "Let's go, Patty."

They all stood around the entrance of the room, blocking the inside.

Magnus spoke softly. "Dean, I'm so sorry. Patty didn't make it."

I reeled. "Then who…"

A more than familiar woman squeezed through the broad shoulders of Slate and Magnus and wrapped her arms around me, kissing me deeply like there wasn't a care in the world. I felt Mary's love and passion all intertwined as our lips met, and when we broke apart, I was crying and barked out a confused laugh.

"I thought you were dead," I said so softly only she could hear me.

Her cool hand rested on my cheek. "Why did you

think that?"

"Oh, Patty didn't tell the Bhlat her real name. When we arrived, she called herself Mary Lafontaine, in hopes it would give them some respect for our group. It made things worse," Clare said, clearly upset by Patrice Dalhousie being gone.

"I can't believe it," Leonard said, wide-eyed, probably conflicted between feeling terrible for killing someone and trying to record everything in his mind for his next comic issues.

Mary was alive, and I was so shocked I nearly forgot what we were doing.

"We have to go. Everyone touch my arm." I held my arms out, the Relocator in my left hand. I nodded to Tres, who kept her distance, and she gave me a grave nod back. With the tap of a button, we all disappeared from the prison cell doorway.

★ ★

"Anyone know how to fly this thing?" Magnus asked as we made our way from the back of the Bhlat drop ship to the cockpit. The craft was empty, so we didn't have to fight our way out.

I grabbed the communicator from my pouch and tapped it. "I need to speak with the Empress." A garbled voice said something unintelligible before the Empress' weak voice carried over the device.

"Dean Parker, missed me already?" she asked.

"We're in one of your drop ships. Have them open the bay doors. We're going to head out."

"Done. We will leave as promised. Good luck." She said another phrase in her native language, and the communication ended.

"I think I can muster some semblance of understanding here," Mary said, and I couldn't help but smile as she sat there, looking confused at the alien controls.

Slate stood behind her suggesting things, and soon, with Clare chiming in, we had the engines running and Mary was ready to give it a go.

"Say a little prayer," she said, and I instantly thought of the Theos. Were they still out there? Could they hear a prayer?

She gently lifted a lever, and we moved slightly.

"We don't have all day," Magnus said, clearly frustrated.

"Do you want to fly?" Mary asked, and jammed the lever back, lurching us toward the hangar ceiling. She pulled down just in time to narrowly avoid crashing. She cringed and smiled back at us before moving the ship toward the open bay doors. The opening was a couple hundred feet across; a dim green barrier glowed as we passed through it, and into space.

We were free of the Bhlat ship. My tight back loosened for a second before I spotted the gigantic fleet ships coming toward us.

"Damn if they don't look impressive," Magnus said proudly.

"When they blow us out of the sky, you won't think so," I said. "How do we contact them and tell them to stand down?"

Nick crowded in behind us, and I got a sense of how poorly they'd been treated. He'd lost a good fifteen pounds, and his eyes had a look I'd never seen in them before. "Is there any way to send a message?"

Clare moved into the seat beside the pilot's chair and attempted to find a communication device. The viewscreen had radar on it: the green lights, which identified the Bhlat master ship and their other orbiting ships, were moving away from Earth. The red lights, showing our incoming fleet, started to move toward us.

"I can't see how to do it." Frustration and panic melded together in her voice.

"They're coming for us. If we don't tell them what transpired, they'll chase the Bhlat and break our peace." I had to think of something. "Magnus, you have the Kraski beams in those ships?" I fiddled with the chain and pendant still around my neck.

"Yeah, you can use the suit's pins to get access if needed. That's just an emergency EVA situation…" He stopped his thought, looking at me and grinning. "One more adventure for old times?"

I smiled back, hiding the stress I was feeling. "One more adventure. Did you leave the pack by the pyramid?"

He nodded.

"Mary, we'll be right back. Magnus and I will get on board the lead warship and get them to stop."

Our eyes met, and a flicker of hope and exhaustion transferred between us. I mouthed "I love you" to her, and she said it back.

"I'll see if I can find anything useful in the back," Slate said, moving out of the cramped cockpit.

"Ready?" I asked Magnus, and touched his arm, hitting the location for the pyramid on the Relocator.

TWENTY-NINE

The first thing we did, when we got the EVA suits Magnus and Mary had stashed near the pyramid, was try to communicate with the fleet in space approaching Earth.

"They're too far for these suits' comms to work," Magnus said, slipping into his suit. Mine was made for Mary, and the fit was tight. They had a little give, so I was able to stand up in it, but not comfortably.

"How do I look?" I asked, serious behind the face shield.

"Like a man that would do what it takes." I'd expected a joke in return.

"I don't think Earth has much time either." The clouds were black, angry, and the air was thin and getting harder to breathe. We needed to get these people off the planet. It was as if all the things we needed to do had severe urgency, but we couldn't save the people without stopping the fleet from attacking the Bhlat.

With a tap of the Relocator, we were back on the drop ship, and I once again thanked Kareem silently for the gift.

Slate jumped at our sudden appearance. "Look what I found." They were backpacks with thrusters. The kind of thing I'd dreamt of flying over the farm fields with when I was a little kid, wishing for something more than canola crops and chicken feed. I guess I'd gotten my wish. Now I wanted to swap with myself and live that quiet life.

"How do they work?" Magnus asked, already trying to put it on.

Our suits had the mini-thrusters Mae and I had used to tether the vessels heading toward the sun almost two years ago. Two *years*.

"Boss, are you with us?" Slate asked, concern on his gaunt face.

"I'm here. Wearing down, and my mind is drifting. Go ahead."

Slate showed us how he thought they worked, and we had nothing to lose. If we flew up to our approaching ships, they would blast us away. We needed to have some stealth.

"Will they show up on the sensors?" I asked Magnus.

He shook his head. "The sensors are for ship drives and radiation, mainly. Whatever's fueling these will be so minuscule compared to their search parameters, we'll be able to slip by with no problem." He looked to me and shrugged. "I hope."

That didn't give me full confidence, but we had no choice.

"I can go instead of you, boss." Slate looked ready to take my place.

"If you haven't noticed, I barely fit into this suit. And even though I'm tired, I haven't been in a cell for months at the hands of an evil alien race."

"Godspeed," he said, clapping me on the back, then Magnus. "Make sure you stay out of their range." With that, Slate left us in an airlock, sealed it, and we opened the doors to dark space.

The jetpack was heavy on the ship, but out here, it didn't matter. My stomach lurched at being out here again, untethered this time. The huge ships from outside New Spero loomed in the distance, and we had some distance to travel to get there. Our suits were made for this, but I still worried something would happen.

"Let's test this out," Magnus said through my helmet's earpiece. He hit the handheld controls and one thruster fired up, sending him into a slow spin. "Damn it," he said, adjusting and getting both going. Soon he'd stabilized himself, and he called instructions to me. After a shaky start, we were both close to competent with the packs, and we started toward our target.

"I think they're moving," I said, thinking they were getting closer to us faster than our packs were taking us.

"You're right. Stay the course."

"What happens if they're going too fast when we cross paths?"

Magnus laughed uneasily, and I wasn't sure I wanted to hear his answer to that. "I have a plan for that."

I really didn't like the sound of that.

We moved this way for almost an hour, the ships getting closer each minute. In the distance, there was nothing but the expanse of space, and my mind drifted to the countless worlds out there we could now access with the portals. What was out there for us to discover? I put the thoughts on the backburner as the half dozen warships grew, until we couldn't ignore them coming toward us any longer.

"There's not going to be anywhere to grab a foothold on them. We have to beam into them." Magnus said this like it was no big deal. Go for a beer, walk your dog… beam into a warship while traveling in the opposite direction in an EVA suit, with a jetpack thrusting you toward it.

"Is there no other option?" I asked, hoping for a miracle.

"Come in, NS-1007. This is your general. Stop where you are. The war is over. I repeat, slow your thrusters and cease your pursuit." He waited and said it again, but still received no reply.

The lead ship was beautiful. The sleek exterior was rounded, giving way from the boxy design of the Bhlat ships or the cube vessels of the Kraski. Our people had found a way to incorporate the size of the vessels but mix them with the slim and smooth smaller ships. They were a testament to how far our race had come in a short period of time. And if we weren't careful, we were about to be smashed like bugs on the warship's windshield.

The ship grew as we slowed our thrusters.

"Crap. They're powering up the cannons." Magnus pointed toward the bottom edges of the ship, where a red light started to glow. "They're going to fire at the retreating Bhlat."

"You sure this is going to work? We won't end up in a wall or out the other end?" I'd used the beam pins on our suit enough times, but not on a target moving so fast.

"The ship's big. We'll be fine." He said it with confidence, but as we got closer to each other, I could see the dread in his eyes.

We were close enough to the lead vessel to see the rough edges that made up the exterior. From a distance, they looked smooth, but up close, they were anything but.

My heart raced as we floated there, waiting for the ship to come close enough to beam into it.

"You're a good friend. Let's get this over with and have a Scotch on your deck," I said, hoping they weren't my last words.

"Deal. Dean, those years we thought you were dead… were the hardest of my life." He looked over at me, and I smiled at his unusual emotional talk. "Enough about that. See you in a minute."

I watched him press the small pin on his EVA collar, and he was covered in green light, the ship now only yards away from us. We couldn't see inside the ship, but I imagined the looks on a helmsman's face when they saw two floating Earth Defense suits outside their cameras.

I pressed my pin, feeling the familiar thrum of the beam's energy. With a deep breath, I blinked as I entered the warship. This time, I opened them sooner and spotted Magnus coming out of the beam, turning solid and rolling to the floor. I joined him, my momentum keeping me moving. I hit the hard floor and flopped forward, hitting the wall with a thud.

"You okay?" he asked, holding his left elbow.

My back was tender and my right knee howled at me, but as I rolled over and tried to stand, I found I wasn't too bad off.

"I think so." I took my helmet off and tossed it to the ground. Magnus did the same. "Where are we?"

"Damn it. In a storage room. They're locked from the outside."

"We don't have a lot of time." I found my pulse rifle on the ground and picked it up, motioning Magnus back. The red beams smashed the door, sending shards outward, opening a hole large enough for us to crawl through.

"Subtle," Magnus said as we emerged in the hall.

"Stop! Drop the weapon!" a female voice boomed from behind us.

"Gladly." I dropped the gun, glad to be away from the enemy and on our own people's ship.

"Turn slowly," the woman said.

When she saw Magnus' face, she did a double take

and saluted him. "I'm sorry, sir."

"Just call the bridge. Tell them to turn the cannons off. Our mission has changed."

★ ★

"You did what?" Naidoo stalked angrily around the room, and I didn't blame her. I'd essentially given our world away. It was far better than the alternative.

"I know you don't like me, but what choice did we have?" I was getting irritated with her but didn't want my heart to talk over my head. I lowered my voice and calmed the erratic timbre. "You tried to make a deal with them, right?"

She stopped in her tracks, turning slowly to look at me. The room in Cape Town was full of dignitaries from around the world, as well as our group. When we'd arrived, the nations were in widespread panic. An alert had gone out over all remaining media that an announcement was coming, and for everyone to gather their belongings and loved ones.

That set off more fear, but after all these people had been through, they were getting used to it. We heard stories trickling in about groups working together, and leaders of communities taking charge, directing people to gather in town halls or city parks.

The air was thin; conditions were far from ideal. Oxygen tanks and respiratory centers were being erected around the world for anyone with pulmonary issues. I was proud of the people of Earth.

"They were coming anyway," was her defense.

"Then you did what you thought best, and they decided to steal our water with us still on the planet."

"How are we going to get everyone off Earth? And where are we going to put them all?" a mature red-haired woman asked. She looked at Mary and me with thoughtful eyes, concern etched on her face.

Magnus took this one. "Our warships have space to transport a large group of people. We'll have to bring more supplies to feed them on the two-month journey, but it can be done."

"And the rest of us?" she asked.

Magnus' eyes roamed toward me, and the whole room set their gaze in my direction.

I looked around the room: tall ceilings. Mahogany wood beams ran across them. Large windows allowed the midday light to cascade down on us at the central table, where we sat at the south end. It would have been intimidating sitting there with all of these people looking to me for answers in my previous life. Now, I was ready for it.

"We walk to New Spero," I said, waiting for a response.

I was about to continue when almost everyone in the room began speaking at the same time.

"Trust me. We have a way to transport ourselves from Egypt to New Spero. We'll send a team there first, tell them what's transpired, and they'll begin to accommodate for the new influx of people." I expected more questions, but that seemed to quiet them.

"How?"

"I'll show you."

THIRTY

"You need to sleep," Mary said as we sat down outside the Giza pyramid.

"I'll sleep when we're home."

We ate sandwiches while watching the procession of people heading into the pyramid, down toward the portal. Clare and Nick were running the trips now, and we'd let the powers that be organize the logistics of getting people from Earth to the warships in orbit, and the rest to Egypt.

The dirt layer separating the bottom of the pyramid from the portal halls had been excavated. It felt wrong to destroy something the Theos had built so long ago, but we had to live another day, and this was the only way.

"What happens after this?" Mary asked, leaning her head on my shoulder as she chewed the last of her roast beef.

I watched the lines of people walking into the Giza pyramid, and spotted a young family with two small children. The mother held her small son in her arms, and the dad held his daughter's hand, leading them to an uncertain future. Life as they knew it was over, for everyone.

"Dean?"

"After this?" I smiled at her. "We help build a new future for everyone."

Leonard came out of a tent set up with food, carrying

a sandwich and a bottle of water. "Mind if I join you?" he asked.

"Not at all," Mary said, patting the unused pyramid stone beside her.

"How are you hanging in there, Leonard?" I asked, seriously concerned about my new young friend. We'd been through a crazy adventure together, one where he'd been forced to kill, and be part of something that turned our people's future forever. His eyes had deep purple bags under them, evidence of the last day's trials.

"You had to do it," I said, knowing he'd understand what I referred to.

"Dean's told me all about you, Leonard," Mary said. "We're both very proud of you."

The man I'd met a couple days ago would have blushed at that, but the new version wasn't the same youth any longer. "I think I'm done with comics."

"You don't mean that. People will want to know what happened." I surprised myself by saying that.

"Really?" he asked, looking at me with tear-filled eyes.

"Really. You're a great guy to have by my side. You'll always have a place on my crew."

His posture straightened up, and he looked up to the sky, the clouds breaking for a moment so the sun beat down on his face.

We sat there in silence, enjoying each other's company in near silence as countless people moved from Earth to our new world. Each one of them with a story: a tale about their pre-Event lives, how they survived the Event, why they elected to stay on Earth rather than travel to New Spero, where fate was bringing them after all.

I wondered where their tales would lead them. For that matter, I didn't know where mine was headed. I sat my hand on Mary's thigh and gave her a light squeeze.

New World

She smiled at me, her hair in a loose ponytail, and a few strands broke free, covering her face. She blew at them, and I loved her more at that moment than ever before.

My future wasn't set, but my fate was now intertwined with hers. We were partners in whatever was to come.

Magnus approached as the sun went down, followed by Clare and Nick when they swapped out with a duo Magnus trusted to make the portal journeys with the people. The room held four hundred at a time, and they could make the trip every five minutes; the people from Earth arrived at the caves near Terran Five on New Spero.

The warships were able to take a quarter of the Earth's population, and because of the distance to the pyramids, the Western hemisphere was being brought to the ships rather than to the portal. All in all, almost everyone would be off Earth in five days or less.

Camps were set up, and all Terran cities were pitching in, taking in refugees and donating food, clothing, and shelter where needed. My sister and her husband James were leading the charge at Terran Five, and I couldn't have been prouder of them.

Slate was the last of my old crew to arrive, and he brought something brown in a clear bottle.

"Where'd you get that?" Magnus asked, taking the bottle and sniffing the contents. He shrugged and grabbed some empty water bottles from around us, filling each with two fingers' worth.

"What are we toasting to?" Nick asked, looking as exhausted as I felt.

"To surviving." I raised my plastic bottle in the air, and everyone joined in. "To surviving." We tapped our drinks and downed some of the liquid.

With that one done, Mary had one more. "To Patrice Dalhousie. One of the strongest and most visionary people I've had the pleasure of meeting."

"To Patty," we chorused, and drank the last, Magnus pouring a splash onto the dusty ground.

★ ★

Mary raced across Africa in the old-style Kraski ship. It had been only six days since we'd made the deal with the Empress, but it felt like weeks.

"Looks clear." Mary lifted up, taking us higher.

"One more pass?" I asked her.

"Dean, we can't save them all. If they didn't make it by now, we can't do anything."

Slate made a tapping motion on his wrist, telling me time was up. "You have a last job to do, and so do I."

Mary nodded and gave the controls over to him.

"Slate, we'll see you in a couple of months. Don't worry, we won't do anything crazy without you," I said, getting an eye roll from him.

"Like you didn't do anything crazy the last time I left you?" He laughed.

We neared the pyramids. After days of commotion there, they seemed eerily quiet and serene on the viewscreen. Nothing was left but some tents and millions of footprints from around the world.

"It's always more fun exploring ancient alien planets with you, buddy. You know that."

He lowered us, and we headed to the ramp in the middle of the ship, opening it to a brisk midnight desert breeze. "You have everything you need?" he asked, passing me a heavy pack.

New World

Mary swung on a winter jacket and tossed me mine, which I caught with my free hand. "I think so. Sad to think this is the last time we'll see Earth."

"You never know," Slate said back. "Especially with you, boss."

Mary hugged our big friend. "Zeke Campbell, you're one in a million. I can't wait to see you back home. Thanks for keeping Clare and Nick safe up there." She kissed his cheek, and I hugged him too.

"I couldn't keep us all safe," he said somberly.

"You couldn't help that," Mary said.

"I guess so. I wish I could just leave this ship behind and come with you, but Magnus is probably right. Every asset should be saved."

"See you soon." I saluted him, and we walked down and toward the pyramid. Slate lifted off and headed upward toward the last warship, waiting for the remaining Kraski ships to join them for the journey home.

We watched him leave, looking at the starlit sky. This was it. No more Earth. I thought about my farm back home, my parents now both gone. With a glance over at Mary, I knew she was thinking about it all too, and a single tear rolled down her cheek.

I stretched out my hand, grabbing hers. "New Spero will be our new home. A fresh start for everyone."

"I'll miss what we had."

"Me too."

We stared into the sky for a while longer before shaking it off and heading toward the pyramid.

"After you," I said, waving Mary into the entrance. We walked along the pathways in silence; recently installed battery-powered LEDs lit our path. The walkway slanted down the whole time, and soon we were at the floor built to separate our people from the portal.

Crude stairs had been dug into it during the excavation process, and we carefully stepped down them, aware of how many feet had walked down them over the last week.

It looked far different than the portal we'd emerged from not long ago. Now the walls had lights mounted on them, and the halls had been widened to fit more people through at once. The entrance to the portal room was there, the round stone door open just enough to allow us to slip through.

I lowered the heavy pack to the dirt floor, thankful for the reprieve from its weight.

"Let's set them down the hall a way too," I said. Mary grabbed a few of the small bombs from the pack and lined the hall with them, one every three yards. They each packed a punch, but we wanted to make sure the portal was gone for good.

Once we emptied the bag of them, Mary took the detonator and slid it into her breast pocket. I tried to roll the door closed, but it didn't matter. None of it would survive the coming explosion.

"What about everyone we didn't remove?" I asked, feeling the guilt weigh heavily on me.

"We don't have the time or resources."

I nodded and moved to the center of the room where the table sat, its gemstone glowing now. We'd run this portal ragged, but it didn't seem to have any limitations. That was good to know for other planets. I'd have to fill Sarlun in on my findings. He'd be saddened to hear we'd destroyed one of them, but I hoped he'd understand why.

With the icon loaded for New Spero, Mary slipped the detonator out.

I grabbed the communicator that was linked to the one we'd left behind on the Bhlat ship housing the Empress and tapped it.

"Empress," I said into it.

"Dean Parker." Her voice sounded stronger than the last time we'd spoken.

"It's done. Earth is yours."

"Thank you."

"Remember our deal. Our conflict is over. When the dust settles, I'll contact you with the locations I promised you." I held my breath, half-expecting a retort.

"Our conflict is over."

With the communicator back in my pack, Mary set the detonator timer to twenty seconds.

"Goodbye, Earth," she said quietly.

I pressed the icon, and everything went white.

THIRTY-ONE

"*I* do," Mary said through a beautiful smile.

"I now pronounce you man and wife." The officiant clapped her hands together.

I leaned in, taking Mary's hands in mine, and I heard the words "you may kiss the bride" after we were already deep into our first kiss as a married couple.

Our friends cheered us on. After a few seconds, I pulled back, not wanting to overdo it.

Mary was so gorgeous, wearing a contemporary wedding dress, her hair in an updo I hadn't seen before. I wore a tuxedo, the dark pink accents matching her flowers, but it all felt a little out of place on our acreage on New Spero. We'd discussed swaying from tradition, but in the end, elected to follow the old ways from Earth. We couldn't lose those types of conventions, not with the loss of our home so fresh in everyone's minds.

We turned to the crowd. I spotted almost everyone we knew, and then some. The day was warm, the planet's summer season in full effect, and some of the guests were using handmade fans to cool themselves.

Natalia stood beside Mary, acting as her maid of honor, with Magnus at my side as my best man. I glanced and smiled at the front rows, spotting Slate sitting with Clare and Nick, all of them smiling widely. I waved and got a thumbs-up from Slate.

New World

"Time to party!" Mary yelled, getting another cheer. Music came on the speakers, and we walked through the crowd again, stopping to chat here and there. I saw Isabelle and James talking with Leonard, who looked great in his new suit.

Suma and her Gatekeeper father Sarlun were there too, beside Leslie and Terrance. They'd all traveled here for the event via the portals.

"I'm really happy for you two lovebirds," Magnus said, wrapping his big arm around my shoulder. "I knew we'd make an honest man out of you."

Natalia was fixing something in Mary's hair, and little Dean ran up to his dad; Magnus scooped him up in his arms.

I felt something on the back of my leg. I turned to see Carey, holding a toy and pushing it against my calf. I knelt down, so happy to see the aging dog still with so much energy. He accepted my incessant petting and eventually rolled over to let me rub his stomach.

The younger pups found their way over when they saw this, and soon I was playing with them all, tossing a ball while they ran after it. After a few throws, Carey slumped his butt down on my shoe, and watched the more exuberant dogs keep chasing the object.

I loved that dog so much, and he knew it. I could feel Magnus' gaze on me.

"I'll be fine. He's your dog. I only selfishly wish that had worked out differently," I said.

Maggie trotted over, and Magnus's son handed me a small bag. I opened it and found a leash, a dog dish, and some food.

"What's this, Dean?" I asked the boy.

"Maggie's going to live with you, buddy," Magnus said, while his little boy shyly hid behind his dad's leg.

"You don't have to do that," I said, looking at the cute dog rolling in the grass.

"Believe me, we have enough going on, and she's never happier than when she's over here with you. Don't say no. You need it as much as she does."

I didn't argue. I just picked up Maggie and got a faceful of licks for my trouble.

As I looked around, surrounded by so many familiar faces, I struggled to remember the man I'd been before the Event.

Magnus set up, chasing Dean and the dogs, and everything felt right.

"We did it," Mary said in my ear as she wrapped her arms around me from behind.

I spun around and kissed her again, this time not caring about first-kiss protocol. I heard James yell, "Get a room."

He had the right idea, but we had the reception to get through first.

★ ★

The night wore on, and soon there were only a handful of us left outside our house. Isabelle and James had gone to our guest room, staying with us while they visited from Terran Five.

Clare, Nick, and Slate all sat down at the outdoor fire pit, where embers were glowing hotly in the night air. So much had changed, but so much about us had stayed the same.

"I need to get Suma to bed soon." Sarlun wore what must have passed for formal wear back home and was as colorful as a flowerbed. He wore it with dignity and grace

New World

befitting a man of his stature.

"Thanks for coming. I'm looking forward to spending our honeymoon in your hot springs," I said, amazed that such a spellbinding place existed. Sarlun had offered his second home there to us, and when he showed us images of the area, we couldn't say no.

"Dean." His translator said my name after he spoke. "There's something I wanted to talk to you about." His eyes narrowed, and his extended nose twitched. He was nervous about something.

I took a pull from my beer bottle. "No better time than the present."

"The Theos may be back."

I spit out the beer I'd sipped and wiped my mouth with my shirt sleeve. "How do you know?"

"One of the Gatekeepers found something," his speaker translated.

"What is it?"

"I cannot tell you. Only Gatekeepers may know."

My stomach clenched, and I looked around at what I had: a wonderful small home on a large piece of land on New Spero, with a newly-wed wife, and a dog that followed me around everywhere I went. That was the dream. It had always been mine.

"We'll do it," a voice from beyond the fire pit's light said. Mary walked over, her dress traded for something more functional. She had a beer in her hand too, and she clinked the near-empty one I was holding.

"We will? He hasn't asked us anything." I wasn't sure we should be rushing into this, but our path had already been forged.

"I will ask you. Dean and Mary, will you join our ranks as Gatekeepers? My daughter was right about you. You *are* special." He looked me in the eyes without breaking the gaze.

My hand found Mary's, and I gave it a squeeze. "We're in."

ABOUT THE AUTHOR

Nathan Hystad is an author from Sherwood Park, Alberta, Canada. When he isn't writing novels, he's running a small publishing company, Woodbridge Press.

Keep up to date with his new releases by signing up for his newsletter at www.nathanhystad.com

Sign up at www.scifiexplorations.com as well for amazing deals and new releases from today's best indie science fiction authors.

Printed in Great Britain
by Amazon

What it was like to be an ...

ANCIENT GREEK

DAVID LONG

Illustrated by
Stefano Tambellini

Barrington Stoke

Published by Barrington Stoke
An imprint of HarperCollins*Publishers*
1 Robroyston Gate, Glasgow, G33 1JN

www.barringtonstoke.co.uk

HarperCollins*Publishers*
Macken House, 39/40 Mayor Street Upper,
Dublin 1, DO1 C9W8, Ireland

First published in 2025

Text © 2025 David Long
Illustrations © 2025 Stefano Tambellini
Cover design © 2025 HarperCollins*Publishers* Limited

The moral right of David Long and Stefano Tambellini to be identified
as the author and illustrator of this work has been asserted in accordance
with the Copyright, Designs and Patents Act, 1988

ISBN 978-0-00-870054-6

10 9 8 7 6 5 4 3 2 1

All rights reserved. No part of this publication may be reproduced, stored in
a retrieval system, or transmitted, in whole or in any part in any form or by any
means, electronic, mechanical, photocopying, recording or otherwise without
the prior permission in writing of the publisher and copyright owners

Without limiting the exclusive rights of any author, contributor or the publisher of
this publication, any unauthorised use of this publication to train generative artificial
intelligence (AI) technologies is expressly prohibited. HarperCollins also exercise
their rights under Article 4(3) of the Digital Single Market Directive 2019/790 and
expressly reserve this publication from the text and data mining exception

The contents of this publication are believed correct at the time of printing.
Nevertheless the publisher can accept no responsibility for errors or omissions,
changes in the detail given or for any expense or loss thereby caused

A catalogue record for this book is available from the British Library

Printed and bound in India by Replika Press Pvt. Ltd.

MIX
Paper | Supporting
responsible forestry
FSC™ C007454

This book contains FSC™ certified paper and other controlled
sources to ensure responsible forest management.

For more information visit: www.harpercollins.co.uk/green

*With love to Rosy,
my favourite classicist*

CONTENTS

1 A HIGHLY ADVANCED SOCIETY   1
Who Were the Ancient Greeks?

2 EVERYDAY LIFE   6
The People and Their Rulers

3 MYTHS AND MONSTERS   19
The Greeks and Their Gods

4 MIND AND BODY   31
Sport and the Arts

5 HOPLITES VERSUS IMMORTALS   44
The Long War Against Persia

6 A TALENT FOR INVENTION   55
Architects, Engineers and Inventors

7 CONQUERING THE WORLD   65
Alexander the Great

8 THE RISE OF THE ROMANS   75
The End of the Empire

9 A LONG LEGACY   83
Greece Today

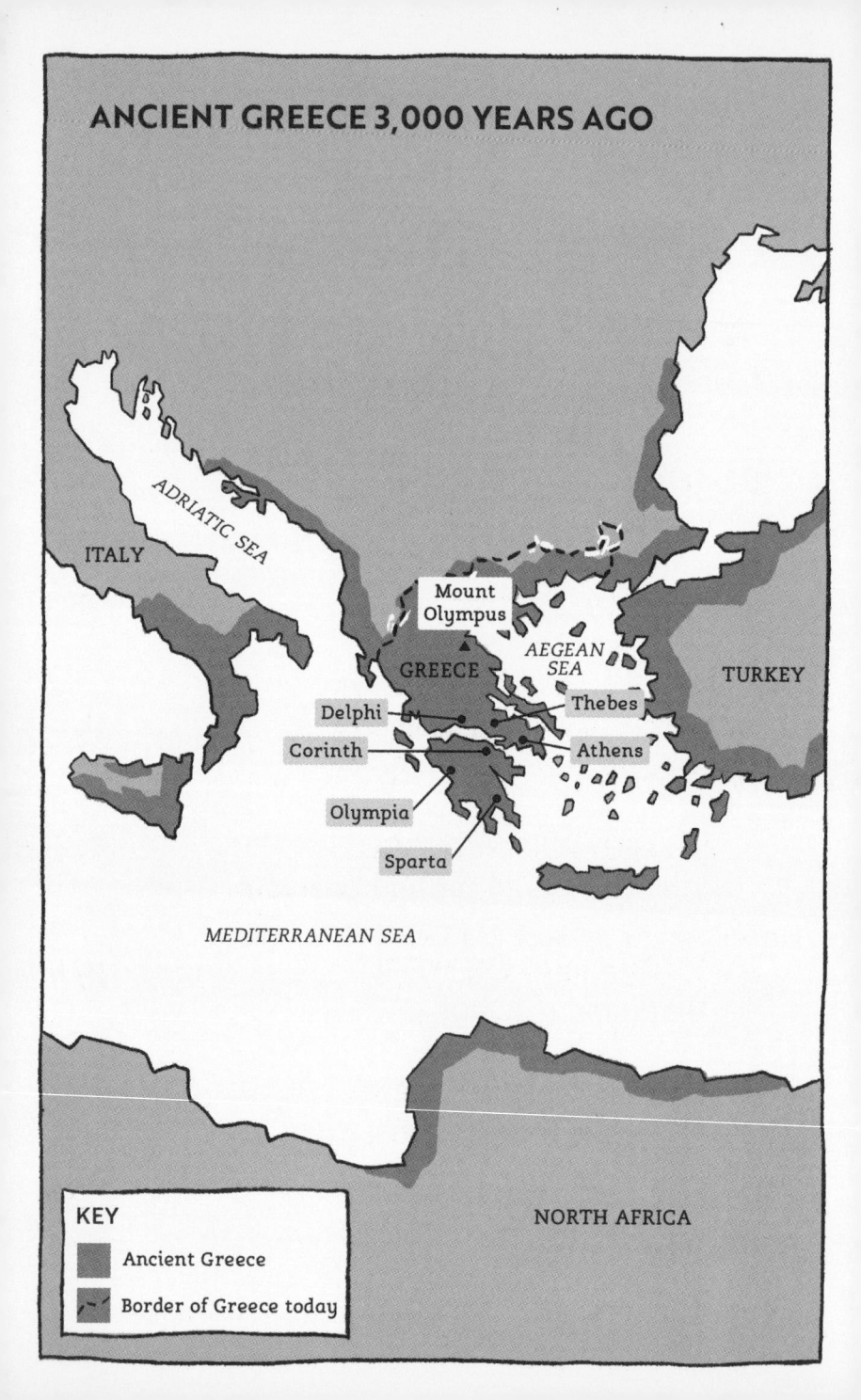

ANCIENT GREECE 3,000 YEARS AGO

ADRIATIC SEA

ITALY

Mount Olympus

GREECE

AEGEAN SEA

TURKEY

Delphi
Corinth
Olympia
Sparta
Thebes
Athens

MEDITERRANEAN SEA

NORTH AFRICA

KEY
- Ancient Greece
- Border of Greece today

1
A HIGHLY ADVANCED SOCIETY

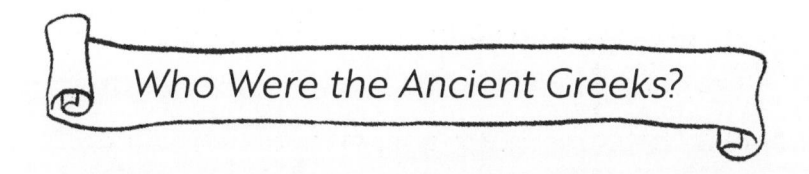

Who Were the Ancient Greeks?

Around 3,000 years ago, the ancient Greeks created one of the world's most advanced and impactful civilisations.

More than seven million people occupied large areas of rocky, mountainous land in southern Europe, which they named Hellas. About half of them lived on the mainland in an area that is now known as Greece. The remainder built their homes along the coastline and on hundreds of small islands in what is now Italy, Turkey and north Africa.

A HIGHLY ADVANCED SOCIETY

At this time, the Greeks called themselves Hellenes. They organised themselves into individual city-states rather than forming one large nation or an empire.

Each state, known as a *polis*, was run separately from the others. The people living in them all shared a similar culture and they spoke the same language, but each polis had its own customs and laws and rulers.

The largest and richest of these states included Athens, Corinth, Delphi, Sparta and Thebes. These cities fought many violent battles with each other until Athens and Sparta gradually emerged as the most powerful.

These two rival cities were at war for decades, and Athens eventually came out on top. It was the most important city in Hellas when the states finally came together in the fourth century BCE. Athens became

A HIGHLY ADVANCED SOCIETY

the magnificent capital of Greece just over 2,000 years later.

Alexander the Great was their most famous leader, ruling from 336 to 323 BCE. Under him, the Greeks established themselves as the dominant power in Europe, Asia and parts of Africa. At one point, his enormous empire stretched from Egypt to India.

Alexander was a superb military commander but a ruthless dictator. His armies conquered so much new territory that it was difficult to rule or defend these areas properly. This meant his empire didn't last very long. However, even when it began to break up, Alexander's conquests across the world meant that many aspects of the Greeks' language, art and ideas spread far and wide.

This is important because the ancient Greeks were highly advanced and sophisticated compared to other countries of the world. Most

4 A HIGHLY ADVANCED SOCIETY

of them worked as farmers and fishermen to feed their families, but others studied hard to become brilliant astronomers, navigators and philosophers.

A HIGHLY ADVANCED SOCIETY

Some Greeks worked as expert traders and teachers, artists and athletes – even scientists, although the Greek language didn't have a word to describe what we think of as science today.

The ancient Greeks' finest artworks and their greatest inventions were later copied by the Romans when they began to establish their own empire. This was even larger than Alexander's and based in the same area.

The Romans weren't the only people to admire the wisdom and learning of the ancient Greek civilisation. Their knowledge and culture spread so widely that the ancient Greeks still influence how we live our lives today, and in some surprising ways.

2
EVERYDAY LIFE

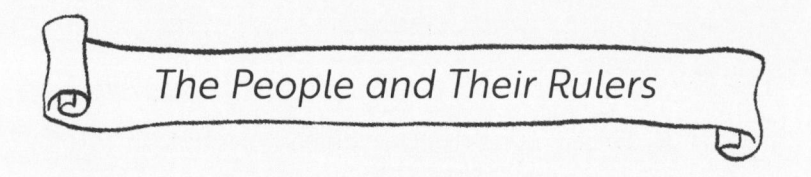

The People and Their Rulers

There were around a thousand city-states in ancient Greece. Most of these were surrounded by strong stone walls for defence, and each one had its own form of government and way of deciding which laws the citizens had to obey. Some were monarchies, such

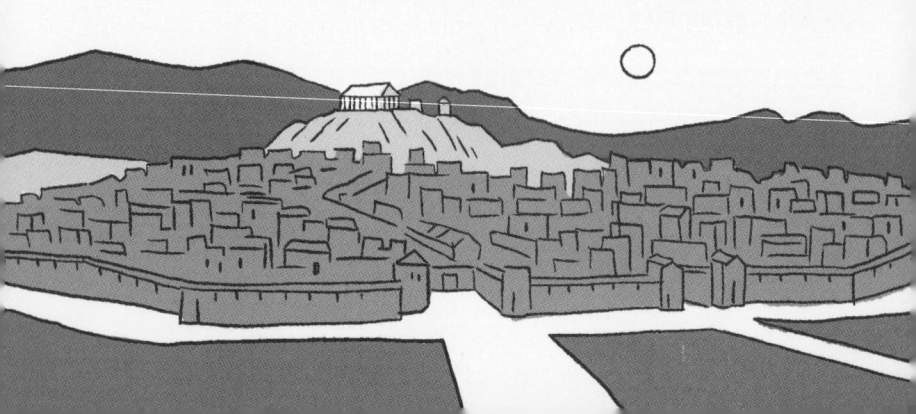

EVERYDAY LIFE

as Macedonia, which meant they were ruled by kings or sometimes a queen. Others were oligarchies, like Sparta, which means the richest, most powerful people take control and run everything to suit themselves. The third type of government was a democracy, such as Athens. This means somewhere that holds elections so that people living there can vote for their favourite leaders.

A democracy was the fairest system; however, not everyone was allowed to vote. Only people known as free citizens could take part in elections. This did not include any women, foreigners, children or slaves, so the lives of ordinary families were often much the same no matter where they lived or how they were governed.

The climate of Hellas was mostly warm and dry, so many of the houses were very simple, with just a few rooms arranged around a courtyard or garden.

EVERYDAY LIFE

The walls were wooden or built with bricks made from dried mud, and houses were often dark inside because the windows were very small. They had wooden shutters instead of glass, and the shutters could be closed during the day to keep out the heat.

Hardly anyone owned any furniture, and only the richest citizens could afford luxuries such as a bathroom. Everyone else washed

A Large Greek Home

Gynaikon

Kitchen

Storeroom

Altar

Courtyard

EVERYDAY LIFE 9

using a bucket of cold water or in a nearby stream. There were public bath houses, but you had to pay to use them.

Adults and children slept on mattresses stuffed with feathers or wool or dried grass, and it was normal for people to go to bed when it got dark. Candles and olive-oil lamps provided a bit of light, but only in households that could afford to buy them at the market.

Bedroom

Bathroom

Andron

Well

EVERYDAY LIFE

People with larger houses often had a special room called an *andron* for men to meet in and another room for women known as a *gynaikon*.

The men mostly wore simple tunics, which were short for younger people and long for older ones. Enslaved men had to make do with a loincloth – a very small piece of cloth that they wrapped around their waists.

EVERYDAY LIFE 11

Women wore a longer version of the male tunic called a *chiton* beneath a *himation*, which was a type of cloak. These were woven using wool or linen (a fabric made from the fibres of a plant called flax). The wool came from goats as well as sheep and was used to make thicker himations for people to wear during the cooler winter months. Rich people normally wore the brightest coloured fabrics.

EVERYDAY LIFE

People often wore hats, but shoes were fairly rare. A lot of ancient Greeks went barefoot because they couldn't afford a pair of leather sandals. But hats were essential for farmers and anyone else who worked all day under the hot sun. Rich men and women also wore hats to protect their faces because they thought being suntanned was unattractive.

Every city-state had enormous numbers of enslaved people. Many were men, women and even children who had been captured after a battle. Sometimes young children were enslaved when their own parents sold them because they didn't have the money to feed a large family.

The enslaved person became the property of a new owner who could put them to work or just sell them to someone else. Alexander the Great's father, King Philip II of Macedon, once sold 20,000 enslaved people after a successful

EVERYDAY LIFE

raid on one of the neighbouring states, but this was an unusually high number.

Owners of the enslaved weren't always cruel and heartless, yet enslaved people often worked extremely long hours in some of the very worst jobs. The most dangerous job was being a miner in one of the silver or copper mines outside Athens. But enslaved people often just worked in their owners' homes. Even fairly poor families had at least one enslaved person, and daily tasks included cooking, cleaning and gardening. Thousands of others were rented out by their owners or put to work on large farms and on building sites.

Unlike nowadays, the rich nearly always ate at home, and the poor went out for their meals. This was because poorer families didn't have a kitchen, so they had to buy hot or cold snacks from stalls in the street.

EVERYDAY LIFE

Men and women ate separately, and everyone used their fingers instead of a knife and fork. The ancient Greeks' favourite dishes included deer, hare and wild boar meat – or fresh squid and octopus for those living by the sea. In Sparta, a special soup made of pig's blood was very popular.

Meat was always an expensive luxury, however, so ordinary families ate a lot of bread made from wheat, as well as fruit and beans. They also had a type of porridge made from barley grains mixed with fish, eggs or cheese. Some ancient Greeks were so poor they only survived by eating acorns.

Women generally organised everything around the home while their husbands went out to work.

Only boys of seven and over were sent to school and then only if their families could afford to pay for it. These schools were very small, with as few as ten pupils and one teacher. The boys learned how to read and write, and sometimes how to play musical instruments. Usually, they left school at the age of 13 or 14 because the Greeks considered them to be grown-ups by then.

Girls from rich families in Sparta were allowed to go to school at one time too, but this idea didn't catch on anywhere else. There were other girls who could read and write, but they were probably taught at home by their mothers.

Boys and girls were often given different toys to play with when they were young. A boy might get a model chariot or some toy weapons. Meanwhile, his sister most likely played with dolls made of clay, wax and even glass.

EVERYDAY LIFE

But a few toys were shared between them, such as yo-yos (a clever Greek invention) and small polished stones that children used to play marbles. Spinning tops known as *stromvos* were also popular, along with noisy rattles.

3
MYTHS AND MONSTERS

The Greeks and Their Gods

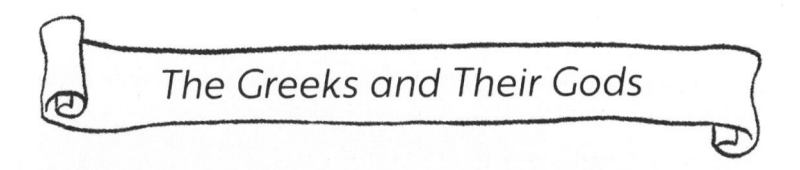

The ancient Greeks were pagans, which means they worshipped lots of different gods and goddesses instead of just one god, like Christians, Jews and Muslims. Thousands of years ago, this wasn't unusual. The people of Hellas had so many fabulous myths and legends about their gods and magical spirits that historians still can't agree how many they worshipped.

The Greeks used to believe that the 12 most important gods lived in a mysterious cloud palace. This was situated at the top of

Mount Olympus, the highest peak in the north of the country.

Zeus was the most powerful god of them all. He was the king of the sky and thunder, so he controlled the weather. His wife Hera was the goddess of women, marriage and family, and his brother Poseidon ruled the ocean

MYTHS AND MONSTERS

and caused earthquakes. Aphrodite was the goddess of love and beauty, and Hades (Zeus and Poseidon's older brother) ruled the dark kingdom of the underworld, where he lived with a scary three-headed dog called Cerberus.

The underworld was where people believed they went when they died, so many ancient Greeks thought it was unlucky even to say the name Hades out loud.

Other gods had kinder personalities. Hermes had wings on his sandals and carried messages down from Mount Olympus. Demeter helped to feed everyone as she was the goddess of farming, plants and crops. Apollo, one of Zeus's sons, was the god of the sun, music and poetry, among other things, and had a half-sister called Athena, who was the goddess of knowledge and war. She was believed to protect ancient Greek heroes when they marched into battle, especially if they carried a shield with a picture of an owl.

ZEUS

God of Sky
& Thunder

HERA

Goddess of Women
& Family

POSEIDON

God of the Ocean

APHRODITE

Goddess of Love
& Beauty

HERMES

Messenger to the Gods

DEMETER

Goddess of Farming

ATHENA

Goddess of War & Knowledge

HADES

God of the Underworld

APOLLO

God of Music & Poetry

Mount Olympus and its gods were very important to both citizens and enslaved people. They were convinced that their gods rewarded good behaviour and punished bad, so religion was a major part of everyday life. Even young children knew they had to please these powerful gods, or at least to try not to make them angry.

To help people do this, every polis had a temple where people went to worship and glorify their gods. Often there were several temples dedicated to different gods and goddesses.

Ancient Greek temples were often very large and very ornate, and many contained statues of the gods that were decorated with gold and ivory. The temples were the most important buildings in the whole of Hellas, and today they are some of the most beautiful and spectacular ruins anywhere on Earth. Every year, millions of tourists visit the temples that

MYTHS AND MONSTERS

remain in Athens and Cape Sounion, and at Paestum and Agrigento in southern Italy.

One way the ancient Greeks tried to please their gods was by sacrificing live animals. This meant killing them, normally by using a sharp knife to cut their throats on or near the altar.

The altar was the holiest part of any temple, but sacrifices also took place in a special, sacred space called a sanctuary or *temenos*. This could be in the beautiful countryside far outside the polis. Any citizen could order a sacrifice, and the priest who cleaned up afterwards was sometimes rewarded by being allowed to share the dead animal's guts or entrails when these had been roasted. On other occasions people gave their gods a liquid gift known as a libation, which made a lot less mess.

Every year, hundreds of religious ceremonies took place in these temples and sanctuaries. Music usually formed part of the rituals, depending on which of the gods the people and their priests were trying to please. People might dance as well as sing hymns, but the music often had names that sound very strange to us today, such as *Prosodion*, *Hyporchema* and *Dithyramb*.

MYTHS AND MONSTERS

Ancient Greeks loved telling each other stories about the gods when they weren't worshipping them in temples. These stories became part of their culture long before any of them were written down in books. Besides gods and goddesses, the best myths and legends included tales of superheroes who fought and killed horrible monsters such as Medusa and the terrifying Minotaur.

The Minotaur was half man and half bull, and he lived in a maze-like cave on the island of Crete. Young boys and girls were sent into the maze to be eaten alive until the brave King Theseus went down into the darkness and stabbed the beast to death.

Medusa was even more terrible. Her hair was made of living snakes, and she had the power to kill anyone who looked at her by turning them into stone. Fortunately, another ancient Greek hero named Perseus found her asleep and chopped off her hideous head before she could change him into a statue.

Not all the creatures in these stories were evil, however. Pegasus was a magical flying horse ridden by a man called Bellerophon, and together they killed the fire-breathing Chimera, which was a type of dragon. Another strange creature was the centaur, a cross

MYTHS AND MONSTERS   29

between a man and a horse. Centaurs were mostly good, but they could be badly behaved after drinking wine.

Many of these myths sound a bit like our own fairy tales, and it's impossible to know whether the ancient Greeks really believed them or simply loved hearing exciting stories of danger and heroism.

Bellerophon

Pegasus

Centaur

MYTHS AND MONSTERS

Thousands of years ago, the Greek myths must have been an enjoyable way for young children to learn about their pagan world. Even now, many of the stories sound so amazing that people around the world still enjoy reading them or watching blockbuster films based on them.

4
MIND AND BODY

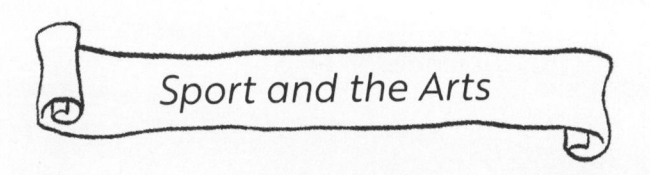

Sport and the Arts

The ancient Greeks famously invented the Olympic Games, which started around 2,800 years ago.

The games were held every four years, just like the modern ones are now, but only men and boys were allowed to take part. Married women weren't even allowed to watch. The Olympics became so popular with spectators that the city-states all agreed not to attack each other while the competitions were taking place.

The Olympics

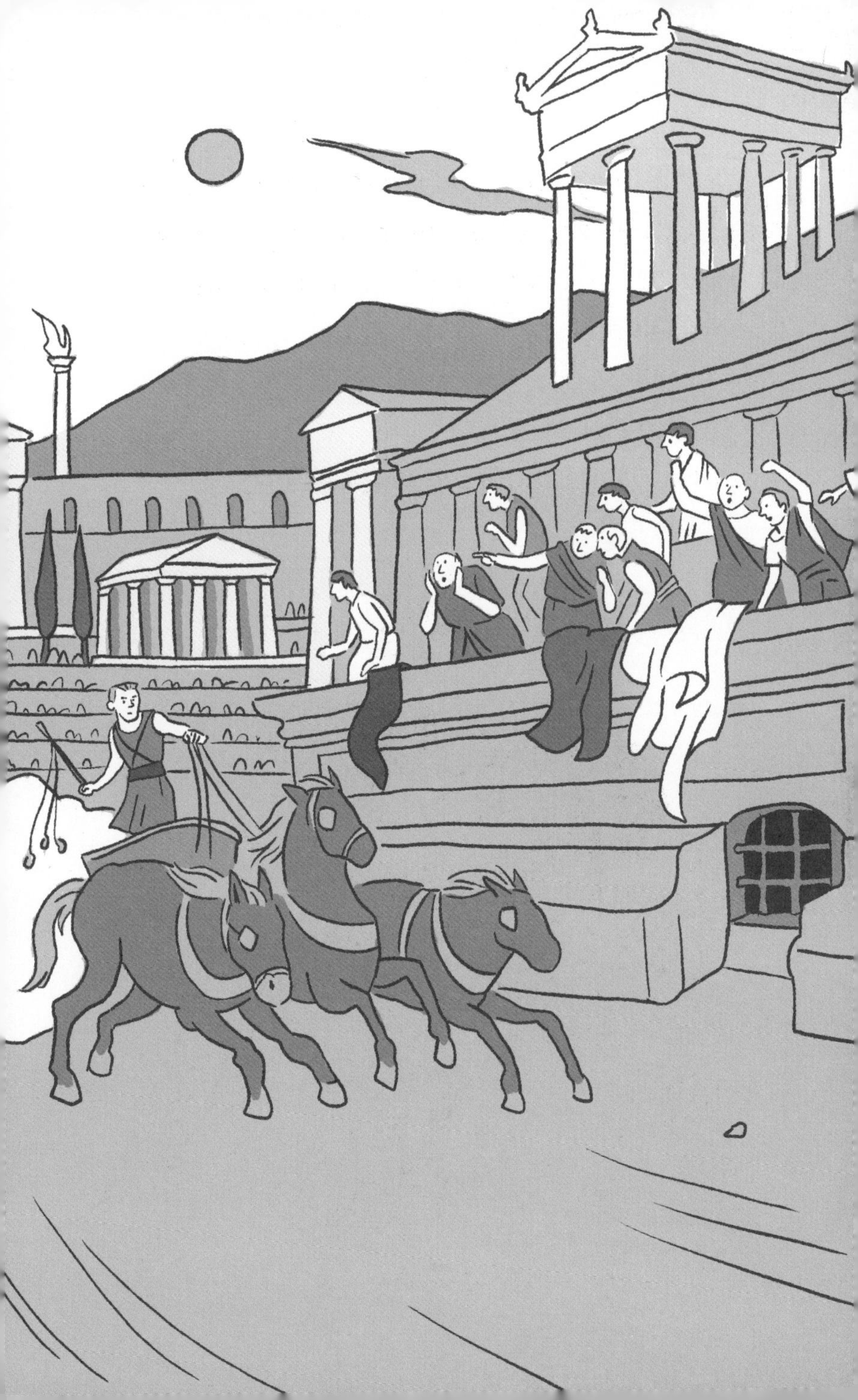

For a long time, the athletes didn't wear any clothes, and even the fastest and most famous ones raced for glory rather than medals or money.

The most exciting events were running, wrestling, boxing and chariot racing.

Each of the winners was awarded a special wreath made of leaves that came from a sacred tree and could be worn like a crown.

Sports formed such an important part of ancient Greek life that the games were named after Mount Olympus, the legendary home of the gods. Artists also honoured these gods and goddesses in their work, often by creating sculptures that many experts today agree are some of the greatest and most beautiful ever made.

The most talented sculptors used marble and bronze, producing striking and highly realistic statues for the temples or to stand in a public place like the *agora*, which was like a town square.

Religious figures were normally shown as larger and more detailed than animals or humans; however, many sculptures showed successful athletes and mythological beasts.

These were often painted in bright colours, but over time the colours have faded or been cleaned off, which is why the statues in museums are mostly plain white or grey.

Smaller figures were also made of wood or clay or solid gold and were meant for people's homes. The very smallest could be worn as jewellery.

Other artists produced highly distinctive vases coloured black and red. These were called *pelikai*, *kraters* and *amphorae*.

| Pelike | Krater | Amphora |

Some of them were purely decorative, but others were used for holding wine or olive oil, or libations for religious rituals. All three types are interesting today because their designs often show realistic scenes of daily life from thousands of years ago. Historians can discover a lot of information about the ancient Greeks and their way of life by studying the painted figures on vases and other pieces of pottery.

The very best potters and painters had their own styles, which are now recognised around the world. This includes men such as Exekias and Makron. Makron's work is so rare that a single wine cup, or *kylix*, made by him once sold for nearly two million dollars. Makron's creations are some of the most collectible, despite us knowing almost nothing about the man himself.

Besides famous artists and athletes, Hellas was also home to some of the ancient world's most important philosophers. These were men and women who studied the world around them, using logic and reason and even science to help them understand the meaning of life.

Philosophers such as Socrates, Plato and his student Aristotle tried to encourage people to think about how a society should work, what justice meant and even the importance of working for a living. Aristotle was one of the first people to suggest that the Earth was shaped like a ball rather than a flat disc. He also started his own school, called the Lyceum, and spent three years as a tutor to the young Alexander the Great. Many of Aristotle's ideas still fascinate philosophers today.

Every city had an open-air theatre as well as a temple because Greeks loved watching actors performing on stage. The theatre was normally semicircular and built on a steep hillside with curved stone benches arranged like giant steps leading up the slope.

Building a theatre in this way meant that everyone in the audience had a clear view of the actors down below. Some theatres were so large that more than 15,000 spectators could watch a performance together. The most famous playwright, a man called Sophocles, wrote at least 120 different plays.

Only men were allowed to act on stage – the same as in England until the seventeenth century. Most of the plays were either comedies or tragedies. There was some painted scenery and loud sound effects such as thunder.

Actors all wore smiling or crying masks so that people in the audience would know whether they were happy or sad. Another way to tell what was going on was the colour of the outfits: actors in a comedy always wore bright colours, and those in tragedies wore dark-coloured clothes. The lines in a play were written in rhyme, and the masks had large holes at the mouth so that the actors' voices could be heard by the audience.

Ancient Greek plays are not performed very often nowadays. However, a word sometimes used to describe actors, "thespians", comes from one of the first actors historians know about: a man named Thespis from the Greek city of Icarius. Similarly, the English word "theatre" comes from the ancient Greek *theatron*, which means "seeing place".

Many people do still read ancient Greek poetry though – especially a couple of very long poems called *The Iliad* and *The Odyssey* by a poet called Homer. *The Iliad* describes events during the Trojan War, which took place in what is now Turkey. *The Odyssey* tells the story of the amazing ten-year journey the victorious King Odysseus took to get home at the end of the war.

These are the oldest known examples of Greek literature and among the most famous writings from anywhere in the ancient world. But no one knows when Homer was born and when he died, or even who he really was. Some historians now think Homer may actually have been several different people rather than just one man, but, despite this, he is still regarded as one of the most important writers who ever lived.

5

HOPLITES VERSUS IMMORTALS

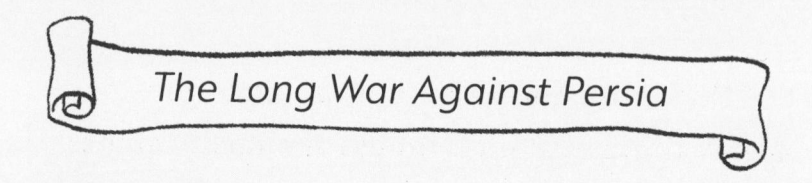

The Long War Against Persia

The ancient Greeks spent years fighting among themselves but were also at war with the much larger Persian Empire for nearly half a century (492–449 BCE).

The terrible bloodshed began after Persian troops invaded several small Greek settlements. The local people objected when the Persian king, Darius, appointed his own military rulers in the settlements. The Greek city-states agreed to fight together to force the Persian army back over the border into the country we now call Iran.

HOPLITES VERSUS IMMORTALS

In 490 BCE, Darius sent a massive fleet of Persian warships carrying thousands more soldiers. They landed at a place called Marathon, which was about 40 kilometres from Athens. The Greeks knew they were heavily outnumbered, but they fought very bravely.

By the end of that day, they had killed 6,000 Persians and lost only 192 of their own men. Afterwards, some of the Greek soldiers ran all the way back to Athens to celebrate this surprise victory. This is the origin of the famous marathon races that are still run today.

Ten years later, the Persians still wanted their revenge. A new king, Xerxes, sent an even larger fleet of up to 1,000 warships. This time, more than 200,000 Persian troops made a second attempt to conquer ancient Greece and

HOPLITES VERSUS IMMORTALS

used a special force of heavily armed soldiers known as Immortals.

Once again, the ancient Greeks found themselves outnumbered when they met the huge Persian army at a place in the mountains called Thermopylae.

The Battle of Thermopylae went very badly for the Greeks until an act of amazing courage enabled thousands of them to escape unharmed. Leonidas, the leader of Sparta, persuaded 300 of his best men to continue fighting to the death, and this gave the other Greeks time to get away.

Spartan soldiers already had a reputation as fierce and effective warriors, and they fought so bravely that up to 20,000 Persians were killed before the battle was over. According to one legend, King Xerxes watched all this happening from his solid-gold throne on a nearby hillside.

HOPLITES VERSUS IMMORTALS

Ordinary Greek soldiers were called *hoplites*. They probably weren't any better trained or even better armed than their enemies, but army commanders have often noticed that patriotic troops fight more fiercely when they are defending their own

PERSIAN IMMORTAL

GREEK HOPLITE

land than when they are ordered to invade someone else's. The hoplites had only long spears and a shield called an *aspis*.

The ancient Greeks certainly weren't going to surrender to their powerful enemy without a fight. The Persians eventually managed to capture Athens, but the Greek navy lay in wait for them with an impressive fleet of its own. Dozens of sturdy warships were moored in a narrow stretch of water called the Straits of Salamis.

The ancient Greeks' best fighting ships were called *triremes* – a type of vessel that had oars as well as large sails. This made them fast and easy to direct, which was a deadly combination for anyone who had to face them in battle.

More than a hundred oarsmen sat in three rows on each side of the ship, which is how the trireme got its name. Each man had to pull on a long, heavy wooden oar, often for hours at a time. They were well paid, but it was very tiring work, so only the fittest and toughest seamen were chosen to do this job.

Gunpowder had not been invented yet, so there were no guns or cannons on the triremes. Instead, each captain had to try to sink enemy ships by ramming them as hard as possible. At the front of each trireme was a sharp metal prow, normally made of bronze. Rowing at top speed, a team of skilled oarsmen could use this to sink another vessel by almost slicing it in two.

Another successful tactic was to position the trireme alongside an enemy vessel. Soldiers waiting on deck could then leap across and attack using their spears and sharp swords.

At the same time, archers on the deck of the trireme would fire arrows at the crew of the other vessel to stop them attacking the trireme. Sometimes the biggest triremes had a tall wooden catapult on deck, which was used to throw rocks and stones to damage the enemy fleet.

The Persian ships sent to Salamis were larger than any of the triremes but also slower. They were much harder to direct too, which gave the Greeks a real advantage in the narrow Straits of Salamis. The triremes began ramming the heavier vessels, sinking one after another and then making their getaway before the panicking Persians could launch a counter-attack.

HOPLITES VERSUS IMMORTALS 53

The exact figures will probably never be known, but the Greeks are thought to have lost only 40 ships compared to the more than 200 Persian vessels that were captured or sunk during the battle. Very few of the Persian sailors knew how to swim, so thousands of them must have drowned.

Xerxes had seen enough by then, so he took his golden throne back to Persia. The fighting continued without him, however – on land and at sea.

Before leaving, Xerxes had ordered his commanders to conquer Hellas no matter how many Persian lives it cost. Unfortunately for King Xerxes, his army was destroyed at the Battle of Plataea in 479 BCE, and the Persian navy lost the Battle of Mycale shortly afterwards. The attempt to conquer ancient Greece was abandoned. Their men were exhausted, and Persia made no more serious attempts at invasion.

A few, much smaller, battles took place over the next 30 years, but in 449 BCE the Greeks and Persians finally agreed to stop. After this, the city-states went back to fighting among themselves.

6

A TALENT FOR INVENTION

Architects, Engineers and Inventors

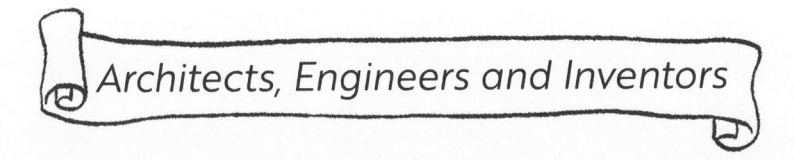

An ancient Greek theatre wasn't just a place to enjoy watching plays but also a breathtaking piece of architecture. Public and ceremonial buildings were designed to impress onlookers with their style, size and grandeur.

They were also cleverly designed. For example, architects made the theatron fan-shaped so that people high up in the back rows could hear the actors down on the stage. This required a deep understanding of acoustics – the science of sound. The ancient Greeks were so good at it that even now, tourists visiting the ruins of these old theatres can hear what is being said by people talking in a normal voice down below.

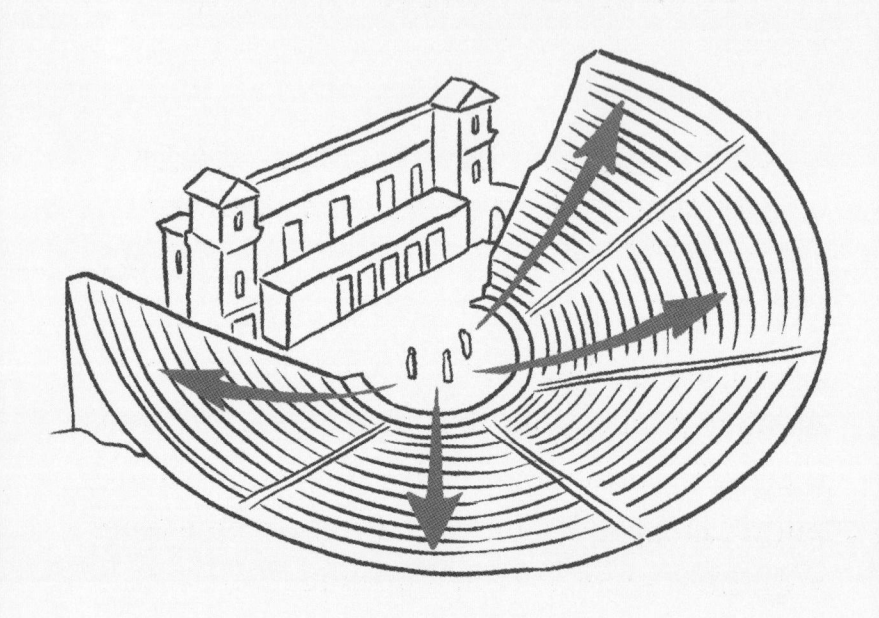

Greek temple design was just as impressive, and it is still admired around the world for its classical beauty, elegance and symmetry. The most distinctive features of a Greek temple were its tall stone columns, which were produced in three different styles or "orders", called Doric, Ionic and Corinthian.

A TALENT FOR INVENTION

Doric is the simplest of the three orders. The columns are a little wider at the base than at the top, and they have carved grooves running their entire length, which is known as fluting.

Ionic columns are normally slimmer than Doric and more elegant. They have a flat, carved stone piece at the top called a capital, which is decorated with scrolls on each side.

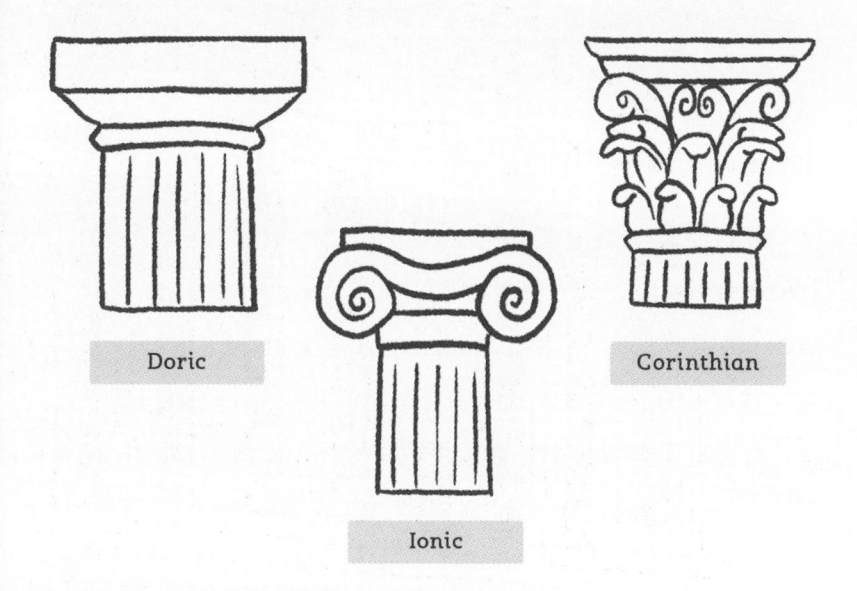

Doric

Corinthian

Ionic

A TALENT FOR INVENTION

Corinthian columns are fluted too and look the most ornate of all. Their capitals have scrolls as well as decorative stone leaves copied from a plant called an acanthus.

These columns were often huge regardless of which order the architect decided to use. The Parthenon, the main temple in Athens, which was built to honour the goddess Athena,

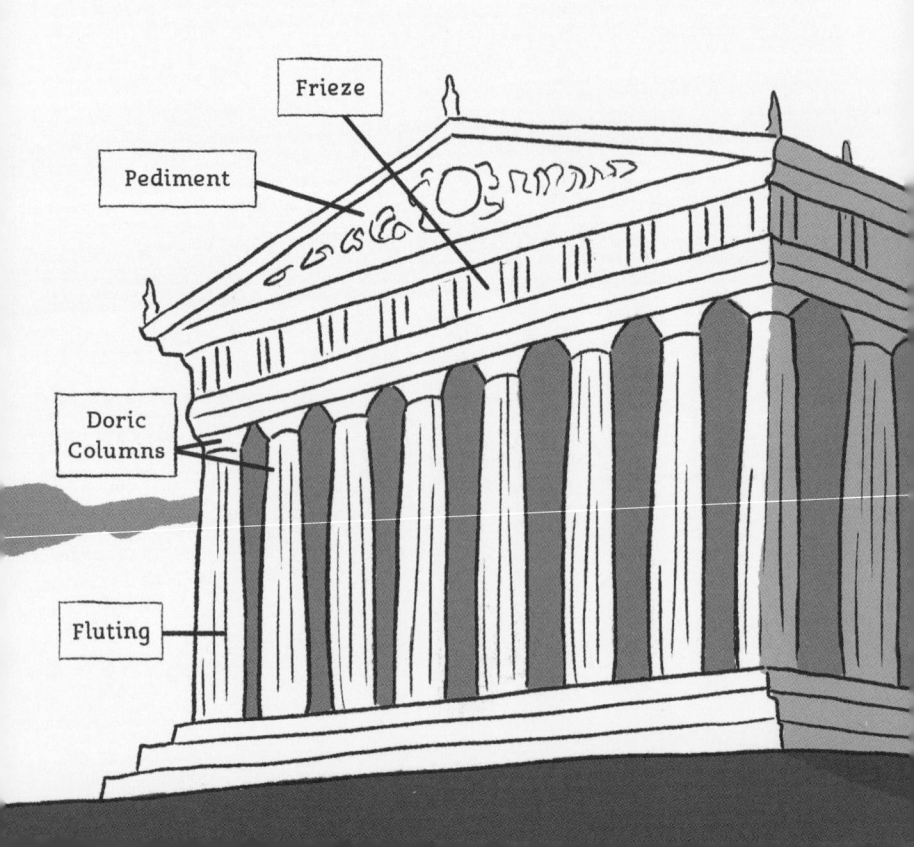

- Frieze
- Pediment
- Doric Columns
- Fluting

has columns more than ten metres tall. It attracts more visitors today than any other Greek temple and offers fantastic views over the city. When it was finished, in 438 BCE, it had 46 outer columns, each of which was nearly two metres in diameter. The ones at the corners were even taller, and inside it had another 23.

At the entrance to temples such as the Parthenon, the line of columns was topped by a long carved panel (also called a frieze) and a large triangular section called a pediment.

This arrangement is still so admired that it has been copied by architects all over the world as well as by the designers of Rolls-Royce cars. In both cases it looks handsome and very simple but requires considerable mathematical skill to get right. For a row of columns like this to appear straight, each one has to be very slightly curved. This is due to a strange optical illusion called *entasis*, which the ancient Greeks were the first people to understand.

Their engineers and inventors were just as clever and as influential as the architects. Many of them spent years studying mathematics, not just because they enjoyed working out complicated sums, but because it helped them design the practical tools and advanced technologies that improved the lives of the people around them.

Examples of this include one of the first alarm clocks, an early water-powered mill used for grinding wheat into flour for making

A TALENT FOR INVENTION

Alarm Clock

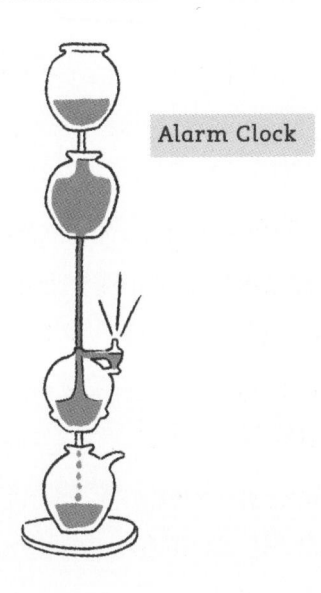

bread, and a device called an odometer, which could measure how far a cart had travelled along a road. The Archimedes screw was a very efficient pump used for watering crops,

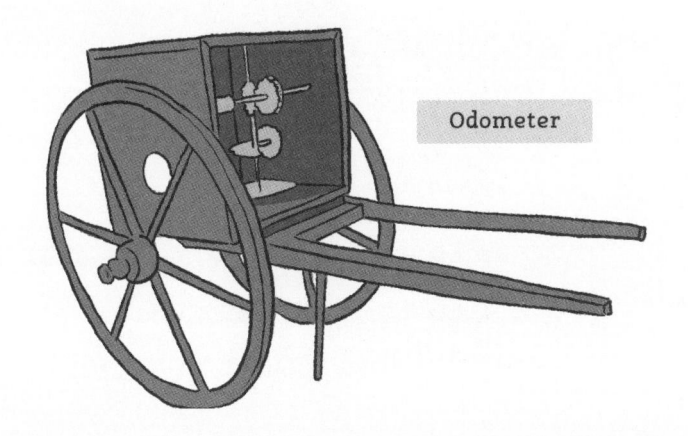

Odometer

A TALENT FOR INVENTION

while the Antikythera mechanism may have been one of the first-ever computers.

This intriguing object was found more than a century ago in an old shipwreck, and historians now think it used more than two dozen bronze wheels to calculate the movements of the Sun and Moon across the sky. Unfortunately, after more than 2,000 years under the sea, it is very rusty, and no one has been able to figure out exactly how it worked.

Antikythera

A TALENT FOR INVENTION

Ancient Greeks were also skilled navigators. A mapmaker called Anaximander, who invented the sundial for tracking the seasons, was the first to draw a detailed map of their world from the Mediterranean to the Caspian Sea. It was also an ancient Greek who came up with the idea that the Earth orbited the sun rather than the other way round. Aristarchus of Samos suggested this in 270 BCE, but it took more than 1,800 years for his idea to be accepted in the rest of Europe.

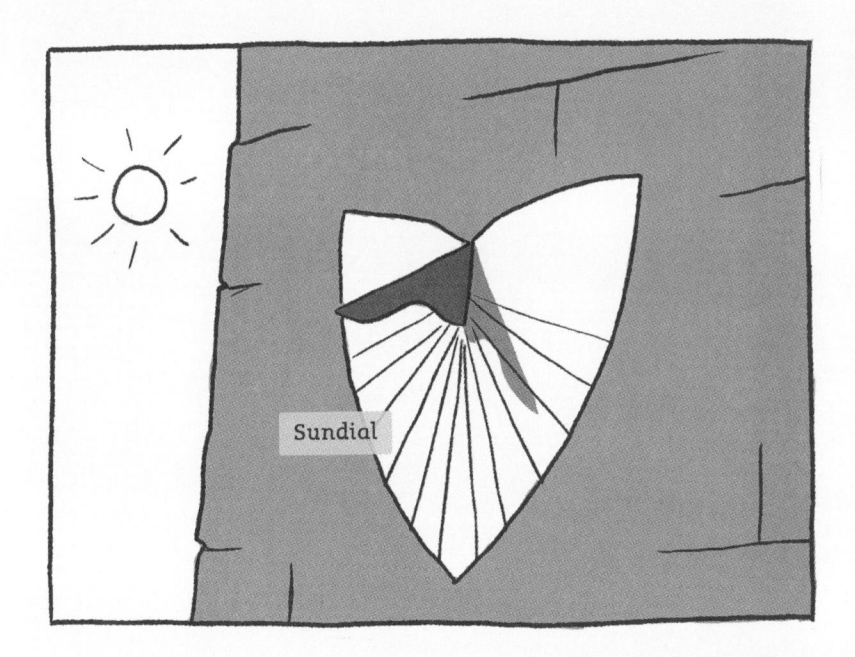

Sundial

A TALENT FOR INVENTION

These are just a few examples of the way the ancient Greeks were able to improve their understanding of science and technology. They also made many important advances in medicine and astronomy by studying plants and animals and natural phenomena such as earthquakes and eclipses.

Often their best discoveries and inventions resulted from a real sense of curiosity and desire to learn more about the world in which they lived.

7

CONQUERING THE WORLD

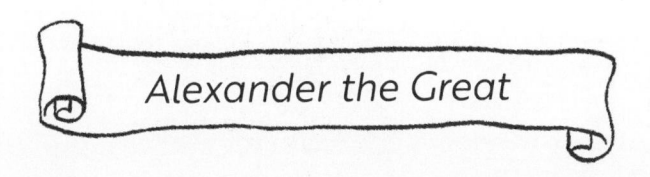

Alexander the Great

Alexander inherited the throne of the Kingdom of Macedonia after his father was murdered in 336 BCE. He was only around 20 years old but was well educated and already had a reputation as an impressive military commander. Soon after his reign began, he decided to expand his father's army in order to conquer Persia, the traditional enemy of the ancient Greeks.

New soldiers were recruited from all over the country, including thousands of young farmers, shepherds, craftsmen and labourers. All of them had to prove they were fit and healthy in order to be admitted to the army, where they learned how to fight with spears and shields. The successful recruits were trained by Alexander's oldest, most experienced soldiers. They practised using an even longer spear (called a *sarissa*) until they could handle it with deadly accuracy.

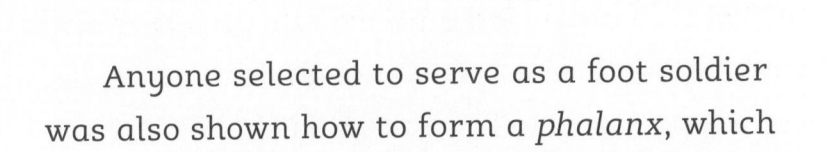

CONQUERING THE WORLD

Anyone selected to serve as a foot soldier was also shown how to form a *phalanx*, which was an important military tactic developed by the ancient Greeks.

A phalanx required dozens of soldiers to stand side by side in tightly packed lines with their shields overlapping to form a protective wall. They would then march in close formation and use their long spears to attack the enemy.

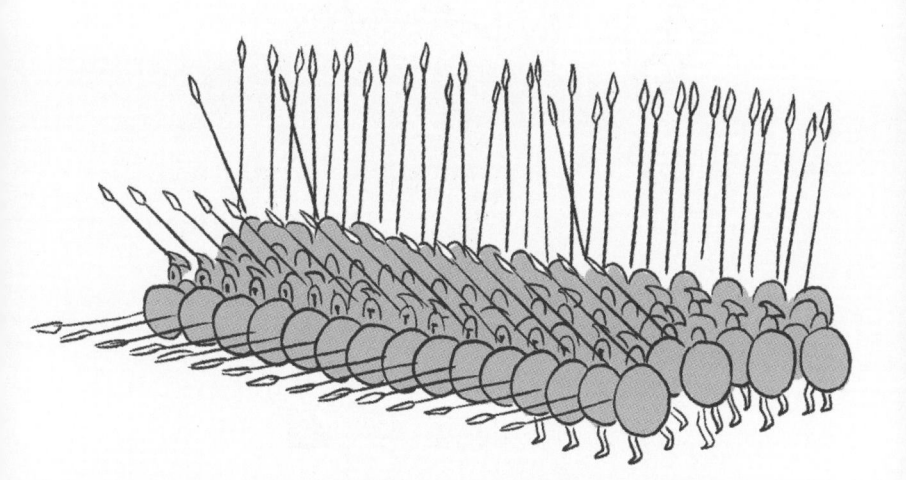

Soldiers in the back rows supported the ones in front and helped to push the phalanx forward. A battle would normally be lost if the phalanx broke apart, though soldiers often continued fighting hand to hand.

Meanwhile, other soldiers were recruited into the cavalry, meaning that they fought on horseback.

CONQUERING THE WORLD

Cavalry units tended to be much smaller than infantry ones because horses were rare in this part of the world and very expensive.

Cavalrymen often wore beautifully made metal armour, including a bronze helmet and bronze plates to protect the legs and chest. All of their equipment had to be paid for by the soldiers themselves, including their horses, so cavalrymen usually came from richer families than the foot soldiers.

Alexander's plan to attack Persia was very popular because the Greeks hated the Persians and looked forward to beating them once and for all. From the start, the young king demonstrated that he was one of the most brilliant military strategists in the history of warfare.

In 333 BCE, his troops quickly defeated the army of Darius III at the Battle of Issus. Then they marched across the Middle East and into

CONQUERING THE WORLD

what is now Iran. Within two years they had captured Susa, which was the Persian capital. At just 25 years old, Alexander became the ruler (or pharaoh) of Egypt in north-east Africa and the powerful new king of the Persian Empire, in addition to being the king of Macedonia and the leader of the Greek city-states.

CONQUERING THE WORLD

However, many of Alexander's most loyal troops were exhausted and wanted to go home to their wives and children. Having joined the army to defeat Persia, they may not have shared their commander's desire to continue in warfare. Most of them had probably never even heard of Egypt or Babylon, let alone thought about invading them. After so many long months on the march – and dozens of battles – they'd had enough.

Unfortunately, Alexander had other ideas. He wanted to push on – to march even deeper into Asia and to extend his territory even further. In 329 BCE, he and his men successfully crossed the Hindu Kush, a deserted mountain range covering more than 150,000 square kilometres of Afghanistan and Pakistan.

In just eight years, Alexander's army had marched many thousands of kilometres, establishing 70 new cities along the way, including several named Alexandria after

CONQUERING THE WORLD

himself. They'd created an empire that spanned three continents, covering an incredible five million square kilometres. But Alexander wanted more and set out to capture India.

In 326 BCE, his army won yet another important battle, against an Indian king on the banks of the Jhelum River. But Alexander's mood suddenly changed. During or shortly after the battle, his favourite warhorse,

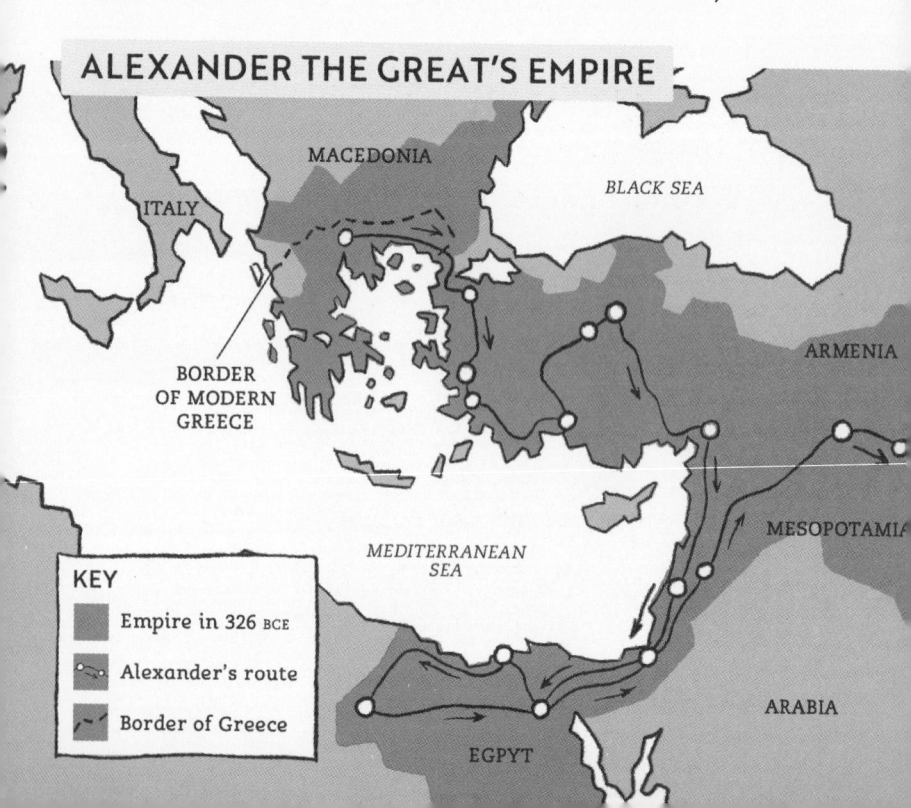

ALEXANDER THE GREAT'S EMPIRE

MACEDONIA

BLACK SEA

ITALY

BORDER OF MODERN GREECE

ARMENIA

MEDITERRANEAN SEA

MESOPOTAMIA

KEY
- Empire in 326 BCE
- Alexander's route
- Border of Greece

ARABIA

EGPYT

CONQUERING THE WORLD 73

Bucephalus, sickened and died. After constructing yet another new settlement (named Bucephala in memory of the horse), a saddened Alexander finally agreed it was time to go back to Macedonia.

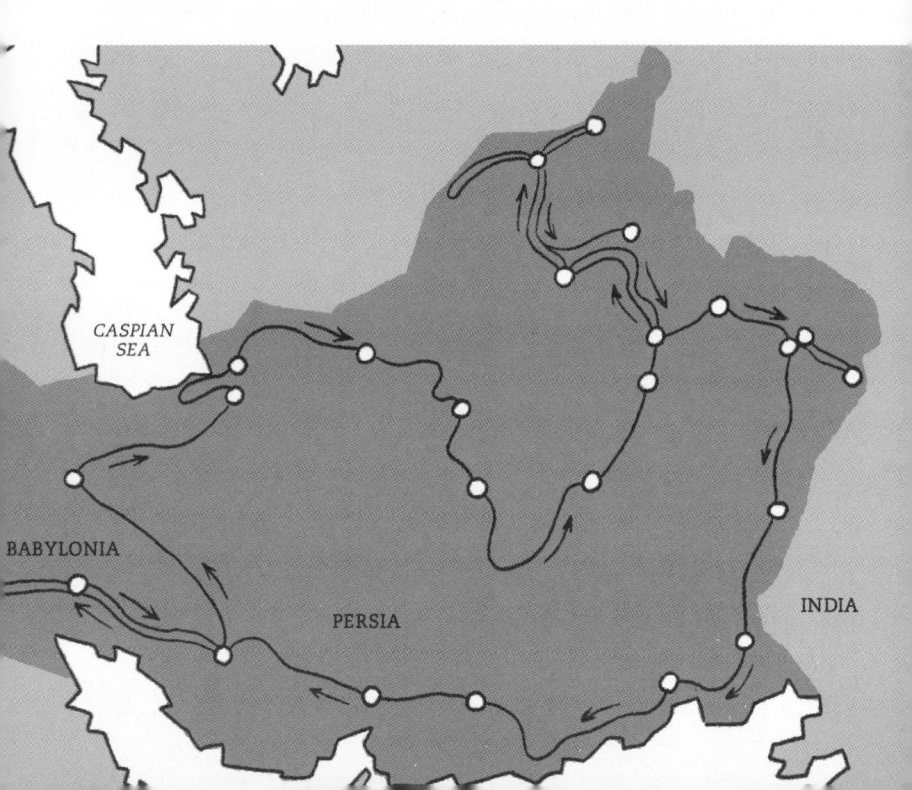

This pleased the troops, but their brilliant commander never made it back home. Instead, Alexander reportedly caught a fever, perhaps weakened by the years of marching and fighting. He died in Babylon in June 323 BCE. He was only 32 years old.

No one knows what type of fever it was, and some historians think Alexander may have been poisoned by one of his enemies.

According to legend, the great warrior's body was placed in a solid-gold coffin and taken to the Egyptian city of Alexandria to be buried. Another legend claims that the magnificent coffin was filled with honey to preserve the remains for eternity.

But his coffin has never been found, so it's impossible to know whether or not either legend is true. Over the centuries, more than a hundred different expeditions have been organised to find Alexander's tomb and its priceless treasures, but the exact location has never been discovered.

8

THE RISE OF THE ROMANS

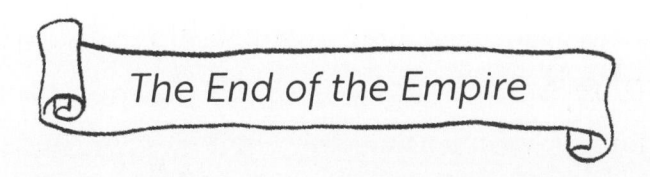

The End of the Empire

The early death of Alexander the Great came as such a shock to the citizens that at first many refused to believe he had really gone. To make things worse, Alexander had left behind three wives and at least one child but no clear instructions about who should take over and rule in his place.

Alexander's son was much too young to occupy the throne himself, so his vast empire was broken up and divided between the army's most powerful generals. These men called themselves the *Diadochi*, which means "successors" in Greek. Before long they had begun fighting among themselves. Each of them wanted to extend his own area of the old empire at the expense of the others'.

The wars over this went on for decades and cost thousands of lives. Eventually, a few of the Diadochi managed to establish their own kingdoms, which they and their descendants settled down to rule.

These were much smaller than Alexander's empire had been but still covered thousands of square kilometres. Other generals were much less successful. Some were forced to surrender their share of the empire to a stronger rival, and they lacked the military power needed to win it back.

During all this fighting, individual communities within the various kingdoms still continued to trade with each other. By exchanging people, inventions and ideas, they also ensured that the language, art, science and culture of the ancient Greeks spread across Europe, north Africa and western Asia.

Still, the break-up of Alexander's empire and the fighting between the new kingdoms had seriously weakened ancient Greek society as a whole. Many communities began to decline, and the most important centres of Greek culture and learning were to be found outside Greece. Mostly this meant they were across the sea, at Alexandria in Egypt, for example, which had the world's largest library, and in the Turkish cities of Antioch and Ephesus.

Meanwhile, much closer to home, many poorer citizens were starting to rebel against the rich and powerful aristocrats who had ruled them for so long.

The kingdoms of the Diadochi had also been weakened by their seemingly endless wars.

THE RISE OF THE ROMANS

A new and more powerful empire began to rise up elsewhere in the Mediterranean – the Roman Empire – and many Greeks worried they might no longer be able to defend themselves from attack. As the Romans threatened to invade the kingdoms one by one, the former conquerors realised with horror that they could soon become the conquered.

THE RISE OF THE ROMANS

In 215 BCE, some of them joined forces with the army of Carthage in what is now Tunisia. But even this was no match for the Romans.

By now, the Roman army was the greatest the ancient world had ever seen, and it must have seemed unbeatable when it defeated Macedonia not once but twice.

THE RISE OF THE ROMANS

Its soldiers were clearly fitter than their opponents had ever been. They had better equipment and training. Roman tactics were also superior, especially a formation of 120 soldiers called a *maniple*, which soon proved to be far deadlier than the traditional phalanx had been.

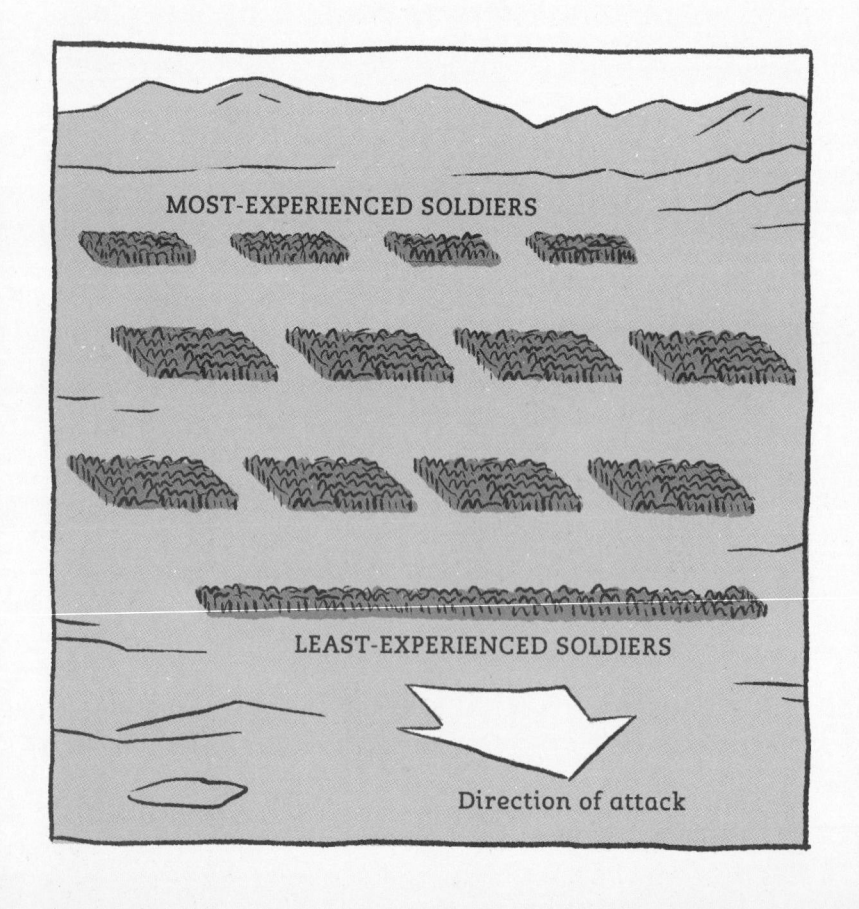

MOST-EXPERIENCED SOLDIERS

LEAST-EXPERIENCED SOLDIERS

Direction of attack

THE RISE OF THE ROMANS

By 146 BCE, the Roman army had conquered the whole of the Greek mainland, completely destroying the great city of Corinth and taking its gold and other treasures. The Corinthians were either killed or sold into slavery – a grim warning to other towns and cities that they were now all under permanent Roman rule. Carthage suffered just as badly the same year when its territories were stolen to become yet another Roman province.

The Roman army had huge numbers of soldiers stationed in north Africa, but it took until 30 BCE for the Romans to take control of Egypt. This was the last important part of Alexander the Great's former empire and a vital source of the wheat the Roman leader Octavian needed to make bread to feed the fast-growing population of Rome.

A year before this, one of the most famous Egyptian pharaohs, Cleopatra, had put together a huge fleet of warships and foolishly gone to war against the Roman navy. The resulting Battle of Actium didn't last more than a few hours because Roman sailors were just as impressive as Roman soldiers. Cleopatra killed herself soon afterwards, possibly by allowing herself to be bitten by a poisonous snake called an asp. After this crushing defeat, the whole of Egypt was absorbed into the rapidly expanding Roman Empire. The golden age of Greek civilisation was finally at an end.

9
A LONG LEGACY

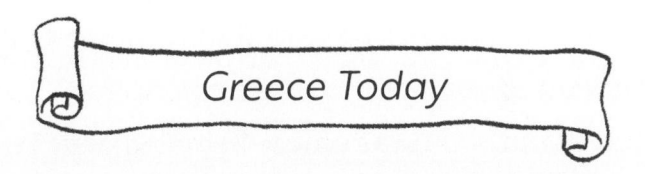

Greece Today

Alexander the Great's empire survived for only 13 years, but its impact on the rest of the world has lasted for centuries. Greece is now one of Europe's smallest countries, with a tiny population compared to Great Britain, yet the influence of its language and rich culture has been unique and very strong.

Two thousand years ago, the Romans spoke a language of their own called Latin. But once they had conquered the ancient Greeks, they copied many things, including their art and architecture. The Romans adopted many of the

Greek gods too and built temples to them which are very similar to the temples of the Greeks.

Since then, many architects around the world have done the same thing, meaning that examples of Greek-style columns, pediments and friezes can still be found on hundreds of famous and important public buildings. These include Buckingham Palace, Birmingham Town Hall and St Paul's Cathedral in London as well as the American Capitol in Washington, DC and the Paris Louvre, which is the largest museum in the world.

But impressive architecture isn't the only thing that countries like Britain, France and the USA have inherited from the ancient Greeks. The first ever Christian bibles were written in Greek, and the letters in our modern alphabet are based on the writing system that the ancient Greeks invented.

Αα	Ββ	Γγ	Δδ	Εε
alpha	beta	gamma	delta	epsilon
Ζζ	Ηη	Θθ	Ιι	Κκ
zeta	eta	theta	iota	kappa
Λλ	Μμ	Νν	Ξξ	Οο
lambda	mu	nu	xi	omicron
Ππ	Ρρ	Σσς	Ττ	Υυ
pi	rho	sigma	tau	upsilon
Φφ	Χχ	Ψψ	Ωω	
phi	chi	psi	omega	

A LONG LEGACY

In fact, thousands of words and phrases that we use every day come from their language. Surprisingly, these include many that people think of as very modern words, such as hyper, meta, acrobat and even helicopter. The word dinosaur also has ancient Greek origins – it is made up of two separate words: *deinos* meaning terrible and *sauros* meaning lizard.

Similarly, the first international Olympic Games in 1896 was inspired by those early men-only races that took place to honour Zeus and the other pagan gods. This is why the organisers decided to hold the first modern Olympic Games in Athens and why every four years a symbolic "Olympic flame" is carried by runners all the way from Olympia in western Greece to whichever country is hosting the games. These events now attract billions of spectators and are shown on television in almost every country on the planet.

Ancient Greek ideas about democracy have been used to establish the political systems in many of these countries too, including Britain and the USA. Women as well as men now have the right to vote in lots of different countries around the world, and both sexes are able to stand for election to sit in parliament or become the next president or prime minister.

Ancient Greek philosophy and mathematics are also very highly regarded in the modern world. Plato, Socrates and Aristotle are still considered to be three of the greatest philosophers of all time. Students study their lives and works closely, and their teachings form the basis of a lot of Western philosophy. Millions of schoolchildren still learn about an ancient Greek mathematician called Pythagoras, who showed how to calculate the size of a right-angled triangle.

These are just a few of the ways in which a civilisation that disappeared thousands of

A LONG LEGACY

years ago continues to affect our lives today. The ancient Greeks may have gone, but their best ideas and inventions still fascinate people, just as they did when Alexander the Great set out to conquer the whole world.